25 ORIGINAL PIECES OF FICTION FRO

ELECTRIC READS
YOUNG
WRITERS'
ANTHOLOGY
2017

First edition

This book is a work of fiction. Names, characters, businesses, organisatons, places, events, and incidents are the product either of the author's imagination or are used fictitiously. Any resemblence to actual persons, living or dead, events, or locales is entirely coincidental.

10 9 8 7 6 5 4 3 2 1

YOUNG WRITERS ANTHOLOGY 2017

CONTENTS

RHEA WILSON-WRIGHT
PAPER BACKED

Rhea Wilson-Wright was an apprentice in patisserie until she realised her true passion for illustrating and writing. At twenty-one, she now studies both subjects in her first year at the University of Worcester. When she's not working, Rhea often visits her crazy, loving family in Manchester, where she curls up with a book from her library-like room. She has been writing for a hobby since she was very young and owns several journals crammed full of ideas.

"What have you done?"

One arm wrapped protectively around her torso, the other bent to hold a thin cigarette towards her chapped lips, she takes a long drag.

"Nothing that wasn't warranted." The smoke she exhales mingles with lighter wisps of condensation. An angry bruise acts as a blush across her cheekbone.

"War is never warranted, Sera."

Two Weeks Earlier

A figure wandered down the early misted streets of London. Camden, usually blazing with bright signs, was muted by its lack of power. The streets were quiet without the usual hubbub of tourists and stall attendants. Cloaked in an oversized green jumper, the faux fur-lined hood shielded the woman's face from the

1

late winter chill.

Her tight clad legs quickly carried her down a narrow alley, enclosed by brick walls and chained fences. A black door flanked by bins was illuminated by the night's only light. It cast a warm orange glow on the hurried paper sign blue tacked to the flaking paint. The doubt plaguing her mind was eradicated by this, so she clasped the handle, twisted and pushed.

Inside the room was a huge circle of chairs; the typical cliché of a meeting for misfits. The faces that stared at the newcomer were only curious, not hostile. The shoulders of the entrant relaxed a little as she pulled down her hood. Her hair was the vivid colour of orange gerberas, shaved underneath and tied up in messy spikes with a tattered scrunchie. Eyebrows as dark at the makeup covering her heavy lids drew down as she looked over the crowd. She then noticed a raised hand.

"Hi, Austin." She said, and her friend beamed in response.

The empty seat he'd saved was marked by a little pink post-it note.

Reserved for Paisley :)

Paisley grinned crookedly as she pulled off her jumper and rested it on the back of the seat.

Absent-mindedly, she ran a finger down her bared arm; the skin rippled like the pages of a book.

A figure stood up and the room's delicate chatter fell to silence.

"Nice to see you all again." The greeting was pronounced in a light cockney accent. "For those of you who don't know, I am the Leader of this assembly."

Paisley thought the Leader looked too short to be in control of such a large group. His expression stopped the thought dead in its tracks.

"The topic for today is more serious than usual, I'm afraid." He drew a hand through his light brown hair. "It's official; nobody knows what we stand for."

A wave of chatter ran through the assembled crowd once more.

"Is that bad?" Paisley asked Austin.

"The whole point is to be noticed." He scoffed in response.

"People only see the name on the backs of our jackets. Nobody knows what we represent and that needs to change. Some physical sign ideally…"

Leader announced this over the murmurs, rolling up his oversized shirt sleeves. His skin whispered like a paperback novel.

Noticing the tattoo on her companion's forearm - beautifully stylised feathered wings that must have hurt even more than usual to have done - Paisley tentatively raised her hand.

"What about wings?" Austin's gaze darted from his arm to her.

"Wings?" Leader's dark eyes settled on her vibrantly haloed head. They briefly flitted to her painted lips.

"This way we're focusing the condition to one area; we're less likely to get hurt than if we had the usual edges of paper running across every inch our skin." Turning in her seat, she silently praised her earlier thinking to wear a tank top with a shredded back. The strange lines imprinted on her skin rustled up and down towards her shoulder blades. Then, just like someone shuffling a deck of cards, the undulations came together, piling atop one another to form a lovely, crisp set of paper wings. As before, she ran a finger over her arm, but it was only skin that time.

"Yes, but why those?" Despite his rebuttal, Leader's mouth had quirked into half a smile; he liked the idea.

"None of the other gangs have them; it's unique."

One Week Earlier

It wasn't.

A newspaper was slammed down with force to the floor. The cover story contained a black and white picture of three people turning away. Every coat covered back had slits cut out to accommodate the wings protruding from them. Emblazoned on each one was a slogan; Paper Backed.

The group assembled around the offending tabloid was a riot of real feathered wings flapping in rage.

"Don't they know who they're messing with?" A vocal member named Seraphine cried out.

"We're not an officially established brand of misfit, yet." One of the quieter, more relaxed individuals offered. He was slumped in his chair, snowy wings resting over its back and brushing the floor.

"Nobody asked you, Paschar."

"Oh, for Christ's sake; use my real name please. The celestial naming bullshit was vetoed last week." Lev, as he preferred to be called, ground out through clenched teeth.

"Well, as long as they stay out of our territory, I'm not bothered." Someone else piped up.

"Same here; we all know what happened to the last freaks that stepped into this place."

"They disappeared."

"Damn right they did!" Sera exclaimed, charcoal feathers ruffling in delight.

"I thought that was just because they were invisible…" Howls of laughter spilled over the Soho rooftop.

"Seriously though, we need to do something about these guys with the medical condition." The group sobered up.

"What do you say?" Sera looked over the gathered souls. "Shall we raise hell?"

The roar of agreement was deafening. Wings spanning several feet lifted, propelling the gang members into the air in a flurry of feathers.

Lev was the only one left; he sat for a long time after, hoping that the others would come to their senses.

All the groups had a common cause; why couldn't they see that?

Yesterday

Hands ripped from each other's grasp, Paisley and the Paper Backed Leader stood side by side.

Despite her nose being bloodied and crooked, Paisley smiled. The blood marring her face was a smudge the colour of her lipstick. To an oblivious onlooker, she'd look like a girl who'd just been ravished. The reality was a lot different.

Surrounded by the newly recognised Gang of Angels, they weighed up their options.

One of them tried to rip her tribe's patch off her fur lined hoodie. Paisley dodged out of the way just in time.

"Don't you dare touch her." Leader snarled.

"You should have thought of that before you strayed into our territory."

Normal pedestrians walked past, muttering behind gloved hands. The theatre district was providing a live show no-one wanted to witness. Some began to hurry, noticing the trouble starting to brew.

The circle tightened, a ring of angry yet excited faces leering in the early darkness.

Sera reached out and plucked a paper feather from Paisley's left wing.

Screaming in both surprise and agony, Paisley lashed out, catching Sera's cheek with her tattily gloved fist.

The group of enraged Angels closed in on Paisley, shouldering Leader out of the way. His attempts to penetrate the mob were useless.

In a matter of seconds, her wings lay shredded in the gutter, rain turning them to a pulpy paste. Every page removed was like a layer of skin; Paisley's suffering was evident on her tear streaked face.

"You were never real, only an imitation of us."

"No more than you!" She yelled, pain breaking her voice.

When Paisley wavered, and fell face down to the pavement, the state of her back was uncovered. It was a riot of deep, page shaped gouges that streamed with blood and rain.

Rounding the street corner, Lev took in the scene. Disbelief clouded his features as he broke into a run.

"You idiots! What they hell are you doing?"

Lev approached with palms outstretched, aiming to protect Paisley's cowering figure.

Leader took it as another attack and rushed at him, the lines of the pages marking his skin slashing against Lev's own. Leader's wings had vanished from his back.

Lev and Paisley were sprawled on the floor surrounded by the chaos caused by identity.

"Huh," Sera muttered as she watched the opposing Leader gather his partner up in his arms.

"What?"

"I guess paper cuts do hurt the most."

~o~

In one of my recent lectures, we watched a documentary on 1970s gang culture in New York. The main thing that caused these people to join appeared to be poverty, but it was the idea of participating in order to belong that caught my attention. It seemed to me that being involved in this kind of culture was considered surviving, and that these individuals needed to be recognised as people conventional society had wronged.

Thinking about how I could make this concept my own, I referred back to some of my older stories and wondered if it would be possible to incorporate the supernatural. I didn't want to over complicate the plot, so I kept the characters and brands of misfit to a minimum. However, the nature of their conditions had to be interesting enough to develop and suggest lives that went beyond the story itself. As a result of this, doodles of lone figures in scruffy winter clothing soon emerged. Paisley was the first; a static figure with book pages trailing behind her.

The Paper Backed gang's medical affliction was thought of as I flicked through a textbook and received a paper cut. I pondered on how people would live if they had skin with the qualities of paper; the consequences of this condition would probably rule their lives, causing pain in everyday tasks.

I felt the inclusion of an opposing force to be incredibly important, especially considering the gang aspect of Paper Backed. Equally as significant was the addition of an individual who didn't wish to fight, but co-exist. This ran parallel to the true events in New York when a peacekeeper from one of the gangs was brutally murdered. The entanglement of so many innocents in something that was never meant to be violent shows how ideas can become twisted and warped by a misguided sense of doing the right thing. This is regardless of the fact that each club has a common cause; the people who ignore and ridicule them are the ones who should be stood up to.

I decided to change the scene from an era I wasn't familiar with to a modern-day setting. I have visited London a great deal and felt more confident in recreating that city's streets rather than the American capital.

HOLLY LOUISE PSALIOU
ROASTED BREATHS

Primarily interested in science fiction, dystopia and the young adult protagonist, Holly Louise Psaliou writes within a selection of mediums. When she isn't writing, Holly is an avid freestyle dancer. Holly is in her final year of studying English and Creative Writing and can no longer binge her favourite American tv dramas without jotting down ideas alongside. She is currently working on a short film. One day she hopes to publish a series of young adult novels. Holly can be followed on twitter - @hollylouwrites.

"Lizzy, I need you to stay behind again tonight," Mark calls from out the back. Probably loitering around the cages, picking at ready-salted crisps or those six packs of juice he sneaks home for his two children. Emma has been lecturing him on cutting back on the sugar. He never listens to his wife. Why would he?

"Okay." I don't look up, because I'm balancing three tasks: registering the takings, checking the stock, and sending a quick text to Katie. Emma doesn't mind me sending the odd text on shift. I remember to ask how Katie's spelling test went, and that I'll be home late. I try to remember the last time I dedicated an entire evening to my sister. I see her less and less lately. Ever since Mark found out about her.

My phone buzzes almost immediately. I tap to open: *Test okay. Rachel said something again 2day bout mom nothin I cant handle. Might make some hot choc now home. See you later. Luv u. K x*

I notice Mark's dirty jeans out of the corner of my eye so I hide my phone under the papers. He drops a six-carton on the counter next to me.

Put those back, Mark! Emma's voice is fuzzy through the intercom. She works from home, in the flat above, but that doesn't stop her from playing Big Brother.

My head snaps up when Mark snatches my pen from my hand. He punctures the plastic, rips out a carton and stabs the straw in. He sucks vigorously, lips puckered as the straw bobs up and down, until he's drawn the life out of the carton. Satisfied, he drops it on the counter. A droplet of juice plops onto the paper. A 1 merges into a 7. He doesn't apologise. I know better than to argue.

"I really appreciate all the overtime you've been pulling in to help me..." Mark says, "And Emma, of course. She thinks the world of you. Good little worker she can confide in."

"It's okay," I whisper, quiet and low-key honest. I look to the red-eye. Wonder if Emma is currently watching. I twist the silicone medical ID on my wrist, trying to refocus on the numbers.

***

Mark is, for once, making himself useful by restocking the Evian. It's unsettling. The way his eyes cast over the bottles, and then to me, as he strokes at their necks.

I rub my sternum. Maybe that liquorice lace I had earlier went down the wrong pipe.

***

Mark has wandered down one of the aisles when my phone buzzes. I finish ringing up the sale I'm currently punching in. "Nineteen-forty."

The customer hands me the exact total. She's gone before I can print her a receipt.

"That lady must be pooping out a kid a week with how she clears us out of whole milk," Mark says, emerging from around back, snacking on a mini pack of biscuits.

"Formula," I correct, jotting down a quick reminder for re-stock of biscuits. "Babies can't digest cow's milk."

Tight-lipped, he nods.

My phone buzzes again. I freeze.

Mark clucks his tongue in his cheek. "Answer it, might be Katie." He smiles innocently. "I'll still let you take your usual toilet break at five." My throat feels like the centre of a doughnut.

I look to the red-eye and then back to Mark. He says, "Don't worry about, Emma. If she says anything I'll tell her I was asking you to look up something for me online."

I smile, and then reach for my phone and swipe to unlock. My stomach twists:

I've burnt my palm. It hurts.

"Fuck."

"Everything okay?" Mark waves a hand between me and my phone.

"Katie's burnt herself."

I reply to her with: *Freeze it with cold water and then wrap with Clingfilm.*

"Nothing serious?"

It could be. "No, she's fine."

"I'm taking Emma to Chiquito. That's why I need you to stay behind," he says through a mouthful of biscuit, crumbs showering over all the paperwork.

"Wait, what?" I say. "Can't you just close up early if it's a special occasion?" The words haven't fully left my tongue when I begin to regret them.

Mark's eyes harden. He laughs like there's phlegm in his throat. "Not special. I can take my wife out whenever. Hopefully will put a stop to her constant moaning about us not spending enough time together-"

I can see the red-eye staring at us. It's a good job Emma isn't able to press a button for a running commentary to go with the silent movies.

"-So I need you to stay and write up the accounts. Bills gotta be paid. What kind of manager would I be to lose a few hours of quality trade?"

You mean just on the off chance Mr Jones comes in for what will be his third box of Marlboros today, I think to myself.

An image of Katie folded up on the sofa in pain suddenly crosses my eyes. And then a clip of her grip missing the kettle and crying out gets stuck on loop.

The weight of Mark's hand on mine knocks me out of my stupor. "Follow me," he says cocking his head around back. I check the clock – 4:45pm; Emma will be getting the kids' tea ready. I wait a beat before abandoning the register and following him.

I find him three cages down with a leg against the wall – his favourite blind spot, where no camera or convex mirror will reach. As soon as I'm in the perfect proximity, he grabs my top and slams me round into the wall – "You need me, Lizzy" – his arms falling on either side – hands pressed into the brick, caging me in. I look to the floor.

Mark pushes off the wall to tuck both hands up under his pits. "I hire you because I care about you, and the welfare of your sister. I don't get how you'd want to jeopardise that by even suggesting I shut up shop early."

We linger in silence until Mark shifts, his eyes trained on me as he digs deep and rummages in his back pocket, pulling out a Snickers bar to wave under my nose, luckily still in the wrapper.

"Wouldn't it be a pity if a crumb of this bar found its way down your throat? Word would get out that you're in hospital. 'Silly Lizzy misplacing her EpiPen. Again', they'd say. And then the social will be knocking on your door because some Good Samaritan tipped them off."

I choke when Mark pushes the Snickers under my chin. "You're going to pretty up all the accounts and lock up tonight."

I weigh up the reality of Katie at home on the sofa, tending to that burn with my measly methods, because I can't always afford to stock our home first-aid kit; and then I line it up against the same reality, but I change the backdrop to a children's home, where she's napping soundlessly, hand bandaged from a quick trip to A&E - the pain has been numbed. Selfish as I am, I know what reality to pick. Every time.

Mark brings my mind back with a harsh, "Capisce?"

"Yeah," I say breathless.

"Have them recorded as a spreadsheet by the time I get back?"

I nod.

He shakes his head with a smile on his face, depositing the Snickers on a cage. "Actually, lock up at ten. Spend some time with Katie."

"Really?"

"Really. Sometimes I forget how lucky I am to have an employee like you. Am I right?"

I can't stop myself from pecking him on the cheek before going for my toilet break. I don't want him to take back what he said. An extra hour with Katie is better than nothing.

***

I'm leafing through a travel magazine when my phone vibrates. I close the laptop lid.

Burn is blistering.

And then:

Dont want 2 worry u.

I close my eyes, sigh heavily. I type, *How big is it?*

About the size of an Oreo, comes the reply.

There's nothing in the first-aid kit, I'm sorry.

It hurts.

I look to the clock. It's just gone seven.

Can you wait until ten? Mark is letting me lock up an hour early.

Please Liz. I'm scared.

I turn on the stool, eyeing the selection of dressings we stock. The cardboard cuboids have accumulated dust. I snatch a box of self-adhesive dressing. I don't get paid until next week.

Please please Lizzy.

I begin pushing together loose papers splayed over the counter, slide the laptop in its designated slot under the counter. I hover for a second, thinking. Surely, Mark will understand.

I'm coming, Katie.

***

The minimart has been open an hour when I rush in.

"Sorry I'm late."

"No biggie," Mark replies from behind the register. "Katie get off to school okay?"

"Yeah." I squeeze past Mark to take my spot on the stool.

"Glad to hear she's feeling better." I stiffen when he begins to finger the medical supplies on the shelf.

"Just a minor burn. She thought it had blistered. Turns out it was just *really* red. That's little sisters for you."

I eye Mark as he walks to the door. He flips the hanging sign on the chain. I hear the lock latch.

13

"Out the back?" I ask.

He nods, and I lead the way.

The odd expression on his face troubles me a little, but I can hear his footsteps behind so I push it to the back of my mind.

When we're clear in our blind spot, Mark pushes a finger to my lips. "I've just had Mr Jones in, throwing obscenities at me that he couldn't get his Marlboros last night. Any idea why that might have been?"

"He must have come after ten."

"I thought so too, until I checked the cameras."

"I was about to tell you. Katie-"

"Can't trust stupid teenage girls." He's patting at his jean pocket. My throat feels like the centre of a Party Ring. "I said close at ten. Want to tell me why the cameras went from you working hard behind the desk to leaving at seven coat-clad and all, and not returning?"

"I-"

"Don't even try it." He pulls a Snickers from his pocket. "I specifically told you to stay here. We're down at least a tenner because of your selfishness... And the missing pack of dressing. You didn't think I'd notice you're stealing from us?"

"Look, I'm sorry," I say, running my hand up his side and underneath his collar. I then initiate a kiss, just how he likes it. There's a dull thump of the chocolate hitting the floor.

Minutes later, something doesn't feel right. My lips are tingling, my tongue feels furry. Saliva is building in my mouth and I can't swallow.

"Oh, that's right, I was feeling a little peckish this morning." He harshly wipes at his lips. Stuffing his hand in his other pocket he fishes out a scrunched wrapper. My eyes widen when I catch a glimpse of that familiar dark-blue, blocked print.

"Katie... burn..." My back slides down the wall until I hit the floor, collapsing onto my side. I have to stay awake. I look down to my hands, the pinky-red hundreds and thousands are spreading.

Mark pulls one of my EpiPen's from his pocket. How did he manage to snatch that from my backpack?

He's crouching. I feel sick. Dizzy. Wheezing. My throat feels like the centre of a Polo mint.

Why is he stalling? Why isn't he injecting the EpiPen in my thigh?

I throw my arm out in front, hoping that the convex mirror reflects my wrist to the red-eye.

His next words are like another peanut to my lips. "You *need* this job, don't you?"

~o~

Roasted Breaths is different to my other works that are predominantly set in a dystopia or futuristic universe. I wanted to challenge myself by writing something that was the opposite of my usual style. I knew I wanted to explore sexual harassment and manipulation aimed at a young girl, who was the sole carer for her younger sister, and I knew I wanted to set my story in the workplace. But I needed something, an image, to higher the stakes. The image of a Snickers bar being used as an improvised-weapon came to me during a supermarket trip. What followed was the idea that would form the basis of my story: What if the young girl had a peanut allergy and was constantly threatened by her boss with Snickers to keep her in line? I vacillated the idea of a supermarket as the setting but soon came to realise that a minimart/corner shop would be more practical due to its minimal staff, and smaller scope - a suffocating environment that would enforce my running theme of asphyxiation.

A recurring motif of juxtaposing the action and feeling of breathing to confectionary soon became apparent as a fitting creative decision to introduce Lizzy's allergy gradually. The similes of Lizzy's throat feeling like a 'doughnut', a 'Party Ring' and then a 'Polo' enhance the constriction of her airways. And assist when I was crafting the language to be somewhat childish. Although Lizzy is older than her sister, she is still legally a child. I found it important to raise questions for the reader on why she is working in such a shop when she should be in school, and where Lizzy and Katie's parents might be. I wanted that sense of ambiguity.

Since starting university, I have branched out in writing within other mediums, such as radio writing and screenwriting. In my second year, I found my love for the short story. I have no immediate plans but I am open to expanding *Roasted Breaths* into perhaps a novel. The young adult protagonist is at the forefront of the majority of my writing, and is the point of view I enjoy reading from the most. The fragility of memory is one of my favourite subject matters to write about and how that sense of memory loss or erasure impacts the protagonist. I plan to continue writing in all forms, focusing on the first of a young adult series of novels I have in mind.

ISABEL MARTIN
WINDOW SEAT

Isabel Martin grew up with a love of writing and storytelling, and now studies English Literature with Creative Writing at the University of East Anglia. She has been included in the 2016 Young Writers' Anthology, and two editions of the UEA Undergraduate anthology.

Day 363

He pulls his sleeve over his hand, gives the window a wipe. All he seems to do is smear the dirt around, but he squints through the speckled glass. Figures hunch over in the rain, crawling like hooded beetles, umbrellas open like wings.

8.03.

Two minutes, give or take.

She has been late four times so far. Three times, she arrived at 8:09. Once, it had been 8:12. Presumably, she had missed her usual bus, and been forced to get the next one. But usually, she was loyal to her routine. His routine.

He watches and waits, hands cupped around his mug – tepid, half-empty. The table is patterned with brown rings. Maybe some of them are his. God knows when they last cleaned the place, and he's never seen anyone else here, in his spot. Window seat, tucked away in the corner, out of the yellow glow dribbling from the low-hanging bulbs.

He tips the mug, contemplates the sandy dregs of the tan liquid.

One minute. Unless she has missed her bus, which would not be like her at all. It has happened before, yes, but normally she is perfectly punctual, and those bad days are the rare ones. Days best forgotten; his pounding heart and sweaty palms, the bile rising in his throat for fear that he has missed her.

He wonders about her name, sometimes. He thinks of her as a Charlotte, but he is not sure why. He has a soft spot for C-names. Maybe she is Christine. Or Clara. Or…

He looks up at the faint rumble, the rattling of the window pane. The stream of commuters pours out, heading off for the station. She is one of the last to leave the bus, as always. She lets others off before her. She is polite.

She must be in a rush today, because she does not stop for a copy of the Metro. She has disappeared into the station within twenty seconds.

He clings to the moment while it lingers. Waits until the ebb of people has died down. Makes his way to the counter for the bill.

He will be back, of course. 6.24pm. Ten hours, nineteen minutes.

It is going to be a long day.

363 days since he began. Since the first time he saw her. She had worn the red coat with the deep pockets, and her black boots. Grey tights – woollen, perhaps, although it had been hard to tell, sat across the road in the café. It would make sense, being Autumn. She has repeated the outfit recently, with the resurgence of the colder months. The purple scarf, knotted tightly at her throat.

Charlotte.

Two days. Two days until their first anniversary. He is going to mark the occasion, although he is not sure how, not yet.

They know him here. They set his tea down, at his place, before he has even taken off his coat. The girl smiles at him as she puts the cup down, but he waves her away impatiently, his heart juddering for the split second that her arm obscures his view. He is not here for them, for any of these little people. They used to try to make conversation. That stopped a while ago. They glance at him from time to time. They pretend they're not doing it, pretend they're concentrating on smearing the grime around the surfaces with the cloth that probably hasn't been washed since he started coming. It doesn't bother him. They may as well take an interest in their only regular.

He almost misses her today. Her head is bent, hat pulled low, her hair covered. He only recognises her by the jacket – the denim one, not the red. She has worn it throughout most of the month, in the mild weather.

He spends his days longing for the evenings. In the evenings there is nothing, usually, for her to rush for. On the worst days, the bus is there waiting, when she emerges from the station. She runs, and his heart catches in his throat and then she is gone before he can register what has happened. When there is a wait, though – those are the days that he savours, the days that he longs for. He will sit up a little straighter, craning his neck and watching her watch the road. When the bus, inevitably, arrives and snatches her away from his gaze, he holds her in his mind until his cup is drained and he no longer has any reason to stay put. Then he goes home and waits for the morning.

Day 364

8.05 comes and goes. 8.06. 8.07.

It is 8.15 when he realises that the back of his neck is slick with sweat. Her bus has come and gone, and another. Another.

The empty cups begin to clutter the table, but nobody comes to clear them.

8.51. She has never been this late before. He waits. He waits all morning, and then he waits some more.

He should be at work. She has delayed him before, on the bad days, but today…today, they will simply have to do without him. She will be here, he tells himself. Perhaps she has an appointment. Perhaps she has taken the morning off. Perhaps…perhaps… There are any number of reasons for her lateness, but she will be here. He will not leave until he has seen her.

She cannot abandon him. She cannot. She cannot.

He is hungry. The emptiness grates away at his stomach under his jacket, but he will not risk the food here. He does not want to change his pattern, in any case. Anything could throw off his pattern. Her pattern. He will stay here and he will wait.

They put another lukewarm mug in front of him without his asking. He ignores it.

He knows that she will not be there that evening. But he lingers until closing time. When he stands up to leave, he has to stamp his feet to regain the feeling in his legs. His tea is cold and untouched.

Day 365

He did not sleep last night. He has to see her. He cannot have another lost day.

Today is the day to make up for lost time.

One year. It is fitting, in a way. What better day to act than their first anniversary?

This morning, he walks past the café. They will miss his custom, but there are other things occupying his thoughts. He crosses the road and makes his way towards the bus stop. Inside his jacket pocket, he strokes the edges of his Oyster card, shivering as he rubs the smooth plastic. He is ready, and he will not move until he sees her.

8:05.

She is on time again today. Perfectly punctual. He springs to his feet as she strides past. He charges after her, terrified to lose her amongst the harried crowd, elbowing his way through suits and briefcases, listening fearfully for the rush of the train. He is red faced and breathless by the time he reaches the platform but – she is there. Stood at the far end, away from the cluster of strategically placed individuals stood exactly where the doors will open. He sidesteps his way towards her, hoping – if her carriage is not too crowded, then perhaps – he barely dares to think it, it makes his throat constrict – he will be able to sit next to her? Or – no – perhaps the carriage will be full, commuters packed in like sardines, and he will have no choice but to squeeze himself in after, to brush against her as her reaches for the bar to balance himself. To smell her hair, to hear her breathing. He shudders with excitement as the train pulls up, steps on after her. She slips into the last available seat and his heart sinks but it is not the end, he is here now, with his sights set on her, and he is not going anywhere – at least, unless she does.

London Bridge. It is not the stop that he had imagined. He had pictured her departing at Kensington, stepping into a little office overlooking the gardens, the palace. She does not belong here, slotting in among the smartly dressed individuals, their worlds of coffee machines and paperwork and computers. He is almost disappointed.

Almost. There are more important matters to deal with.

He does not lose her until she disappears into the office building, swiping a card against a panel by the door. He cranes his neck, looking for another way in. He takes a tentative step towards the crowd, wondering whether he can squeeze through the barrier after one of the power-walking office workers...but the doors are too fast, sliding shut within seconds, the gleaming glass taunting at him with its smart little click as it shuts him out again. He is locked out, yes, but at least he is close to her – this will have been the most time they have spent together, he realises – and she will leave the building eventually. When she does, who knows what will happen? He quivers at the thought.

It will be worth the wait. It will. He will make sure of that.

He settles himself inside the bus shelter. Barely ten paces from the entrance, he has a clear view of the door. When she comes to him, he will be ready.

As the hands of his watch edge towards midday, his heart begins to race. He gets to his feet. She will be out soon, surely. He makes his way back to the entrance, sidestepping a man who is stood blocking his path, holding a bag from the sandwich shop on the corner. He should have brought her something, he realises now, but it is too late to do anything, in case he misses her.

The crowds begin to leave the building.

They spill from the sliding doors like ants, piling out to cafes and parks and sushi bars. It is 12.37 when she steps out of those doors. She has left her bag behind, holding only her purse, and she is glancing around. She looks up, smiles, and there she is, walking, walking towards him and he is ready, this is what he has been waiting for and somehow, somehow, she knew, and –

And she is not looking at him. Someone nudges past him and there is a man, a man in his way, blocking his view of her and – no, he is with her, he is with her, his hand clinging limpet-like, to hers.

He flinches and recoils, sickened. They glance at him, warily, and he wonders if she knows, if she can see his pain, if she knows what she has done, what she is doing to him. The slimy bastard his arm around his companion (her name, what is her name?) and she does not pull away. Bile rises in his throat as they hurry past. Still, he watches. He watches until they are gone. She is gone. More than that; she is stolen. He cannot scrub that bastard from his mind, his slimy grip, his smug smile, as if he knew, knew that he had taken what did not belong to him.

He had planned to linger, to cram himself into her train at the end of the day, but he cannot bear the thought of seeing the two of them together again. He tries to think of her, of her alone, as she should be, but it is them now. Them.

He boards the train, heads back to the café where his tea is waiting.

He watches from his window, of course he does. But it feels different today. Hollow. When the waitress sets down his second cup, he looks up to grunt his thanks. She has a pretty face. He has never noticed before; he has had other things occupying his mind. He glances down to her name tag. Carla.

He has a soft spot for C names.

Day 1

He heads down the street propelled by a new purpose. In his mind, he repeats her name like a mantra. Carla, Carla, Carla.

~o~

Window Seat started with the image of the café in the opening of the story. I played on the idea of people-watching, on what would happen were this to be taken to extreme lengths. The diary layout came from this, and I was able to get into the mind of someone whose perspective of reality is entirely distorted. His day revolves around a woman he has never met, to the point where he feels that he has complete ownership over her – but when she "betrays" him (in his mind at least), he is able to switch to a new victim as though she never existed. He is entirely arbitrary, his next inevitable obsession based solely on a name. It was a bizarrely enjoyable experience to write a character who is decidedly creepy, particularly cycling back to the start of a new fixation with somebody else – one of what could be an endless stream of victims.

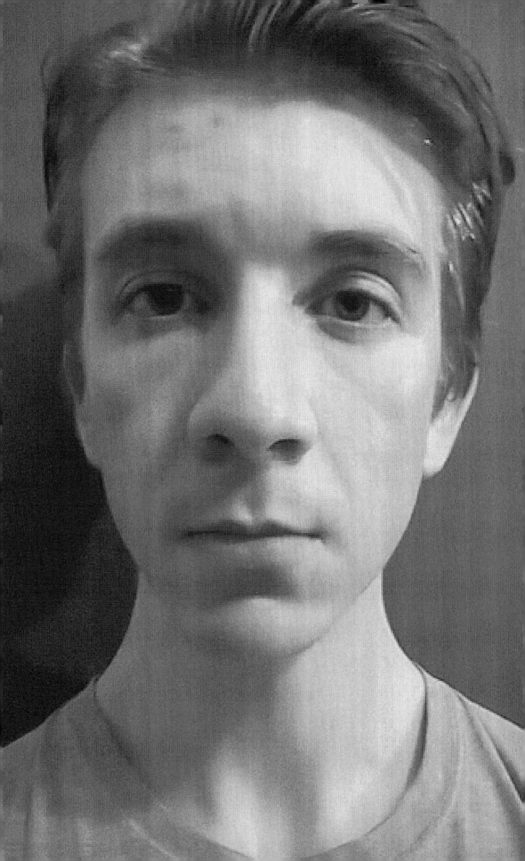

MICHAEL CONROY
NO PLACE LIKE HOME

Michael Conroy is a 22-year-old writer studying Creative Writing at The Manchester Writing School. He is currently working on what he hopes will be his magnum opus, however, his tendency towards procrastination, plus his many existential crises, often get in the way of his writing. Unfortunately, he can't give you any details as he's afraid you might steal his ideas. It's nothing personal. He plans to one day go insane, like Poe, or turn to the bottle, like Hemingway. Whether he finishes his novel or not remains a mystery. So the story goes.

"Dammit!" the Old Man curses, feeling his thumb crushed between hammer and nail. He drops the hammer. It lands with a soft thud against the grassy earth. He sucks his thumb and winces.

Like a damn baby. Can't even swing a goddamn hammer anymore.

He shakes his hand about, trying to cast off the pain. It subsides to a dull throb. He leans forward against the fence and sighs.

The sun casts its warm glow over everything. The scent of fresh air, corn and wheat, and grass is all around. Horses nicker and canter about the field, others grazing, some drinking from the trough. Behind them, the plains go on forever – the yellow and brown wall of trees, just the suggestion now of that which was verdant and green a few months ago.

The mountains stand over it all, silver peaks surveying everything that is beneath the great blue expanse overhead.

He turns around, leans back against the fence, watches the small circular windmill on top of the house turn gently in the breeze. He shields his eyes from the sun and marvels at how tanned his arms are. Scratching his head, hair white as a cloud, he wonders what his face must look like. A damn Injun or some such thing.

For a moment, he thinks he sees something in the cornfield a little way from the house. But it's nothing. He doesn't notice the dog strolling up to him until it stops, looks up at him expectantly.

"Hello there. What brings you all the way to these parts, eh?" he laughs. The dog ruffs at him and wags its tail, tongue hanging from its mouth.

The Old Man ruffles its furry head and pats it on the back, admiring the mix of black, white and tan, colours all here and there like on a paint palette.

"Shall we go, Mac? Are we done, boy?" The dog barks and jumps up at him. "Well, that's that then. Let's go, boy." Springing back to the ground, the dog bounds off in the direction of the house. Turning back, it stops and waits for him.

Picking up his hammer by its wooden handle, the Old Man moseys towards the house as well, though not too fast because his joints are hurting again.

"Let's hope I don't injure myself anything serious on the way back," he says, knowing the dog won't understand the humour behind the remark.

Inside, he sets the hammer down and kisses Norma on the cheek. The dog enters the kitchen as well, and pads about, snaking in and out under the chairs and table and around their ankles. The dog returns outside.

"Hey, there, handsome. Did you mend the fences?" Norma says, preparing lunch. The hot stew casts off steam into the air, trailing the scent of herbs, meat, and vegetables.

"Why, yes, I managed to make some room in my busy schedule to fix the fences. Is there anything else I can do to please you, wife?" he says, hugging her from behind.

"Oh, well, so many things, but you could call the girls in for lunch – if you can find the time in your *busy schedule*," she says, and smiles.

He smiles too. Leaning outside, hanging from the door frame, he calls out to his two daughters. They don't hear him at first for their laughter, but he calls again. Playing on the tree swing, the older of the two jumps off, while the other, a little younger, stops chasing the dog around on the grass, and both run inside after their father.

They sit down at the old wooden table to enjoy their stew, but first thank the Lord before eating.

"I wish you two would be more careful outside. You'll ruin your dresses," says Norma.

"But we can't help it if they just get messy," says Abigail.

"Now don't talk back to your mother," the Man says, tickling his daughter's neck.

"Stop it, Daddy," she giggles.

"Tickle me too!" says the younger daughter Maddie, her mouth full.

"Not at the dinner table, girls. Now eat your food," says Norma.

Mac the dog barks and stands up against the Man's chair, panting.

"Mac wants some too," giggles Maddie.

"Down, boy, down. Mac has his own food," says the Man. Mac whines his assent, drops down to the floor, wanders off outside.

"Daddy, can we play with the lambs later?"

"No, Maddie. What have I told you? Remember? They're livestock, not pets."

"Yeah, Maddie," says Abigail, sticking her tongue out.

"Shut up, Abbie," Maddie retorts with a sour face.

"Now, girls, quiet, and don't be mean to each other. Eat your food before it gets cold, then you can go back outside and play."

"Listen to your mother, girls," the Man says.

He smiles at Norma. She smiles back.

After lunch, the girls play outside again, the dog as well. Like a good husband, the Man offers to help his wife with the dishes, but she insists he go and relax. She appreciates the thought, though, and kisses him.

He enters the living room, but looks back at his wife. Watches her, loves her from a distance. He likes the way she ties her hair back with a scarf like older women do.

The girls are 6 and 7, and, yet, Norma still looks like one herself. So youthful, so beautiful. That gingery hair, those russet-olive stones for eyes, like a forest at dusk.

He hopes she won't leave him when he gets older.

The rustic living room is filled with all the lovely small things they own, and that make his wife so happy. In the cabinet, the good china and silver cutlery – both gifts from Norma's mother. On the floor, the beautiful area rug she loves so much, which she had bought from a Native American man who wove it himself, expending many tireless hours for its making, or so he told them at the time. The many plants she likes to tend, orchids and cacti and evergreen – and outside, even more, roses and sumacs, honeysuckles and salvias. And then the Man's modest collection of books, plus the wireless radio that sits atop the mantelpiece, and all the happy pictures of himself and his family that adorn the walls.

A glint of light catches his eye. He moves closer, squinting to see what it is.

A broken window. Glass crunches beneath his boot heel. It litters the floor under the pane, and the sun streams in, glinting off it all rainbow-like. "How the hell . . . Norma, we've got a broken window here."

No answer. "Norma?" He turns around.

The kitchen is empty. He moves forward but stops again, stares at the strange wooden box with the glass window that has materialised in his living room. "What in heaven . . ." What is it? Where had it come from? He's never seen anything like it, but— No, of course.

The television set.

He scratches the back of his head. Turns away. Turns back. Runs a hand through his brown hair. It doesn't belong there. "We don't get a television until 1950 . . ."

He turns around.

"I – I don't live here anymore . . ."

"Yoo-hoo, Francis, be a good boy and put your toys away, will you?"

"Mother?" he says, as he does as he's told.

"What's wrong, baby? You look all confused," she says as she picks him up and kisses him on the cheek. The fabric of her dress is coarse, not like her skin, so soft and warm against his own. He inhales the floral scent of her perfume as she holds him tight.

She puts him down and disappears into another room. He looks around, puzzled.

His father enters the room. "Hey, sport, how ya doing? You put your toys away like your mother said? There's a good boy." His father grins, and the corners of his moustache turn up. He tussles the boy's hair and pats him on the shoulder before disappearing into another room.

". . . I don't live here anymore . . ."

A sound, of something approaching him from behind. He spins around to face it, but there is nothing there. "Girls? Norma?"

"Yes, honey?" asks Norma. "You all right?"

He looks at her.

"Honey? Why are you staring at me?"

"Uh, nothing. It's fine, darling."

She smiles, leaves him. He can't seem to remember what she looks like.

He looks around. The house is different now. The furniture is different, everything modern, chic, as they say. He has the impression that there are many other houses just like it. The television is in the same place. *I Love Lucy* is on. In their black-and-white world behind the screen, Lucy, who doesn't speak Spanish, as her mother-in-law does, tries to find the words for chicken and rice.

"Daddy, you're in the way of the TV," says Abigail.

"Yeah, Daddy," says Maddie, and both girls shriek with laughter as Lucille Ball starts strutting about like a chicken.

Static. The channel changes. Dramatic western music. John Wayne with an eyepatch. An old man now. Not a cowboy anymore. *Bold talk for a one-eyed fat man.*

The music fades.

"Daddy!" the girls whine.

He turns around. "Sorry girls, I— Oh god!" He retreats from the two small skeletons on the couch. Bones old and weathered. Posed like people, curled up, holding one another.

"Girls . . ."

Empty eye sockets. Faint scent of burnt hair. Burnt meat.

They don't answer. Sit staring. At nothing at all.

"Oh my god!"

He turns, looks around. The television is gone. So is most of the wall. Demolished. So is most of the house. Scorched black. Dust pervades. He looks

31

back at the couch on its side, up against one of the few walls left standing. The skeletons are gone.

He can see outside, but there is too much dust to make anything out.

He rushes into the kitchen. "Norma?" No answer. Kitchen just rubble, ceiling collapsed, table gone, cabinets ripped out. Nothing left. Debris clatters as he treads over it.

He goes back. Fallen bricks clop and thud against the floor as he pushes through. But he can't get out the front door for fallen timber and toppled bricks. He heads back into the kitchen, runs outside through the back door, and around to the front of the house.

The empty streets mutter to themselves. The wind blows away the dust and ash that saturates the air.

Standing on the dusty lawn, where the grass no longer grows, his legs become weak, almost give out under him. He steadies himself.

His eyes run over the many duplicate houses in their ruined suburban neighbourhood, blackened and reduced to cinders, frames exposed and collapsed. His eyes sweep down the street at the cars turned over and destroyed, a lone bicycle, scorched black, red with rust, in the middle of the sidewalk. Rubble lies everywhere, concrete and asphalt cracked and torn up, as if by the power of God.

He brings his hands up to his face, shuts his eyes, shakes his head as if to make it all go away. He runs back into the house. Finds himself inside another one.

He steps back, gasping. Steps forward again, looks around.

His childhood home. Not for a very long time. But he knew it would be safe here, somehow. Safe from what? He doesn't remember. He's old, older than he knows now. He forgets so many things. But he survives. That's all you can do. The only thing he's sure of anymore.

A thick layer of dust coats the floors and furniture inside the old building. What little is left is broken or falling to pieces. The windows that aren't smashed are boarded up. Glass, paper, leaves litter the wooden floors. The dull sepia light from outside permeates the gloom. Dust motes shine like dying stars in the murky atmosphere.

He heads to the kitchen, and out through the back door. The front is boarded up.

Outside, the house is decrepit and worn with age. A dusty fog sweeps all around him. Not much left of the old homestead. But the land is not completely barren. Some of the farmhouses he's seen are still intact. Not like in the cities.

Some trees survive, starved of sunlight, dying of thirst. Beneath them, long yellow grass sways in the wind, whispering. The crops are all dead. The horses are gone.

He hears a familiar bark. The dog emerges from the brush and wanders up to him.

The dog stops before him, panting.

"Are – are you real?" the Old Man says.

The dog looks at him, tilting its head to one side.

He draws his pistol, points it. "I said, are you real, dammit!"

The dog whines and runs off.

He calls after the dog, "Come back, please!" Hears only the wind. Beyond that, only silence. He holsters his gun, hesitates, rushes forward.

He runs through the trees and the brush. Grass rustles and branches shake as he pushes on through. He stops at a clearing, thinks he can hear the dog for a moment, but it's just him who's panting. He starts forward again. Twigs and dead leaves crunch underfoot as he hurries on through the wood to then leave it behind, coming to the foot of a large hill.

He clambers up, boots scraping and sliding against the earth, struggling in the steepest places, though he knows he could have done it with ease when a younger man. Over rocks and roots, and the bones of some dead animal like a fox or coyote, only larger, until he reaches the top.

He looks down on the wasteland below. Skeletal trees dotted about on the plains. The ruined city and crumbling highways in the distance. Skyscrapers toppled and reduced to powder, not a light to be seen now, a city of dust and shadow. Faint impressions remain where the roads used to be down on the plains, winding about far below, threading across the earth like ley lines.

The landscape is muted. There are only suggestions of colour.

The clouds hang like dead things, spectres of decay, grey-brown, tinged with green.

The Old Man cannot see the sky beyond.

"Now I remember," he says.

The wind whistles past his ears on the hilltop as he looks down. Wondering how far up he is. How far the fall would be.

He looks towards the horizon. Not knowing what to do or say, or whether to do or say anything at all, he remains quiet. It all seems unreal, a background painting in an old film.

The wind is bracing on the hilltop, but he does not move. The light is fading, yet he stays. He finds himself tired, awful tired.

The Old Man and his spidery legs are wracked from all the exertion.

He doesn't quite know how he got here.

It doesn't matter. He enjoys getting away from it all, just being alone with good old Mother Nature. He breathes a sigh of satisfaction, smiles to himself, doesn't feel up to heading on home just yet.

So he sits there a while, and wonders where the dog got to.

~o~

When it comes to writing, my interests are very literary and speculative. While I have a soft spot for certain genres, I tend not to limit myself to writing within their conventions. Writing is amoral and can be about anything or nothing at all. Some of the best books are.

I marvel at the work of Vladimir Nabokov, Virginia Woolf, Franz Kafka, and Kurt Vonnegut, among many others, but I'm also fascinated by anything Western or post-apocalyptic. Cormac McCarthy's *The Road* and Charles Portis's *True Grit* are two of my favourite books, both of which had an influence on my story 'No Place Like Home'. The title, of course, comes from *The Wizard of Oz*, which, like my story, also explores ideas of dreams and the nature of reality.

I've written my fair share of rubbish, but this piece is one of the better ones. I find free writing to be useful when stuck for words and this story is a product of such an exercise. The idea came to me, as they often do, out of nowhere. An old man struggling to hold onto the past in a bleak post-apocalyptic landscape. I went with it and now here we are.

Whether or not the story is successful is not up to me to say, but I wanted to explore the malleability of memory and perception through a story about loss and loneliness. The ending, I think, is bleak yet poignant. Art, particularly stories, allows us both an escape and an experience of catharsis in our unhappy world.

HANNAH RETALLICK

SEARCHING THE SLATE

Hannah Retallick is a twenty-three-year-old from Anglesey, North Wales. She and her two brothers were home-educated by their mother. Hannah is working on her second novel, writes short stories, keeps a journal and a blog, and would love to be a professional writer. She plays the trombone, piano and clarinet, has taught brass since she was fifteen, and has conducted her local training bands for five years. Hannah studied with the Open University, graduating with a First-class honours degree, BA in Humanities with Creative Writing and Music, and has begun an MA in Creative Writing.

The day is slowly waking up, sun breaking through the thick clouds. Rachel and her family wander from their house on the high street to a path which runs along the edge of Llyn Padarn. The slate-grey lake is turning blue. Llanberis nestles behind them, crowded with cafés, B&Bs and brightly coloured houses.

'Mum, can you tell Cariad to share?' says Joe.

Cariad, a five-year-old with strawberry-blonde hair, munches Rainbow Drops, and Joe nearly trips over her heels.

'Joe, please stop walking so close to her. Go the other side of me,' says Rachel, flicking a long strand of brown hair out of her face.

Cariad strangles the top of the packet as her brother lunges for it. 'No,' she whines.

'Hey, you've had loads already!'

'They're mine!'

'Joe, stop it,' says Rachel. 'Leave your sister alone.'

'Please!'

'I said stop. They're hers – she bought them with her own money…Your lips might fall off if you keep pouting.'

Joe stomps on ahead and he responds with his favourite refrain: 'It's not fair.'

'What's not fair?' asks their father, Terry. 'You've already spent your half-term money.'

'Yeah, but the yo-yo broke…'

'Well, that's too bad.'

Joe isn't much bigger than Cariad but it seems as if he is. His light-brown hair needs a cut – it creeps far down his neck, spilling over the red polo shirt collar. He keeps hitching up his jeans, which Rachel hopes he'll grow into soon, and Cariad skips after him as she always does. He turns when she catches up and grabs at her hair. She squeals.

'Right, enough is enough,' says Terry, squeezing Rachel's arm before jogging over to the quarrelling pair. He pulls them apart and takes them strongly by the hand. Cariad nuzzles into his side. Joe quietens.

'Now, your mother's going to have a nice birthday. So we'll have no more arguing – got it?'

'Yeah. Sorry, Dad,' says Joe. 'Please can you let go?'

Terry releases his hand and squats down to their level. 'Right, listen up, troops. I need you to go on a mission. Mum would love a perfect white stone for her birthday and I want you to look on that little beach over there. Let's see if you can find one in all that slate!'

'Okay,' they say.

'Off you go, then – and keep together.'

'Don't go too near the water,' Rachel calls after the running figures as her husband returns. 'Thanks, Terry.'

Terry has taken the day off from Padarn Watersports Centre to spend it with the family. A long lie-in had been in the plan but the children wouldn't allow it. Terry had kept them quiet for as long as possible. When Rachel finally admitted to being awake she was greeted with a tray of breakfast and shouts of, 'Happy birthday!' They jumped onto the bed, slopping weak tea onto the tray, while their amused father watched from the doorway.

Rachel and Terry stroll along, hand in hand. She looks at his mop of light hair flopping back and forth in the wind. He wears a T-shirt, as always, though Rachel is bundled up in a navy-blue parka. His skin, with its deep all-year tan, is goose-bumped, which doesn't seem to bother him.

When they had first met it was Terry's warm-brown eyes and dark lashes that drew Rachel in. She had never thought they could look more beautiful but today they do, as he looks towards his children who search the slate.

'You're an amazing dad,' says Rachel.

Terry looks like he did when she complimented Liverpool FC.

'What?' she says. 'Why do you look so suspicious?'

'I'm not suspicious. Thanks…'

Rachel takes her hand away and warms it in her pocket.

'Are you okay?' Terry asks. 'Is there something you want to talk about?'

'No, I'm fine.'

Cariad crouches, studying the pebbles beneath her one by one, occasionally shuffling forward. Joe is overseeing the operation, leaning over to check on her progress, and filling up the front of his polo shirt. He wanders nearer the shoreline and flings a few stones as far as he can, as though trying to get them to the other side. One skims three times. His face shines as he turns to look at his father.

'It's been thirty-three years since…you know,' says Rachel. 'I was six. Six. The same age Joe is now. Can you imagine?'

'He's not going to lose me anytime soon, Rachel. I'll hang on for a little while longer!'

Rachel smiles and hooks her arm around his. 'If only we were in control of these things. You know, I was thinking last night how terrible it must have been for my mum. She had to work so hard to support us, and it was all so sudden…'

The two collaborators come running. Cariad reaches out her cold-reddened hand to Rachel, cupping a small white stone.

'Oh, that's beautiful!'

'Well done, sweetheart,' says Terry.

'Hey, that's not white,' says Joe, stones still sitting in his polo shirt hammock.

As water begins to dry from the stone's surface Rachel sees that there are veins of grey running through it.

'Oh, no, it isn't. Not completely,' she says, taking and rolling it in her palm. 'But thank you, Cariad, it's still beautiful.'

'It's not,' mutters Joe. 'It's ugly.'

Cariad's eyes fill with water and she pushes him. 'I hate you!'

'Mum! Now I've dropped all my stones, stupid girl!'

'Please don't start…'

'But Joe's being mean.'

'I said stop!'

'Come on, you two,' says Terry. 'If you want some of Mum's birthday cake you'd better stop fighting. Look, that's a perfect skimming stone – could you find me some more like this?'

Rachel's pocket vibrates and she draws out her ringing phone. Private number.

'Aren't you going to answer that?' asks Terry, picking up a piece of slate and skimming it across the water.

The mobile lies in her palm. 'I don't know who it is.'

'Answer, and then you will. Come on, don't be silly – if it's a cold-caller you can just hang up. Hey, kids, a bit further from the water, please.'

She takes a deep breath. 'Hello? Yes, Rachel Palmer speaking…Right…Oh my goodness. Okay…Okay, I'll be there as quick as I can.'

Rachel meets three pairs of concerned eyes.

Helen's eyes follow the tiny crack across the ceiling. Part of her still wants to get up for work. She stretches her arms back and taps the headboard with her fingertips, then curls back into a ball, wrapping her arms around her head. Beside her is an open work diary, filled with tiny writing. She has drawn a cross over the day.

Helen's bedroom is fitted with white wardrobes and drawers. The carpet that runs through the small house is pale grey and thin. Her feet are heavy as she climbs out of bed, walks into the adjoining bathroom and up to the big mirror. There is a smudge. She takes a cloth and polish from the glass-doored cabinet above the washbasin and wipes it clean.

Now Helen can see herself clearly. She stares into her green eyes and touches the dark rings beneath. No expensive eye-cream is a remedy for a naturally-deep eye-socket. Her fingers catch on knots as she runs them through her wavy bob. She picks up a hairbrush, slowly untangles her hair and replaces the brush parallel to the edge of the shelf, checking the time on her phone – 10:08.

She walks across the hall to the kitchen and boils the kettle, dipping a teabag into a mug of hot water and laying it on the teapot-shaped dish to use later. Three spoonfuls of sweetener.

Helen freezes in the hallway, her feet feeling pinned to the floor, as in a bad dream. The ceiling is low, far too low, and a dim bulb hangs from its centre. She feels as though someone is pushing down on her forcefully and she crouches down to the floor, leaning her back against the wall. The pale tea ripples.

The hallway is not unlike that of her childhood home, the dark hallway of the hostel her parents ran for walkers and climbers. It looked out towards an imposing slate heap. Helen sometimes thought she saw it creep closer at night, and when she screamed her dad would come and sit with her until she slept again, however long it took.

She remembers the day when they were to go on a family trip. She had gone upstairs to get Dad but he didn't want to come. Mum told her not to bother him anymore and promised that they would still enjoy themselves. The hostel had been quiet. It seemed to become quieter every day.

They returned early, Mum fumbling with the key in the big brown door. 'That lock…' she muttered, as always, flicking her long hair out of the way – it was so long she could almost sit on it. Helen had waited, pulling the white cardigan tightly around her shivering body, and drawing her hands into the sleeves. The door had finally opened with a creak. The keys had hit the floor and Helen inhaled sharply. She was turned around by her mum's strong hand. Then all she could see was slate.

There is a loud knock and a splash of tea jumps onto her pyjama trousers. She waits a moment. The knocker is persistent. Helen eventually opens the door to a tiny woman with energetically curly hair, and a large bunch of lilies wrapped in cellophane.

'Oh, hi, sweetie. I didn't mean to wake you – did I wake you?'

'No,' Helen replies, flatly. 'I was up.'

'So sorry to hear you're not well – Mr. Lewis told me.'

41

'News travels fast.'

'Only because I asked where you were,' says Kate. 'I can only stay for a sec – I'm on a double yellow.'

She pushes into the hallway and faces her. 'Now, Helen, what's the matter?'

'I'm just not well – I'm sure it'll pass.'

'Are you?' She tilts her head, eyes fixed on Helen. 'Look, I could barely clean your desk today – papers all out, just left in a mess. That's not you, sweetie, so don't try and tell me there's nothing to worry about.'

Helen's hands whiten as they grip the mug.

'These are for you,' says Kate, thrusting the flowers at her. 'Everyone at Russell & Russell sends their love.'

'You really didn't need to.'

'Look, Helen, I need to go, but I think you should talk to someone in your family or go to the doctor.'

'I don't have any family.'

Kate blinks repeatedly. 'I have to go,' she says, as she walks out. 'Please call me if you need anything.'

Helen shuts the door. She returns to her room and sits down on the bed, picking up the phone to check for messages, many of which have collected over the past few days.

Her heart jumps as the phone begins to ring. She recognises the number. It rings five times before she decides to answer.

'Hello.'

'Oh, Helen, thank you for picking up!' says Rachel.

'What do you want?'

Pause.

'I had a call from Ysbyty Gwynedd.'

Helen's whole body shivers.

'Helen…Mum has had a heart attack. Please come to the hospital.'

Helen bites the skin around her little finger. 'I don't think I can.'

'Oh, please. I'm sure you're as busy as always, but can't you put work aside for once?'

'Not really. You don't need me there.'

'No, you don't understand. Mum asked me to call you.'

Helen is quiet for a moment. 'She asked for me?'

'Yes, she asked for you, Helen…' Rachel's voice breaks. 'Helen, please come.'

'I…I suppose I can – if you really want me. But I won't be there for at least two hours.'

'Yes, I want you. Thank you,' she says. 'And Helen?'

'Yes?'

'Happy birthday.'

Helen's mouth dries up. 'You too.'

Rachel reaches out to touch her mother's hand. It's wrinkled and the nails are split and yellowing. Sue is a small woman, in every way. Her head is surrounded by white curls and rests on a clean pillow, eyelids flickering open and closed, as though not able to focus.

'Rachel…' she says.

'Yes?'

The curtains surrounding Sue's bed are drawn back, letting in the sunlight – most of the other patients have them closed. The light room smells of cleaning fluids and hand sanitizer, which churns Rachel's stomach.

Her mum frowns. 'I had such a strange dream.'

Rachel gets up from the armchair and kneels beside the bed. 'What was it about?'

'I don't know. There was grey, a lot of grey. I think perhaps I was trapped in a cave…or tunnels. There were memories…' She screws up her face. 'Dark and cold.'

The door opens slowly and a slight, pale figure enters, searching the Coronary Care Unit until her eyes come to rest. She is Rachel's reflection.

Rachel rises from the floor, her knees clicking. They stand looking at each other for a moment. Helen's hair has grown out since they last met, which suits her better than the cropped style she used to have. She is dressed in a fitted black jacket, with dark-jeaned legs, and walks slowly through the ward until they are face to face.

'Hello,' says Rachel. 'Thank you for coming.'

'Helen?' says Sue, squinting.

'Yes,' she replies.

Helen walks towards the bed and shuffles onto the hard cushion of the armchair. She sits down with her legs crossed and her back straight.

'How are you?' Sue asks.

'I'm okay, thanks. How are you?'

'As good as can be expected…'

'Yes, of course.'

The ward is hot and airless. Rachel rolls the sleeves of her loose, beige cardigan and gathers up her thick hair into a messy bun. They are next to the window and she watches the car park fill up, as visiting hours have begun for the rest of the hospital. They look like Joe's toy cars, sprawled across the carpet. The window is shut and the sun exposes circular smears from a cleaning cloth.

'How are the children?' Sue asks, suddenly, staring at the ceiling.

'Err, very well, thanks,' Rachel replies, with a glance at her sister. 'They've been on their half-term break this week. I'll be relieved when they go back to school on Monday. We had a walk by Llyn Padarn this morning – it's as beautiful as ever. We've been out and about as much as possible – they bounce off the walls and are at each other's throats all the time otherwise, which can be…'

'It's only natural,' she interrupts. 'It's their way of showing how much they love each other. You and Helen were like that once.'

'Were we?' asks Helen.

'No, I don't suppose you would remember. You were only little.' She sighs and shakes her head. 'So stupid…stupid and unaware.'

'Mum?' says Rachel.

'You ran about so freely, getting everything you wanted, while the world crumbled around you…' Sweat glistens on Sue's forehead.

Helen leans forward, resting an elbow on her thigh. She supports her head on a trembling fist.

Rachel steps forward. 'Maybe we should leave – she needs a rest.'

'She's the cat's mother!' says Sue. 'I'll rest when I'm buried in the ground.'

Helen smiles for the first time since she arrived. The skin around her eyes creases and it doesn't bounce back instantly. The smile disappears much more quickly.

Sue props herself up on the pillow, ignoring Helen's outstretched hand. 'Have you any idea what it was like? It's all very well for you, high-flying woman, and you, with your lovely Llyn Padarn walks.'

Sue begins to weep and Rachel crouches by the bed.

'I think I'll go,' whispers Helen.

'No, please don't,' says Rachel. 'Mum will be okay in a minute.'

'Llanberis…' Sue murmurs. 'I loved it too – the mountains, the lakes, the sunshine. He never told me it usually rained… and all that slate…cold, grey slate.'

'It's not so bad,' says Rachel, stroking her arm.

'What the hell do you know?' snaps Helen.

Sue barely seems to hear them. 'Oh, if only I'd kept quiet, suffered in silence, but no…'

'What are you talking about?' asks Rachel.

'I had to tell him every little grievance – foolish girl!'

A nurse enters the ward and walks over to them. 'Excuse me,' she says, with hands on bulging hips. 'It's supposed to be patient quiet-time now, so if you wouldn't mind…'

The hospital restaurant is busy. It's filled with doctors, a few visitors, and nurses dressed in blue or green. Rachel and Helen are sitting at a four-seat table, hands wrapped around cardboard cups of tea. They have placed themselves next to a partition with pale wooden slats, which cuts the restaurant in two, giving them some privacy from the busier half of the room. Rachel has a plate of chicken curry.

'It's been a while,' she says. 'How's work going? How are things in family law?'

Helen tucks a lock of hair behind her ear and tears into her yellow sweetener sachets. 'It's fine. Everything's good.'

'Are you sure?'

Helen leans back in her mint-green chair. 'What do you really want to know?'

'Okay…' Rachel says. 'Why did you answer my phone call?'

The green eyes flicker away for a moment and then settle on Rachel. Helen stirs her tea with a plastic spoon. 'What do you mean?'

'You know exactly what I mean,' says Rachel, hands shaking as her voice strengthens. 'I mean, why did you answer my call this time? I've been phoning you for weeks, months – you never answered or replied to my messages.'

One of the restaurant staff, dressed in an eggshell-blue uniform and mottled apron, passes them with a tray trolley.

'I'm sorry,' Helen whispers. 'I've been busy.'

'Busy,' says Rachel. 'You've been busy for as long as I can remember – too busy to talk to your sister.'

An old man at a nearby table turns to look at her. She lowers her voice. 'Look, Helen, I can tell you don't want to talk, but at least tell me why.'

'It's not that simple.'

Rachel's food is untouched. The grey tray has warped slightly, so she spins it gently with her fingertips as she watches her sister, who chews the edge of her cup.

'Rachel,' says Helen, a moment later. 'Do you remember Sara Brown?'

'Yes. I wonder how she is…Why do you ask?'

Helen shrugs. 'The two of you were really close when we were little, but you drifted apart. It happens.'

'If I saw her again she would still be my friend, she would still answer my calls…' Rachel shakes her head. 'It's not the same.'

She picks up Helen's plastic spoon and bends it back and forth. She faces a large window and looks up as an ambulance drives past. The curtains are old-fashioned and faded, topped by a frilly pelmet, and seem to belong in a cosy living room rather than a hospital eating area. They look strange against the wall's grey bricks. Dark and cold.

'I was thinking about Dad earlier,' says Rachel. 'It's thirty-three years today.'

'I know.'

'I was at Sara's that day, wasn't I?'

'Yes, you were – without me.'

Rachel's cup is full but the tea has stopped steaming. She takes a gulp. 'It was unkind of me to leave you on our birthday. When I found you crying on our doorstep I thought it was my fault.'

'You were wearing your little white dress, the one with the red sequins. You looked so happy. Then Mum came and…' Helen stops suddenly.

Rachel bends the spoon too far and it snaps in half. 'Brain tumour,' she whispers. 'I didn't even know what that was.'

'Neither did I. Rachel, have you never wondered how Mum found out the cause of death so quickly? How could...' She stops. 'But that's all in the past now.'

Rachel takes a deep breath. A single teardrop ripples her tea. 'No, it isn't.'

Helen stacks their used milk pots, pushing her three empty sweetener sachets into them, and begins to scrape bits of ingrained dirt from the wooden partition.

Rachel hits the table. 'Helen, stop!'

Her sister's hands freeze.

'Something else happened that day. Nothing has been the same since then, nothing – not you, not Mum...' She can't restrain the tears. 'I've always told myself it was the shock and the grief, but there's more to it, I know there is.'

Helen bites her index finger. There are tears in her eyes too.

'You know something I don't, don't you?' says Rachel, reaching out and grabbing her hand. 'Tell me what it is.'

'Oh, Rachel...' Helen leans closer and takes both of Rachel's hands in hers. They're cold. 'I didn't know how to say...'

'Tell me,' she repeats, in a whisper.

There is a clattering sound from the kitchen behind her as the staff clear up but it doesn't break their gaze.

'It was the day Dad died. Mum unlocked the door and began to walk in. Before I could follow she turned me around and pushed me outside. It was too late. I've never told her, Rachel.' Helen's lip trembles. 'I saw.'

'What? What did you see?'

'His body.'

'Oh, Helen, how horrible!'

She shakes her head. 'That's not it.'

'I don't understand. Tell me what else.'

Helen squeezes her hands tighter. 'His body was hanging from the light in the hallway. Hanging.'

'He...' Rachel blinks tears from her eyes.

'I have to talk to her,' says Rachel, striding down the corridor.

'It won't do any good,' says Helen, stopping her by the arm.

'She lied, Helen. Now look at us! What right did she have to keep us in the dark? What right did you have?'

'How could I have said?' says Helen. 'I was a child – I didn't understand.'

Rachel makes her way to the ward and pushes open the heavy doors. She enters and walks to the bed, feeling Helen's hand on her back. There is fear in her mother's wrinkle-surrounded eyes.

'I need to talk to you,' says Rachel.

'Oh!' says Sue. 'Oh, you're back. I was scared that you might have gone. I'm so sorry.'

Rachel swallows with difficulty. 'Mum.'

Sue's body relaxes into the pillow as they approach the bed. 'I thought you'd left without saying goodbye.'

'Of course not,' says Rachel.

As Sue's eyelids begin to droop her mouth pulls into a smile. 'That's all right, then,' she says. 'You wanted to say something, Rach?'

'I…' She stops. In front of her is a woman who is worn-out and attached to a monitor. Every movement puts pain into her face. 'No, it's nothing. You have a sleep now.'

'Just rest,' says Helen. 'Goodbye, Mum.'

Sue nods gently and her eyes shut. 'I love you…' she murmurs. 'Very much.'

The corridors are quiet and they walk together in silence until they reach the hospital entrance, where visitors trudge past.

'Helen…' says Rachel, stopping and turning to her sister. 'Are you going to come back?'

'I think so – hopefully tomorrow,' she says. 'You were right not to confront her.'

'Well, she seemed peaceful…'

'She did,' says Helen. 'It's best to leave her that way.'

'What about you?' says Rachel.

'I feel…relieved.'

Rachel takes her twin by the shoulders, drawing her in for a hug. The scent of Chanel No.5 drifts into her nostrils as they linger there for a moment.

Helen smiles as she pulls away. 'Goodbye, Rach,' she says. 'I'll see you very soon.'

Rachel watches her leave through the revolving doors. She sits on one of the seats which line the entrance, and breathes deeply and slowly to calm herself. Her pulse throbs.

Terry, flanked by Joe and Cariad, enters the hospital. The children laugh their way through the doors. Terry leans down and whispers for a moment and their faces become solemn. Rachel stands to greet them.

'How is she, love?' Terry asks, giving her a hug.

'Sleeping now. I think she'll be okay – the doctor seemed hopeful earlier.'

'Should I take the kids in?'

'Not now. She's asleep – I don't think we should disturb her. I'll go back after quiet time.'

'Okay, maybe we can all come tonight too…How are you holding up? You look pale.'

'I'm…tired,' she says, sitting down again. 'In shock still, I think.'

He rubs her back and then winks at Joe. 'We need to get your mother a nice cup of tea from the machine.'

'Mum,' says Cariad, gently, putting a little hand on Rachel's knee.

'Yes, my love?'

'Look.' Cariad uncurls her hand. A stone lies in her palm. It is smooth and pure white.

'Oh, wow!' says Rachel. 'Where did you find that?'

'Joe found it on the verge of the car park,' says Terry.

'I gave it to her.'

'For sweets,' Cariad adds.

'It's perfect,' says Rachel. 'Found in the car park…Who would have thought it?'

'I know – after all that searching by the lake…She'll just have to make sure she doesn't lose it, won't she, troops?'

'Yeah, keep it safe, Mum,' says Joe.

Rachel smiles at the three earnest faces of her family, running her fingers through Joe's straggly hair and pulling Cariad close to her. Terry walks over to the vending machine. He smiles at Rachel as he puts coins into the slot. She takes out her purse and places the perfect white stone in a zipped compartment. 'There. It can never get lost now.'

~o~

Searching the Slate was written for the final assessment of the Open University module 'A363 Advanced Creative Writing'. The story was inspired by considering different types of isolation, and the thought of twins who are suffering from loneliness, despite being nothing alike in character or environment. I know a pair of identical twins, and I began to wonder what it would take to separate them. This led to the idea of a close family being broken up because of trauma, dishonesty, and unawareness.

When I was little, our neighbour killed himself. My parents were reluctant to tell me the details, but I managed to find out that he had hung himself from the light in the hallway. I was familiar with their house and had played with his daughter occasionally, and so the image never left me. The plot for *Searching the Slate* came from asking 'What if?' questions. What if his daughter had walked in and seen him hanging? What if no one knew she had? How would that affect her?

The answers became aligned with the isolation and family themes; one twin saw, one twin didn't, but the trauma of the event pulled the family apart. I then had to search for the catalyst to resolution, which was as problematic as the children's efforts to find a white stone in the slate! As with the white-stone search, the answer came when I'd stopped looking. The twins' reconciliation following their mother's heart attack signified good things coming from a bad situation. This inspired me to write about the children finding a perfect white stone in the car park, to symbolise that theme and to conclude with a sense of hope.

Short stories are a powerfully concentrated form, and mine usually start with two or three ideas converging – ideas that produce a 'spark'. The dark scenery of the Llanberis slate heaps in North Wales, along with its beautiful lake, influenced the *Searching the Slate* story, teaching me that plot, character, and setting are inextricably linked. It was the final piece of the puzzle.

I love character-driven stories, with simple language and complex emotion, particularly as I have a fascination with psychology and what makes people tick. A story can have the best, most clever plot in the world, but if I don't connect with the people then I'm not interested. I have noticed recently that I'm drawn to the topics of death and trauma too, perhaps because of some difficult experiences my family have had recently.

Art can create beauty from hardships. Although *Searching the Slate* is a fictional story, it was cathartic to write because the subject-matter meant a lot to me. Real life was my inspiration, Kate Bush was my soundtrack, and writing is my perfect medium.

MADISON WHITE
THE PLASTIC SAX

Madison White is a twenty-three-year-old Creative Writing master's student, illustrator and travel lover. During the final year of her Bachelor's degree she spent nearly four months studying and living in Bangkok. While she was in Thailand she worked on her first ever colouring book. She loved the drawing style so much that she went onto create a colouring book for Redditch, the town where she grew up. Creativity is so important to Madison that she tries a variety of different things, from cooking to embroidery. All of these things make up her life and it's from life that she takes inspiration for her fiction pieces.

The little blue suitcase had reappeared and once again it lay upon the mattress, open, its empty insides clear on show. Gradually though, with each carefully folded item it began to fill, its sides bulging out with its ever growing load. The clock on the wall ticking away the time until it would be zipped up and hauled away. What was so often a bright and happy home was cloaked in a haze of misunderstanding and sadness. It had started with a knock and a welcoming hand, but it soon spiralled down into a deep conversation with a tone of despair.

The little girl so full of joy only moments ago, now sat on the stairs clinging to her new favourite toy, a little plastic saxophone. Her cheeks wet with confusion, yet a determined stare remained fixed in her eyes. The strangers in their fancy clothes sat in the chairs below, their complicated words picking away at her beautiful world, while up above the suitcase kept on growing.

What could she do to stop such destruction? She put her saxophone to her lips and blew and blew and blew, until there was barely a breath to blow. She needed to summon the cavalry to her side to keep the queen in the castle. The broken noise of the plastic tune filtered up through the house to the suitcase room. There it settled on the ears of the queen, her face too featured gentle streams glistening in the light from the oblivious world outside.

No cavalry came to the princess's side. Not a sword or a horse or a footman to be seen. She was all on her own sat on the stairs. It was only the sound of the zipper that pulled her away. Slowly she got to her feet, her saxophone still held tightly in her grasp. The traces of her failing still present on her face, still dripping off her chin. The blue suitcase was now full to bursting, the queen's hands resting on its tight surface. Both could see how the other was breaking and yet neither could mend the rapidly growing cracks.

The voices below grew louder and closer. This seemed to refuel the little girl's momentum and commitment to fight. She put her saxophone once more to her lips and yet once again her efforts failed. No one was coming to the castles aid. The queen gripped onto the princess with all her strength, it was as if she was trying to absorb her very being so they would never be apart. The voices were strong though and they fought harder than the little girl could ever dream of fighting. With one final bang, the little blue suitcase was gone and the little princess was left with only her little plastic saxophone and her father's strong hand resting protectively on her shoulder. He too had streaks of despair running down his cheeks, it would seem that the princess was not the only one who lost the queen.

~o~

I wrote *The Plastic Sax* one evening while in Bangkok. It focuses on the impact a parent suffering with mental health has on a child. I chose to write about the tough subject of mental illness but from a different perspective and putting a different spin on it. I took inspiration for this piece from passed experiences and so I feel it has more of a real and raw feel to it because of that. The fairy-tale aspect helps to make it feel more childlike since many little girls are the princesses in their families and their mothers are the queens of their castles. I wanted to avoid the stereotypical portrayal of mental illness and I also didn't want it to be too dark or overly depressing. Normally I would spend more time on a piece and re draft it a few times however this one I just sat down and started writing. I didn't plan on submitting it for anything, but then I found out about the young writers anthology and I decided to tweak my piece a bit and submit it. If I have learnt anything from this process and from my creative writing master's course in general, it's that just letting the words flow and not thinking about it too much may be the best way for me to create my best work. I have also realised that I definitely want to write a novel at some point in my life. I have heard it said before that everyone has a novel in them, perhaps I will eventually get mine down on paper.

KELLY GREEN
TAMING THE CREATURE

Kelly Green is a twenty-two-year-old university student from Birmingham, pursuing a Bachelors in Creative and Professional Writing, while volunteering as an assistant for a Young Writers program nearby. She spends a lot of her free time in a crowd, soaking up the atmosphere of live music, until returning to her studies. Other chosen escapism is gaming, visiting Disneyland and reading.

2006

I've never had similar interests to my friends. I didn't care for Power Rangers, or the latest Gareth Gates single. The 'hottie' factors mentioned in *Girl Talk* magazines were something I could never relate to, so I tended to indulge myself in the latest pop band release... but for reasons other than Harry Judd's mullet or Matt Willis' *dreamy* smile.

"I'm thinking of asking Josh to see the Garfield movie with me this weekend," Sarah informed our circle one summer lunch break, looping the stems of daisies together to form a chain, which we all assisted in creating the largest flower crown possible in forty-five minutes. "Greenie, you should ask David and we can double date!"

I shook my head, pulling the petals from my own innocent weed. Weekends were reserved solely for Tomb Raider and reruns of Raven. I'd been rehearsing the final challenge with broom hurdles and my sisters slide; I could almost reach the top backwards if I had a running start now. Sometimes I'd get extra practice if I completed my homework by Saturday afternoon and eaten enough dinner.

"David? But he picks his nose with his tongue!"

I was soon excused, a chorus of giggled disgust echoing around the group. I found myself forming excuses of why I shouldn't meet with David, and Ryan, and the boy from the top of my street, outside of school every few days. They were relatively easy to create, considering boys' hygiene had always been an unforgivable issue within my friendship group. Back then I was innocent and oblivious to the creature that grew inside, much like a child should be. Its scaly spine and sharp talons only tickled my stomachs interior, whilst it's beak-like crevice remained unopened.

However, leading into secondary school the excuses gradually began to get harder, while their accusations cut harsher, and the monster ate on my misery, becoming fully grown.

2009

No one seemed to understand that there was hardly any time for dating while Valkyrie Cain was soon to master necromancy in the next of her series, or how Emma Watson had posted online about the upcoming *Harry Potter* film and I was hardly prepared for the trailer release. Inexcusably, they cared more about how Chris' latest profile picture was of him and Naomi from 10B1, while also messaging some other girl during Math.

"So, Kelly," I heard Anna mumble from behind me, her practical partner's recognisable snigger following. I swivelled my chair once ensuring Miss Vince had left the room, past attempts at feigning a lack of hearing having proved useless. "You have Facebook?"

"No," I mumbled in response, clicking the pen still in hand from notetaking. "Not allowed."

Anna sighed, her eyeroll hardly subtle considering her butterfly pinned fringe. "But there's a guy who goes down Pigeon Park on a Saturday that I think you'd like. He saw Fall Out Boy last weekend."

"I'm not really interested." I replied, shrugging and going to move my chair back around to shield my throbbing cheeks. Since beginning secondary school a gnawing had formed, one that never seemed to pass long after the conversation of a potential boyfriend was over. The creature had awoken and made its existence known by nibbling on my stomach, occasionally scratching at my organs as it crawled up my body towards my throat, where it'd cut off any wetness and dry up my mouth, until I was physically incapable of communicating my feelings properly.

"Why?" She replied, tone near accusing, caused my head to throb as I tried to concentrate on replicating a molecule diagram. "You a Les or something?"

The creature continued, appearing to find more leverage as it moved faster, my kidneys, stomach and lungs acting as step ladders.

"No," I ignored my lab partner's chuckles from beside me. "No, I'm not a Les." Admittedly, I didn't fully understand the apparent insult, having no indication from anything other than laughter as to what she meant by the term. The creature knew perfectly, however, seeming to bounce within stomach acid in excitement as it settled once more. I wasn't sure what a 'Les' was or why those around me continued to snigger and repeat it long after the conversation was over. Having my friend Natasha inform me of how I was the topic of conversation during English after lunch also didn't assist my understanding.

"Everyone agrees," She informed me during final registration, shrugging. "They either think you're a Les or racist." I stared to draw out further information. "Well, the only guys you ever talk about are the Weasley Twins." It didn't help. My understanding was still limited. However, it wasn't until those around me added 'Fag' to the list of titles that it finally clicked; gay. They were calling me gay. I had no oppositions towards those who identified as such, however, the label seemed to impact my social status more than I would like. I soon frequently found indecent images scribbled across my exercise books of badly drawn female genitalia, Blu-Tak thrown into my hair as I left the premises after classes, and having large gaps between myself and others in changing rooms. The creature didn't seem to care for their antics, merely huffing while I spent my evenings pulling the blue substance from where it was embedded into my skull, having to resort to scissors on occasion.

It wasn't until I fled school that I began to fully analyse myself. The creature began to build a den deep within my insides, deepening the scratches made in the past whenever I was in contact with a male, hissing at my life choices whenever I believed in something more. It approved of isolation if there was a boy involved, its growling rumbling like hunger pains. Eventually, we came to a pact. With the comfort of knowing there was no reason for those I feared in school to hunt me down on social media I delved into it, setting up a few well-known websites and somewhat learn more about those around me. Although, many around seemed more interested in the latest tweets from celebrities or what films were being released soon, Sexuality was also something discussed often. The creature seemed to approve, curling up within the acid of my stomach, content with the warmth that engulfed it. It slept.

2012

Submitting to my sister's request of finally creating a 'Facebook' account didn't take much persuading, admittedly, it didn't take any at all. I was curious of what my old peers were up to; in relationships, starting college, a new job. Not much different to myself, except the odd high school dropout who uploaded multiple photos of her baby girl. Setting up a profile took no longer than two minutes, adding my name, age and a profile picture of a band logo I found online, before adding more information into my 'About' section: *Interested in: Women.*

The creature purred in content, snoozing some more.

Thereafter, many of my other social media accounts stated the same, identifying myself for anyone who seemed to stumble upon my page as a lesbian, and it felt good. It felt right. I'd managed to snuggly fit myself into a labelled box and not feel claustrophobic; I could still breathe. Admitting it to those online seemed one thousand times easier than admitting it to those around me. It wasn't too bad for my sister, her seeming to understand and already kind of 'know' before opening my mouth.

"Well, you're always talking about that singer you like," She answered with a shrug. "it's cool if you are." For that I was thankful, she was right; it wasn't that big of a deal. My Mum seemed to respond the same, telling me immediately that she'd known for years, 'a mother's intuition', she said, seeming overbearing mysterious. I thought it was more horrifically Disney. However, those seemed to be the only ones around me who agreed; others were less accepting.

I'd never enjoyed visiting my Grandmother. If it wasn't the outdated wooden furniture, or the lack of heating regardless of how often she'd tell us it was on.

It was the conversations. She never seemed to understand that visiting her on a weekly basis wasn't a scheduled hour of rants and rambles about things that, in the whole grand scheme of things, didn't matter. They'd overflow from the minute we'd enter the kitchen, the rumbling of a kettle boiling water failing to overpower her arguable words, until we'd submit to hearing of the man who cursed her werewolf of a dog for trying to bite him. It was my sister who changed the topic to myself, deciding to mention in conversation of the 'gays' down the road and slipping it in as a joke that I was, in fact, one of the gays.

"No! You're joking, no," was her response. "No, no, no, not my granddaughter, no." I managed to force my small smile in place, rubbing my knees a little in attempt to divert my attention elsewhere. I heard a small 'Mary, c'mon' from my Mum, yet nothing more during that visit. I felt the creature hiss, sending signals to my brain to snap back, or demand reason from her, but the smile caged in the words: *Interested in: Men and Women.*

After a few years of claw marks gradually healing, the creature began to climb once more, reopening the wounds. Its beak dug into organs, ripping and pulling in rage, yet I ignored its outcry.

2015

We met in college, having a mutual interest in a band who was somewhat rejected from the mainstream scene, and things gradually began to evolve into more than friendship. He expressed his feelings to me via social media, thankfully blind to my conflicted turmoil on the other side. I somehow managed to respond, describing how I felt the same way, regardless of how although it was true… it also wasn't. I wasn't sure. However, the creature did, clawing at my stomach in hope of tearing its way out. It was easier to conform, there'd be no 'no's at the mention of my preference, or odd stares, or space between myself and them whilst changing clothes. He was my first partner, and things were bound to be scary in the initial few months… or eighteen. I managed over a year of confliction, telling myself that things would settle soon and I'd adjust. For the first few months I managed to divert the kisses to my cheek, force myself not to stiffen too noticeably when he'd wrap his arm around the curve of my waist, and skilfully avoid any mention of the word love by diverting the conversation to anything relatable around me.

"Why won't you kiss me? We've been together for nearly six months." He eventually confronted, leaving me stranded on the other side of the table. My fingers thumbed at the corner of the menu, picking the laminate away from the paper. For the first time the creature roared up at me, forcing me to choke as it fought against my brain for control. With a deep gulp, I drowned it in saliva, the sticky substance acting as chains as it wrapped around its wrists, bounding it tightly.

"I'm just nervous." I managed to croak out, feeling a clawed punch to my gut. He seemed to understand, and I eventually did kiss him, multiple times in fact, yet each time the creature seemed to shave my self-love apart, leaving me with nothing more than shreds by the end. It was easier, that I'd admit. Walks with entwined hands were welcomed down the streets, and at the mention of a boyfriend to people around me I'd receive an 'ooh' and further questions on our relationship. There was no fear of disgust. However, things didn't last, my form left in tatters by the creature, and I eventually submitted. We broke off after those long eighteen months, myself doing the honours by mentioning how uncomfortable I was. Every touch felt dirty, every kiss like it was flaking the skin off my lips. He wasn't okay about it, and we never brought it up since, but it hurt too much to keep living isolated and chaining up the creature; it didn't deserve it.

Interested in: Women.

2017
The creature moves up, sitting higher and pokes its head out of my throat, glancing around at the bright light of the world. I hear it hum in approval on occasion, nuzzling against the rough surface of my tongue, before shuffling back down to rest.

~o~

My inspiration for *Taming The Creature* was primarily my history and reaction towards my sexuality. As someone who has been surrounded by various levels of homophobia from an early age, the idea of myself being homosexual was initially rejected and ignored. This created a deeply unsettling lifestyle and I have only recently accepted and found peace with myself. This piece was the beginning of my recovery and acceptance of my sexuality, and within the story the creature personifies my self-hatred and doubt whilst experiencing years of neglect. The creature progresses from an antagonist to a protagonist through the years explored within *Taming The Creature*, until I accepted myself and allowed it to experience the world first-hand.

Taming The Creature was first written for a module entitled 'Life Writing' at university, and was given the advice that if a piece was difficult to create, then we weren't ready to write it yet, and is something I've held close in the process of completing this story. It's been one I've had waiting to write for a long time, and my university module prepared me for the correct way to express it, and I feel it was told in the way it needed to be. The scenarios within were difficult to express, but I knew I wanted to tell them in the hopes of inspiring people on the difficulty for members of the LGBT community, and I feel extremely grateful that I pushed myself to complete it.

#FRAMEDINVENICE

ROBYN WILSON
SEV HELDER

In her final year as an American Studies student at University of Leicester, most of Robyn's writing has consisted of essays and job applications. When she does get the chance, she aims to challenge and explore our relationship with society in her writing. She asks questions that confront people with their privilege, amaze them with their potential, and send the windmills of their mind into cardiac arrest. People and words are the two most difficult things in the world. Unfortunately, they're also Robyn's favourites. She hopes someday to understand both.

Far be it from me to force my tongue between foreign lips, but some stories are best told by others.

Picket signs surrounding a television studio, for example, told a far more visionary version of Sev Helder's Saturday morning than anything the novelist herself would later say on the matter could've.

Forgive my being flowery: I'm trying to distract you. This is not a story about beautiful things, this is a story about ugly things. But I didn't want to put you off.

Well if it's a story at all, I suppose I'd better tell it.

***

Hostile chanting of an indeterminate nature filled the green room. For me? All for me? Sev Helder addressed the voices inside her head as she swirled around

65

the green room, delighted with the turn-out. She was to appear on television for the first time ever, and was excited. An employee of the station told her she had five minutes. She finished her drink. For weeks now, she'd been rehearsing, dutifully stationed in front of the silver-tongued mirror, her responses to the inevitable questions whirling around in the blustery shitstorm surrounding her latest novel. Sev Helder did not much care for listening, and didn't mind whether or not people chose to do so. Secretly, though, she hoped they would, because she had been rehearsing these responses for weeks.

The green room, which really did have green walls – well, a murky grey-green like a lake that does not invite swimming – was cohabitated by Sev Helder and the morning's 'musical guest'. He had dreadlocks and a pork-pie hat and seemed out of place, with his tatty boots resting on a soft, pink rug. Once or twice, he had attempted to initiate conversation with Sev. Her responses had been brief, because she was primarily concerned with remembering how she was to address the impending interrogation. Now he spoke again. Was she, he wondered, the target of all that toneless shouting outside? Indeed, she confirmed, she was. It was all for her.

Now a familiar presence, the studio employee came in to tell Sev she was on in two minutes. She drew a deep breath and rolled her shoulders vigorously. Something cracked. Satisfied, she told the employee that since she was ready, she could go on now if he liked. With an unexpected earnestness, he replied that no, that wouldn't be necessary. But he was glad she felt ready. Two minutes later, Sev left the lofty musician and the murky, green walls and the soft, pink rug, and walked through a door beplaqued 'studio'. Once inside, the din of the outside crowd was inaudible.

One of the invariably irascible things about life is how often we have to change our plans. You'd wonder why we still bother to make them. It was with a dull ache in the back of her throat that Sev Helder spoke the *new* answers that dissolved weeks of practice on the tip of her tongue. It became apparent that she'd somewhat overestimated *Saturday Morning Gibberish*: the questions weren't nearly demanding enough to demand the answers in her arsenal. Rather, the host wanted to know about the death threats Sev had received, and the publishing contracts that lay desecrated, and the husbands that had stormed out. Sev told the host that she didn't have a husband. The host requested a brief, brutal summary of the novel. Rumbling tongues behind her, she acquiesced. It was not nearly so terrible as she'd anticipated. She was disappointed. Many other novelists, I'm sure, would've been relieved. Novelists aren't very good at answering questions. The only questions we know how to answer are rhetorical ones. Perhaps, that being the case, Sev Helder was not like many other novelists. Certainly, as she watched the flashing of the chat show host's eyes with a rolling pair of her own, she thought about how much better she would be at answering these questions if they were asked by a sharper tongue. That musician in the grey-green room, for example, had asked her a question and her tongue had practically rolled out of her lips before she had time even to consider alternative answers. Wasn't she a genius? (One wonders, at this point, how the crowd outside the studio would've answered that question. We'll never know.)

We now came to the final question. Of course, it promised to be the most provocative, designed to sharpen minds and numb senses. By this point, Sev was cocooned in a gossamer sheen of sweat, but this could be attributed wholly to the hot studio lights, not to any mental workout or flame of passion. In my dreams, thought Sev snidely, as the host gently cradled her good opinion in the curve of a smile, laughing at something she hadn't said. Sev smiled back. What could this final question hold, she wondered. It was sure to be something related to this novel's apparent controversy. Sure to be. Sure to be. The host had barely touched on it, more concerned with the successful five years that Sev had left where they belonged, five years ago, and the future, which lay too far beyond the tip of her tongue to contemplate. Briefly, as the host filled the space between them with small-talk, Sev experienced a sudden shock of nerves that caused a shudder to pass through her. How would she look on television? Would she ever find out? That morning, dutifully in front of the mirror, she'd observed the greyness of her skin and reddened her lips in an attempt to offset it, but since then she'd drank coffee. What if the entire nation – well, some of the nation – saw her on television – her first ever appearance by such medium – with smudged lipstick? Lipstick on her teeth? The radiant translucency of her face would serve as a veritable red carpet on which to display the disaster. How horrible it would be. She shrugged. We came to the final question now anyway; far too late to become concerned with a sinking ship when the lower decks were already submerged. Horrible as it would be to be *humiliated* like that, on the television of all places, it would be worse to lose oneself to distraction, and miss this final opportunity to answer with *gravitas*. The host's pupils slipped and slid around, eyes flashing with the reflection of the autocue. It was sure to be about the controversy.

It was. And when Sev opened her mouth to answer it, her tongue fell out.

She screamed, of course, but, of course, it was a pointless endeavour. There it was, a cold slab of meat on the ground. It didn't flip-flop about like you might hope or expect. It simply existed there on the flecked linoleum of the television studio, a soft, pink, pathetic ornament. Wild eyes torpedoed around the room. The audience gawped. The host gawped. Sev gawped madly back with wild, wild eyes. She grasped at her tongue but her hands could not contain it. She called for help (obviously in vain). It was no use. Perhaps they were as shocked as she was, tasered into inactivity. Perhaps they just didn't care. They didn't say anything either way. They all just *stared*. Making a series of slurping noises that could not possibly be interpreted, Sev unhinged her mouth and gestured erratically around the studio, pointing inside of it, its emptiness apparent. Why won't you help me?! Sev demanded this, as well one might, but internally only. Tears started to drip into her crimsoned mouth: salty ones, probably, though obviously, she couldn't tell; desperate ones definitely. The host was whispering to somebody. It was the employee from the grey-green room. He stared too. The show was a disaster. This was 1000 times worse than being caught with lipstick teeth. For a prolonged number of minutes, there was nothing but silence and staring and whispering, then the show was over. What the crowd outside thought of it, we'll never know.

***

People were talking over her. Popular opinion would've liked Sev Helder to black out after her tongue fell out and the interview was terminated, and wake up somewhere completely different. That's not the case. She did collapse, but only as far as her knees, fingers scrabbling against the studio linoleum to grasp at her absent appendage. Security removed her. She was taken to hospital. Her tongue stayed behind on the studio floor. People were talking over her now, as she floated on the thin grey cloud of her mattress, suspended on a metal framework and staring alternately up into a rouged open mouth on her left and a darker one on her right. Even though the woman on Sev's right wore a white coat, she did not have the weary lilt of a doctor in her voice as she discussed Sev's fate with the other woman. But surely she was a doctor, because here we are in a hospital, and she was wearing a white coat. Perhaps the other woman was a nurse. Sev didn't know. She didn't care. The heavy emptiness between her lips occupied her entire imagination. Whatever terror awaited her in the operating theatre was beyond her concern. Perhaps they were going to stitch it back in, if they'd managed to peel it off the linoleum. As painful (not to mention unhygienic) as that might be, it was better than no tongue at all.

Sev plucked her attention away from the conversation above her head and focused it on the thick grey walls that arched upwards into the very backs of her eyelids. A very tall ceiling for a very small room. Pallid yellow bulbs illuminated it, their icy sunbeams trickling down the walls and pooling pathetically in the shadows on the floor. Sev wondered briefly if she would have to spend eternity here. When her lower lip rolled nervously backwards into nothing, though, she was abruptly reminded of the facts of her detainment in that high-ceilinged cell, and was intensely depressed.

The women continued to talk over her. She wished they would stop it and look down. Though if the one on the left were to look down, Sev mused with amusement, would she even be able to see her toes? How could she even get past the end of her chin if it was so impossibly hard to find amid the folds of her neck? Like the snap of a que on black, the woman's head wobbled round to look down into Sev's face, red lips jangling above a mass of undulating skin, eyebrows knotted into a question-mark and framing a gaze of unanswerable queries. Did she read my mind? Sev wondered, coloured momentarily by a flush of genuine concern. If she could've laughed she would've. Of course not. People don't read minds. By the time she'd righted her thoughts, her cupcake-shaped dominatrix was waddling away to attend to someone else's wailing. Above her, the doctor (if doctor she was) told Sev they needed to address the elephant in the room, and Sev quietly begged for the right to laugh.

***

There were no windows. Pastel coloured electricity crackled in its wall-mounted incubators, but the light it shed was minimal. Natural light seemed a luxury in *Casa del mudo*. If there was a lightbulb in Sev's brain – the one that popped out in moments of cartoon inspiration – let it shine now. Her empty mouth longed for flavour. Something to eat would distract her from the itch in her throat. Or something to read. Yes, a good book to chew on. Something whimsical and fantastical; a chance to digest someone else's words for a change. Nothing too heavy, mind you; something light enough to consume in a single sitting. Sev didn't imagine she would have much time for anything resembling a tome anyway. How long did it take to fix a tongue? She wasn't expected to lie there and wait for a new one to grow, was she? Mercy. With no food, no company, no entertainment?! Mercy! And *oh* how it burned. It was as though somebody has set off fireworks down in the overgrown jungle of Sev's throat and they were wrenching their way through the thickets of phlegm and charring the very fabric of her trachea, such was the burn. In desperation, she opened her mouth and thought temporally that she saw a coil of smoke wisp upwards from between her lips. A trick of the watercolour lighting, no doubt, no doubt. So fiery was her boredom that she almost wanted the doctors to come back and ignore her again. At least it would give her some amusement, something to keep her invisible tongue occupied. Alas, nobody returned for Sev Helder, bearing edible gifts or otherwise, for what was probably three hours or more. When the waddling Wonder Woman did reappear, she was the one consuming edible gifts. She spoke with her mouth full of cupcake crumbs and Sev glared jealously. Hardly professional conduct, she thought. I don't believe I would ever want to be seen by a patient in a hospital putting myself so openly at risk of diabetes. Whatever the nurse said remained above her head.

***

It did not become the hospital staff to let Sev Helder starve. Eventually, she was fed. Liquid mush was cannonballed down her throat and she was required to sit very still and make sure it all went in. The taste was not altogether to her taste, but it was surely better to be nourished on nonsense than allowed to disintegrate (after more than one day of this mush-munching, admittedly, Sev was forced to question this philosophy). It occurred to her a number of times to question why she was bed-bound. Wasn't it her tongue she had lost, and not her legs? She assumed the doctors knew what they were doing though, and she couldn't make inquiries even if she wanted to, so she relaxed into her figurative chains. Maybe the fat nurse had explained it to her, but Sev could never find the motivation to listen. Besides, the woman's voice grated. It had a nasal quality akin to a rusty foghorn attempting Bach. When she caught wind of its honking approach, Sev made sure to tune her brain to a different channel.

Occasionally she heard impossible sounds. Nights tended to be very dark and very quiet, and with nothing to do but listen, Sev would spend her evenings entertained by the unlikeliest of soundtracks. Breathless moans seeping through the walls. Avian wails dripping through the ceiling. The roar of a tiger once – she'd swear it under oath. That, of course, would not make it true. Sev did not care for probability, so she allowed the melodic romance of noise to continue its nightly efforts to lull her to sleep. She was a writer, remember, so facts meant little to her anyway. And though she did not much care to listen, she had no choice in the circumstances, and was grateful to have something warmer to her senses that the metallic scraping of the nurse's voice. If nurse she was. Sev noticed, for the first time, that the woman was dressed in a nurse's costume because she was struck one day by how much she remined her of the Stay-Puft Marshmallow Man. Ever since she came to this realisation, the image haunted her, and whenever the nurse was nearby, she focused the entirety of her vision on the naked lightbulb sizzling above her head, so as not to be blinded by the extreme, vast whiteness of the nurse. Or Moby Dick. The Stay-Puft Marshmallow Man or Moby Dick. Either was a fitting point of comparison.

The impossible sounds, I'm afraid to say, did not get louder, or closer, or more vivid in any of the ways they were supposed to. They remained constantly on the other side of whatever physical barrier held them. A train passed below Sev's bed without shaking the floorboards. A Chinese opera was performed without a cast or stage. Rain splattered the windows of the windowless room. On went the noises, symphonic to Sev's silent brain. Crescendos became increasingly imminent. Sev grew agitated. Nights no longer contained the impossible sounds. Before long, they drowned out patient complaints, whirring machines, and the nurse. They could strike up at any moment, and all Sev could do was listen. Day after day she lay in a circle of sounds. They sliced through her like typewriter ribbon or razor-wire, marking her mind with deep, empty crevasses then pouring in the pulsating molten noise that plucked her every brainwave with guitarist's fingers. Painful as I have made the experience sound, it was really an immersive one. As long as sound's echoes filled the caverns of Sev Helder's brain, the yellow pallor of hospital noise, of blathering nurses and slathering psychopaths, was kept from exerting its dismal influence. There was an uncomfortable numbness in all that noise; one that Sev Helder feared she, as a writer, would struggle to communicate in words when the time came to publish the sensation. Writers are frequently unwoven by the loudness of living. Such a bizarre story, though, could not, as far as Sev Helder was concerned, go untold. Eyes narrowing instinctively, she watched the nurse's busy blubber bustle between patients and wondered whether this was a story she would ever be allowed to tell. Their eyes met over a blink. The nurse looked swiftly away. Sev smiled a little. There is no monopoly on storytelling.

***

It would've been poor conduct to allow Sev Helder to starve. The daily waterboarding continued, the drip drip dripping of regurgitated mush, as far back into Sev Helder as it could reach. It was still preferable to starvation. She found hunger more damnable than almost any other feeling. Often, though, she found that the noise in her head diluted the feelings closest to the surface of her skin. Hunger's furious *growl* – which had previously often been the very noise in Sev Helder's head – registered now only in quiet moments, and these were so few and far between that when the time came to absorb her mushy meals, she found herself wandering where was the hunger that necessitated this torture? Drowned out, it seemed, by a more insistent orchestra. And 'drowned' is appropriate because, as though underwater, everything blurred and rippled beneath a crushing tsunami of sound. Even the nurse took on a kind of wibbly-wobbly beauty as a watercolour artwork in the gaze beneath Sev Helder's skewed eyebrows. From the tense rumbling of untold stories, to the faraway fizzling of critical voices, Sev's brain was awash with pure, beautiful *noise*. Nothing else seemed to matter. Hunger? Pssh! Fear? Pain? What of it? The heavy invisibility of Sev's tongue dissolved on its non-existent tip. Her mind made noise for her. Outside of it, the quiet world simpered on not with a bang, but with a whimper.

And yet she still let that fat nurse feed her hospital pulp.

Where was the silent dignity in that? Sev wasn't hungry – she *gorged* herself on sound. Yet she allowed herself to be humiliated: manipulated and force-fed by a voiceless intruder. Her tongue was still pending maintenance, but was she helpless? No. She had five other senses, and a whole jukebox of pure sound to fuel them. The nurse gazed on from the doorway. Her eyes, to Sev's mind, seemed to become wider and increasingly unprofessional as the hospital lost its power to supress Sev's senses. They lacked a stern decorum and took on a cloudy lightness that throbbed with one-million emotions unfit for a hospital. Chief among them was *uncertainty*. It chewed on her gummy lower lip and echoed beneath the ripples of her flesh and the mush she force-fed Sev Helder was no longer a question of conduct but of *power*. It was a game the nurse's squashed, inefficient senses would not win: the uncertainty that was all over her betrayed her knowledge of this fact. Wearing her victory in her smirk, Sev lifted her electric eyes, set deeply in the useless blue of her face, and fixed them on the nurse's. Sev smiled and the nurse, frantic with swarming emotions, left in a hurry. She sang along with the intensifying orchestra in her head: Tchaikovsky's *1812* carried on the swooping wings of bats. The incommunicable nature of victory occurred to her all at once, in a crescendo of cannon-fire, and that night she stayed awake whilst the bats filled the attic of her mind.

***

Once more, the nurse's panting blubber loomed over Sev Helder. Beside her, on Sev's unexplored right, the doctor's eyes stayed on a level with the nurse's, and the two of them held their counsel in the air above their patient. It was feeding time. Sev had made her protest loud and clear, with the flash of an eye, and here was the nurse to tell the doctor: the game was up. Time for the torture to stop. The power had vacated the doctor's latexed palms and had been restored, in a colourful explosion of jukebox noise, to Sev Helder's sharp mind. But Sev frowned. She had blinked, had missed a key point in the conversation, and now the nurse approached with her hospital apparatus once more. But we agreed. Didn't I show you yesterday? I won. Can't you see that? I won.

Beneath thundering brows, her scowl darkened as the nurse got near. I don't need to eat. I'm not hungry. I'm not hungry. I'm not—

"I'm not hungry."

There was a moment of tranquilised silence. Then the echo of a gong as the symphony crashed to a halt. Sev glanced downwards. Pink and plain and as real as a chainsaw, her tongue hung between her lips. She glanced upwards, suddenly speechless, with desperate eyes as the nurse's quivering expanse pulled a vast shadow across the pallid, yellow hospital lights. The hospital apparatus she held was close enough to Sev's face now for her to identify it. She opened her mouth to scream, and the nurse's scissors descended with a *snip*.

~o~

Everyone has a story inside them. Our right to tell our story, and our responsibility to listen to the stories of others, is central to the parable of Sev Helder, a controversial novelist whose sharp tongue tickles a nerve too far in her latest book. What we do or do not say changes everything. To say nothing changes everything as well, as Sev Helder discovers, as without speaking we can rely only on what we think, hear, and see to understand the world around us. As Sev struggles to collect her mental, aural, and visual clues into a coherent whole, she starts to lose control of the story inside her. When narrative control of your story is placed in somebody else's mouth, you become utterly powerless.

'Sev Helder' explores what it means to be voiceless. This is the story of a novelist, but everyone is a storyteller. When our ability to tell our story is compromised, the world ceases to bloom in full colour for us. There are certain experiences and pleasures that we cannot access when condemned to voicelessness. It challenges the reader to confront the power they wield by their ability to speak, and consider the struggle of those from whom this ability has been stolen.

JESSICA FARROW
THE RIDINGS

Jessica Farrow is a 24-year-old writer from Boston, Lincolnshire. She has recently completed a Masters degree in creative writing at Edge Hill University which is also her Alma Mater for her bachelor's degree. She is a lover of stories, whether they be told through the medium of books, film, music or theatre and is keen scrapbook artist. Jessica is a previously unpublished writer but hopes her short stories will one day appear in literary magazines and anthologies nationally or, dreaming big, world wide. She is also currently working on her first novel in the genre of dystopian fiction.

Charlie and I turned the corner, our usual route home on the way back from the park. He was tired today. All the energy had been zapped out of him, spent when he'd tried to chase the pigeons in a futile effort to keep up with the other, much younger, dogs. Sometimes he forgets how old he is. I do too. When I saw him scampering across the grass with the other dogs, his tail wagging with unrestrained excitement, it was easy to see him as the young pup I took home to my wife thirteen years ago. But when I called him back I was instantly reminded that he was no longer a puppy, the arthritis which is a Labrador's painful inheritance upsettingly clear. My heart broke a little as we slowly made our way home.

As we walked the last stretch of path home, we passed the houses of my neighbours who I knew little about. Years ago, my wife Ellen and I knew our neighbours relatively well. It was a new development and it seemed that everyone who moved to The Ridings wanted a friendly neighbourhood. Whenever anybody moved in people would offer to help unload the van, bake cookies, or bring them a bottle of wine – the last was mine and Ellen's usual calling card.

We took the Littman's a nice budget bottle of Merlot. We'd only moved in ourselves a few months previously and had just bought a new sofa set - Charlie had torn ours to shreds within minutes of me bringing him home. Nevertheless, the Littman's seemed grateful for the wine and we quickly became friends.

They had a dog too, a Rottweiler - Jazz. Ellen was afraid of her at first, those preconceptions that most people have about those breeds stuck in her head, but after a few dinners at the Littman's, she could see she was nothing but a big softie. She used to feed her bits of chicken under the table.

Our dogs became as close as we did. Myself and Herman Littman would walk them in what used to be Grange Woods before the accident and they would run around and play. It was sweet and, considering how close we became to the Littman's when they lived across the road, it was a damn good job. If one of us was going away, the others would look after their dog for however long was needed. Ellen and I hardly went anywhere, so the Littman's offer of dog-sitting was never used - but they went on holiday every few months. Jazz was at ours a lot, so the friendship and the very nature of that friendship of the two dogs was hardly a surprise. Nevertheless, I suppose that Charlie and Jazz's affection for each other was why our friendship with the Littman's crumbled.

"How could you let this happen?" Herman said.

We were sat, late one evening in our kitchen. Charlie was in his bed by the fridge, the humming of the appliance comforting him, but Kate was holding Jazz back by her collar. Kate stared at Charlie like he was diseased.

"They're dogs Herman, it's just in their nature," I said.

Ellen was bustling around in the kitchen. She'd set herself the task of making everyone tea, though no one had requested a drink. Her unsteady clatter with the kettle filled the tense moments of silence.

"I don't care if it's in their nature, you should have prevented this! I told you to prevent this. Jazz was promised to a breeder in Devon, a damn good breeder."

"I know."

"You should've had him fixed."

I blinked at him but didn't respond. To this day I don't know what I should have said. I've gone over it in my head countless times but nothing I come up with ever seems good enough. All I know is in that moment, that sentence effectively ended our friendship. For me anyway. For Ellen that moment came later, when the puppies were born. She was still trying at that point.

She brought over everyone's unwanted tea. Out of duty and respect to her, I picked mine up and took a sip but this only enraged Herman. He slammed his fist on the table, tea spilling on the table, instantly staining the cloth.

"How can you sit there and drink tea? You've just lost me thousands of pounds!"

The loud noise scared Charlie who whimpered and scarpered through the kitchen door. We heard the stairs creak so assumed he had hidden under our bed, his favourite spot when there were loud noises. After Bonfire Night, we can't tempt him out for a good day or so afterwards. We have to leave his food and water bowl under the bed.

"It's only one season," Ellen said softly. Her voice wavered as she went on. "Surely she will still be able to breed in her next?"

"No breeder worth a damn will take her when they hear she's been defiled by your mongrel."

"Charlie is not a mongrel!" I said standing up. "We could take him to a breeder ourselves if we wanted but we don't look at him like a fucking bank account."

"Tom," Ellen said, tugging my shirtsleeve.

"No, he's not talking about Charlie like that."

"We should go," Kate said, pulling poor Jazz by the collar as she stood up.

"No, please, we can work this out," Ellen said. She moved over to the door hoping to stop them from leaving. "Please Kate, we can talk about this."

Herman pushed past Ellen and opened the door. "We're done talking."

"But what about the puppies?" Ellen asked. She was close to tears.

"We'll drown them."

We found out the hard way that they weren't kidding. Ellen knocked on their door every day after they had told us what they were planning to do when the puppies were born. I think that she wanted to try and stop them, ask them to give us the puppies when they were born instead, bargain with them by offering to pay the extortionate vet's bills they were sure to have racked up through the whole ordeal, but they never answered the door.

The last morning she went over, she only got to the end of our driveway when she saw Herman coming out of his house with a canvas laundry bag. It was moving. Ellen became hysterical - she hadn't said she was hysterical but I knew she had been. She ran over, begging him to reconsider, to give her the bag, but he didn't listen. He moved her out of his way and dumped the bag in the passenger seat of his car as he got in. He pulled the car door from her grip, ignoring her as she banged on his car window. Ignoring her still as he started the ignition and drove off, leaving her standing heartbroken in the middle of the street staring after him.

She told me that evening, her eyes red and puffy, that she'd sat on the curb outside our house all day waiting for him to return. Charlie kept her company, knowing she was upset. He sat with his head in her lap until he heard the roar of Herman's engine, at which point he ran back inside the house to hide. Ellen had stayed and watched Herman get out of his car the empty laundry bag in his hand. Ellen swore that he knew she was there, but he spared her no glances.

Three weeks later the Littmans moved.

The house was empty for a while, the silence of the structure echoed in my marriage. Even Charlie was quiet, constantly looking out the window as if searching for Jazz. Ellen was cold. She blamed me for not doing more to stop Herman, but what else could I have done? It took a couple months for things to return to normal.

By that time, a new family had moved into the house. We offered our usual bottle of wine and sat with them for one evening to drink it, learning enough about them to make small talk but not enough to be as close as we were with their predecessors. There were three of them; Malcom, Maggie and their son Henry. Malcom and Maggie were in their late forties; Henry was seventeen and studying at the local college. He wasn't there when we visited and, from how often we saw his racer-boy car, he wasn't there often.

"He has a girlfriend," Malcom explained, handing us a picture they had already dug out of the boxes that cluttered the living room we had come to know so well. The picture was of Henry and a pretty girl, round in the face, dark straight hair and clear blue eyes. Malcom smiled as he spoke. "Her names Amara. Her family own that restaurant in the centre of town."

"They're going to give Henry a job when he finishes college," Maggie continued.

"He'll need it," Malcom said with a sour face. "Boy's going to be a father."

Ellen couldn't keep her surprise to herself. You could see it in her face. And when she said, "How lovely," it was also clear in her voice.

Maggie picked up on Ellen's tone. "It was a shock to us as well," she said with a slight shrug, "But what can you do?"

"We've just got to focus on the child now," Malcom said.

"And a new baby's always so exciting," Ellen contributed.

I said nothing. I just sat there nursing my glass of wine and looking at my watch every so often. Charlie needed his walk at 7pm. Ellen kept shooting me disapproving looks for not making conversation.

"Well we're just across the street if you need anything," I said as we left. It was courtesy rather than a real offer. They only ever knocked on our door once.

The news that the young lad across the way had impregnated his girlfriend wound its way around the neighbourhood quickly. It was a point of conversation for most people. I paid no attention to the chatter but it seeped into Ellen's mind. I waited until she brought it up, knowing what she wanted.

"Let's have a baby," she said one night when we were in bed.

"Are you sure we should?" I asked, feeling her deflate in my arms like a puncture in a tyre. "I mean, we don't have a lot of money saved. And then there's Charlie…I don't think he could cope with a baby."

"Just think about it," she said

I was surprised by her response and was even more surprised when she didn't broach the subject again, though I knew she wanted to. Every time she heard Henry's racer-boy car she would watch through the window as Amara, her belly swelling as the months went by, was greeted by Malcom and Maggie with proud hugs. She'd busy herself cleaning after. The mood she exuded effected both me and Charlie. Charlie would follow her around and when she would finally sit down, lay his head on her lap. I just felt an overwhelming sense of guilt and feigning work, would go on the computer so that I didn't have to be confronted by her depression. After four months, I caved.

We started trying straight away. When I came home from work, Charlie would have already been fed and walked, and there would be candles lit in the bedroom. I saw no need for candles but Ellen liked them. For a whole month, I was treated to nightly sex and I began to think this trying for a baby malarkey wasn't so bad after all, that is, until Ellen took her first pregnancy test.

She was biting her hangnail and pacing back and forth nervously whilst the pregnancy test sat by the bathroom sink calculating its results. I leant against the door frame, watching her anxiety come to life.

"They take a couple minutes," I said.

Ellen didn't halt in her stride. "I know."

"It won't be long then."

"Tom will you just…please?"

I fell silent. Charlie sat at my feet, an invisible barrier keeping the pair of us out of the bathroom. After two minutes Ellen scrambled to grab the test. She seemed to shrink when she saw the results.

"These things take time love," I said, walking into the bathroom and wrapping my arms around her. "It'll happen."

It didn't happen. Over the next couple months, all Ellen's pregnancy tests came back negative. I could always tell if she had taken one. When I'd come home she'd be curled up on the sofa, Charlie resting his head on her lap as she cried. I tried to be supportive, tell her it was still early days, it could still happen, but she wasn't comforted by my words. She went to her doctor for help but they said they couldn't intervene until we'd been trying for a year. What depressed her even more was seeing Amara and Henry bring home their baby girl.

Ellen bought a card and wrote it out but didn't want to see the baby, so asked me to drop it off. As I approached their house, I heard raised voices. Not wanting to interrupt a family issue I dropped it silently through the letterbox and walked back across the street to our house.

A few minutes after I got back, the argument I'd heard escalated to the point that the whole neighbourhood could hear. Ellen peered through the curtains, (the other neighbours doing the same), and saw Maggie running across the street carrying a bundle of blankets.

Charlie barked loudly as she banged on our door, not stopping until I answered.

She shoved the screaming blankets into my arms. "Please," she said, breathing heavily. "Just please keep her here until we sort things out."

Ellen came into the hall and took the baby from me.

"What's happening?" she asked Maggie.

Everything was so loud at that moment; the argument across the street was louder with the door open; Charlie was still barking; and the baby was screaming.

Maggie didn't answer Ellen's question. "Please. Just for a few hours."

The slamming of a door across the street cut through the noise like a guillotine. We all looked to see what was going on. Henry was storming out of the house, wiping his face with his jacket sleeve. He got into his car and the engine roared to life. The sound snapped Maggie into movement.

"Henry!" she screamed, running across the street with reckless abandon as she tried to stop her son.

We knew we shouldn't be watching, that we should take the child inside and shield her from the noise, but it was like a car wreck – we couldn't look away.

Henry reversed out of the drive, narrowly missing Maggie who was begging him to stop. But he revved the engine and sped off with a loud squeal of the tyres.

Amara and Malcom stood in the door way. As soon as Henry's car was out of sight, Maggie turned on them. She yelled profanities which I wouldn't have believed she knew, and the closer she got to them, the angrier she seemed to get. We watched as Amara tried to hide behind Malcom, and then stood in shock as Maggie grabbed the girl's arm, pulled her out of the house, threw her to the ground, then slapped Malcom clear across the face.

An almighty crash in the distance stopped her obscene shouting. The air was still. An unrivalled silenced enveloped the entire neighbourhood. Seconds later it was pierced by Maggie's shrill screech. She took off, running as fast as she could down the street which Henry had disappeared down. To this day, I don't know how she knew what had happened before seeing the wreckage. Ellen said it was maternal instinct.

The funeral was a couple weeks later. Malcom didn't attend. Instead he cleared his belongings out of the house as it went on. We heard later that he and Amara had moved in together with the child.

Maggie moved not long after that. Ellen and I helped her pack the house up and move things into the van. She didn't tell us where she was moving and we didn't ask. We just said our farewells, went our separate ways.

Things returned to normal quicker than I expected, Henry's suicide and his family were soon forgotten. Grange Woods which the boy had crashed his car into was levelled and the park was created in its stead. The only reminder that they had been there at all was the once again silent house across the street.

Ellen and I continued to try for a baby. We had taken a short break after Henry had died - Ellen hadn't felt right about trying for a child of our own when a mother we had known had lost her own so abruptly - but after a few months we were back on our normal schedule.

But nothing happened.

After a year Ellen went to get tested. She was nervous; thinking the worst. I found it better to let Charlie quell her anxiety – at least he wouldn't say anything that would upset her. He just snuggled into her stomach.

When Ellen's results revealed she was completely fine, she asked me to get tested, to see if it was me.

"If you're ok I'm sure I am," I argued. "I don't see why I have to go through this humiliation."

"It's just a precaution. If there is anything wrong, then at least we'll know."

"Nothing's wrong."

Ellen paused. "Please just go to the Doctor."

My results came back quicker than Ellen's did, though they weren't as positive. I was fertile, which was good; I just had very docile sperm and it was going to be difficult to conceive naturally. But as we couldn't afford any other option, all we could do was to keep trying.

When Charlie was eleven, a new family moved into the house across the street; mother, father, a daughter, no more than eight years old, and her butter coloured Labrador puppy.

We offered no wine to them.

Charlie sniffed around the hedges outside our house and, revelling in the last Ellen free minutes I had left, I left him too it. He was old. I owed him the chance to enjoy nature whilst he still could.

We had tried for five years. Nothing happened. We never discussed it but we gave up. It was a futile endeavour. And just as she had with the puppies all those years ago, Ellen blamed me. Over the years she grew colder and more resentful, though she tried to hide it. At first, I tried to make her happy again. I would surprise her with flowers, jewellery, shoes and chocolates but I should have realised that material gifts would never fill the void of a child. It was unspoken between us, and I couldn't say when we both realised it, but we knew that we were only staying together for Charlie.

I looked over to the house across the street, thinking about the neighbours we knew in that house and the ones we now chose to ignore when I saw the little girl coming up the street. I often saw Ellen looking at the little girl with longing, wishing she had a daughter of her own.

The girl was crying, streams of snot and tears lining her face. In her arms, she carried her puppy, it's head lifelessly lolling over the crook of her elbow. Her hands were covered in the dark blood that was matting the dog's butter coloured fur, her shirt and the pavement she had walked stained with it as well.

Through all the things that had happened in the neighbourhood, that image would be the one to haunt me.

~o~

The Ridings is a piece of fiction I completed during my Masters. Its creation was born out of the final image at the end of the story; a young girl, distraught, holding her dead puppy in her arms. It is a powerful image which I believe makes a lasting impression in a reader's imagination. Going forwards, I collected more images that I found similarly striking and wove them as snapshots into a story which takes place in a single neighbourhood over a period of years.

The first section of *The Ridings* concentrates on Tom and Ellen's first neighbours, the Littman's and their relationship with them. In a lot of ways, their relationship and its demise is the most important part of the story as it sets them up for their own self-destruction. If they had not befriended the

Littman's, then their marriage and the history of the neighbourhood may have been different.

Something I really focused on when writing this section of The Ridings was the characterisation of the dogs, specifically Charlie. As an integral part of the story, I wanted to ensure that he was more than just an animal and have tried to achieve this by fleshing out his personality, giving him individualistic traits such as the comfort he finds by the humming of the fridge. I love dogs, but do not have one myself so, in a way, I created in Charlie the companion I wish I had.

When the second set of neighbours move in, the neighbourhood is subjected to a volatile and dramatic event. The scandal of Amara and Malcom's affair and Henry's subsequent death sow the seeds for what I believe is the second most striking snapshot in the story; Maggie's unearthly scream at losing her son. The whole event is something that effects Tom and Ellen in their relationships, not only with any new neighbours, but with each other.

Tom and Ellen's marriage is shaped by the happenings in the neighbourhood and I tried to show this during this section. Seeing Amara pregnant pushes their marriage into a new and difficult place. In trying for a child, something Ellen hopes will bring them together, is eventually the thing which breaks them apart.

I saved the striking image of the girl for last, hoping the abrupt end would mirror the impending sudden end to Tom and Ellen's Marriage. The image is made stronger still by Tom's reaction. If his past relationships with previous neighbourhoods hadn't been so distressing and hadn't taken such detrimental blows to his marriage, he might have stopped and helped. Instead, all he does is observe and comment offhandedly on how haunted he will be by what he has seen.

Typically, many of my short story's flick between focusing on psychopathic protagonists or dystopian fiction. In diversifying my focus with The Ridings, I feel more confident in myself as a writer and would like to continue to tackle different genres in the future, perhaps even in novel form.

DANIEL MORGAN
ONE QUIET NIGHT

Daniel is a twenty-four-year-old writer from South Wales. He's currently studying English Literature and Creative Writing in Swansea University, and is also working as a Freelance writer. Despite writing mostly in various nonfiction niches for work, Daniel still pursues his own aspirations of becoming a published novelist, and has several novels currently undergoing refinement process in preparation for submission. He believes that the only way to find success in this industry is to never give up, and to continually strive for improvement, something which he always endeavours to do.

It was just past three fifteen in the morning when the call came in.

Within twenty minutes, Uri was sitting in the emergency room waiting area of Hope Memorial Hospital. It was a fairly quiet night all in all, and he sat with his head hung back over the remarkably uncomfortable chair that he'd chosen. He let out a long sigh of boredom and tapped his phone against his fingers, drumming out the rhythm of some long forgotten song.

'Uri? Is that you? Damn, it is you. I thought your days of ambulance chasing were over!" came a jovial, and familiar voice.

Uri didn't look up, he just smiled at the ceiling tiles and shook his head. He'd not heard that voice in years. 'Mike,' he cooed in reply, finally standing. 'Long time.'

They embraced like brothers and held each other for a drawn out moment. When they finally broke apart, both straightened their tailored blazers and ties in reflex. They caught the other doing the same and exchanged a smirk.

'Humph, don't think I'll ever get used to this monkey suit,' Mike huffed.

'Tell me about it.' Uri chuckled. 'Not like the old days any more, is it.'

Mike stared into space with a look of melancholy spreading across his pale blue eyes. He ran a hand through his tousled blonde hair and forced himself back to a more upbeat expression. He clapped Uri on the shoulder suddenly. 'So what the heck are you doing here? Thought you left all the grunt work behind - moved onto bigger fish. This is a little small time for you, isn't it?'

Uri checked his phone again and then met his old friend's eyes. 'You know how it is. Cut backs, holidays. We're understaffed, so I'm pitching in. You know, it's kind of nice to get back into the muck and the mire - get my hands dirty again.'

Mike smiled warmly, measuring Uri from behind a set of pearly white teeth. He brushed off the shoulders of Uri's pristine black suit and pursed his lips. 'Doesn't look like you've been dirty for a long time. This is a nice suit.' He put his hands on his hips and surveyed the man who, once upon a time, had been among his closest friends. 'Least they pay you well.' He tutted.

Uri's grin waned with sadness. 'You know I didn't leave for the money.'

Mike swallowed hard, trying to keep the venom from his voice. 'Then what was it? You never told me why you left - didn't even warn me. All those years together, I didn't deserve that, huh?'

'Mike,' Uri sighed quietly. 'It wasn't like that-'

'Oh, wasn't it, Uri? Tell me what it was like then,' Mike growled, his eyes sparkling with the fire of an ember that had long since burned out.

'I wasn't happy.'

Mike set his jaw and narrowed his eyes. 'But to go and work for them? I just never expected it. We always used to talk so much crap about them, about how shady their practices were - about how dishonest and *disloyal* they were. I just didn't think they would ever be a good fit for you.'

Uri blinked slowly. That hurt. 'Neither did I, but...' He rubbed his head and checked his phone again. One new message. 'Look,' he said quickly, grabbing Mike by the shoulders. 'Let's just let sleeping dogs lie, yeah? I've got work to do, and... Wait. Who are you here for?'

Mike held his chin high. 'Christopher Santos.'

Uri stepped back and looked at the ceiling. Silence fell between them for a second, broken only by the low hum of the halogen lights above. 'Oh no,' Uri shook his head. 'This is my client. It's already a done deal.'

Mike stared hard at Uri, looking for any waiver. 'That's not how I see it. I'm under strict orders to-'

'To hell with your orders. This is my client, and I'll be damned if I'm gonna let you poach-'

'You're already *damned!*' Mike suddenly roared throwing his hand out. 'You sealed your fate the second you walked out the door. We were brothers once, but that doesn't mean that I'm gonna let you have this one, or anyone for that matter. Now get out of the way.'

Mike took two steps before Uri's palm found the flat of his chest. There was a dull thud as they met, neither prepared to give an inch. 'Don't make me do this,' Uri snarled.

'Do what? Wait for me to walk past and then drive a knife in my back? You should be pretty good at it now. Had enough practice.'

Uri's mouth twitched and his loose hand curled into a fist. Mike cast a quick look down and then returned his gaze to Uri's brimstone glare. 'You do that, and you know there's no coming back.'

Uri smirked. 'You think I'd ever come back? To you. To him? He'd never let me set foot inside the door.'

Mike softened and he dropped to a whisper. 'Things have changed, Uri. He's not the same guy he used to be.'

Uri scoffed. 'Yeah, right.'

'It's true. He'd forgive you, take you back. I know he would. But not if you do this. If you use that.' Mike nodded to his still balled fist. 'And if you stand in my way now, that'll be it.'

Uri narrowed his eyes to slits and stepped back, taking a hard breath. 'You *knew.*'

Mike raised his eyebrows and feigned ignorance. 'I knew what?'

Uri's ran his hand through his hair in disbelief and turned away. 'You knew I'd be here. That's why they sent *you.*' He laughed now, annoyed that he'd not seen it earlier. 'You came in here, all high and mighty, saying that this was a lousy meal ticket for me, and you expect me to buy that they sent you? You're not here for Santos at all, you're here for me.'

Mike looked down and opened his palms. His fingers shook a little. He closed his hands slowly and looked back at Uri. 'I heard you'd be here, yeah. I wanted to come. I wanted to come to ask you to come back. Things haven't been the same since you left.'

Uri smirked falsely, the emotion roiling high behind his walls, a seething sea of rage and regret. 'I'm *never* coming back. Now, piss off, I've got work to do.'

Mike stood in silence, a suit clad statue, as Uri disappeared into the emergency room. He waited a second, shook his head, huffed, and then took off after him. Uri was standing by Christopher's bed when he found him, filling in a form, his face gravely carved and shaded from the light above. The scraping of the nib on the paper echoed around the room as if they were the only ones there.

'Uri,' Mike began.

'Shut it,' Uri breathed.

Mike reached out across the bed and grabbed Uri's arm. 'Stop.'

Christopher wheezed laboriously between them. His face was covered in bandages and his arm was in a sling. The bleeping of the heart monitor was incessant and fast. He didn't have long.

'No, Mike. You stop,' Uri spat, snatching his arm away.

'This isn't your call.'

'The hell it isn't.' Uri clapped the folder shut and dropped it callously onto Christopher's legs. He groaned almost inaudibly.

Mike glanced down at it for a second, and then at Christopher's blackened and bloodied face. 'Why not let him decide, huh? It's his call at the end of the day. Or are you *afraid* he might choose me?'

'You think I'm twelve? That you can gode me into this? No chance. The deal is done, and there's nothing more you can do,' Uri snapped, smiling victoriously.

'There's *always* hope. For him. Even for you.' Mike's eyes never left his as he knelt at the bedside and leant in to Christopher's swollen cheek.

'What the hell are you doing? Mike, *stop*. That's not fair. For God's sa-'

Mike's hand suddenly leapt into a fierce point. 'Don't. Don't do that.'

Uri raised his hands and sighed. 'Sorry, I forgot.'

His eyes left Uri's and he returned to Christopher, whispering into his ear in a voice so quiet that not even the dead could have heard it.

Christopher stirred a little and raised his one good hand. It was covered in scrapes and bruises. 'Dios... Dios...' He began to mutter.

Uri stepped back and exhaled hard. 'You bastard,' he hissed, whirling on Mike, who was now standing, and straightening the hem of his milky white suit. 'He was *mine.*' Uri's eyes glowed red and his voice fell into an unearthly register. 'I had him. You can't do this.'

Mike stood quietly and cast his gaze skywards. 'You'll never understand, will you.' He shook his head slowly and took one last look at Uriel, at the thing that had once been his brother. 'Goodbye Uri. I hope we meet again one day, although I don't know that we will.'

Uriel's teeth ground together like the rending metal of a car crash.

'Dios... Dios...' Christopher cried louder.

Doctors suddenly began to swarm to the bedside. One pulled out a stethoscope and put it against Christopher's chest. The other checked his pupil response with a pen light. 'What the hell's happening?' The first asked, her eyes wide.

'I don't know,' the other gasped. 'He fell three stories! There was no brain activity. He should be dead!'

'Well, clearly he's not!' she half shouted, checking the readings on the monitor.

'I don't understand! He was barely alive a second ago - there's no way he should be conscious!'

Uriel and Michael kept their eyes locked on each other as more nurses and medical personnel began swarming to the bed between them, driving them further apart.

Uriel sneered, baring pointed teeth, 'I'll see you in hell.'

Michael smiled softly at him with a last flourish of fleeting warmth. 'No brother, you won't.'

And then he was gone.

~o~

One Quiet Night is a deviation from my usual writing style, and strays into the supernatural/fantasy genre. The piece begins in a hospital waiting room with a little bit of literary misdirection, showing off two characters who at first glance appear to be ex-coworkers, though from their conversation, it's revealed that things didn't end on a positive note. The fantasy elements are withheld as the piece progresses, and it's instead intimated that both characters work in either the legal, or insurance sectors, and that they're both here to cash-in on a patient's misfortune. As the story comes to its resolution, the twist is segwayed into abstractly, and only in the final lines is it revealed that this is not in fact the story of two disgruntled co-workers, but instead an angel and a fallen angel come to claim the soul of the patient in question.

The piece aims to blend humour and poignancy, providing a route into a genre that can be selective in its audience. As the piece comes to a head, it's clear that the roles of the two protagonists are filled by two of the angels who feature in the bible; Michael, an archangel, and Uriel, a fallen angel. What at first glance was a story about an old colleague trying to convince his friend to return to his previous employer, suddenly becomes a story of good and evil, of forgiveness and embitterment, of a friendship lost to time.

I always tries to take the familiar and make it strange, or to present something other-worldly in a package that's accessible by all. Universal themes link all literature, and a fantastical short story is no different. While there may be little of interest in regards to the biblical and supernatural elements, everyone has experienced loss and betrayal at some point in their life, and if nothing else, that part of this story may speak to you.

It's in that way that no genre, no writer, and no story should be overlooked of cast off without being given a fair chance. Writers write from their hearts, and it's in their writing that you'll discover the things that make them human - the things that make them smile and the things that make them cry. Maybe it'll be the simple story of a person trying to rebuild their life in the wake of a tragedy. Maybe it'll be a sprawling sci-fi epic set in a distant galaxy. Maybe it'll be a comedy about a talking dog. Or maybe it'll be a story of angels and demons. Nothing is ever written for no reason, and it's one of the great joys of reading to be able to discover that reason, because without doubt, it's there.

REBECCA METCALFE
SHOES ON THE DANUBE

Rebecca Metcalfe is a 22-year-old writer and student from Essex. She studied English Literature with Creative Writing at the University of Chester and whilst there had some of her pieces published in student and university publications. She is currently studying for an MA in Victorian Literature at the University of Liverpool. When not studying or working, she spends her time writing both her own fiction and for a student magazine, reading, swimming, drinking tea and befriending local cats, as hers is still in Essex.

December 1944

Eva and Laszlo stood on the bank of the Danube. In front of them lay the winter river, swimming in ice. Above them stretched the morning sky, drained of all colour and sound. The endless white space of it encompassed everything above their heads. And its blankness pressed down upon them in a cruel mix of freedom and suffocation. Behind them lay Eastern Budapest. Behind them lay twenty years of happy memories and terror. Eva felt Laszlo's hand brush against hers. He couldn't openly hold her hand, that would not have been allowed. But it had been years since they had last seen each other, and time could not always let go.

Behind them, the officer barked.

"Remove your shoes!"

Eva, Laszlo and the other Jews all did as they were told.

October 1931

Eva Gerde and Laszlo Sarakany first met during their shared childhood in the streets surrounding the Kazinczy Street Synagogue. Although they were the same age, and grew up playing with all the same Jewish children in that area, they did not become aware of each other until they were eight years old. Their relationship began one night in an unlit alleyway that connected the streets they lived on. A large group of children had been playing out in the streets, as children do at that age, and one of the other children had decided they should all go off somewhere. So off they all ran, but Eva and Laszlo fell behind and found themselves alone in the dark alleyway. They looked at each other.

"I don't think I've seen you before," said Laszlo. "Who are you?"

"Eva. What's your name?"

"Laszlo."

They smiled at each other as they stood in that high-walled unlit alleyway, the night sky shimmering above them in majestic blackness.

"Where do you live?" asked Laszlo.

"Nagy Diófa Street," said Eva, pointing towards one end of the alleyway. "Where do you live?

"Nyàr Street," replied Laszlo, pointing in the opposite direction.

"My friend Margit lives there," said Eva, excitedly.

"What, you know her too?" answered Laszlo.

The two stared and smiled at each other for a moment under the dense night sky. They smiled at the thought of familiarity, at the thought of a shared friend, a shared culture and heritage. A shared life.

"Do you think it's strange how we've never met before, because we live so close together, but we've never seen each other, that's strange, isn't it?" said Laszlo, with a nervous splutter. Eva smiled.

"I suppose it's a little bit strange," she said, "but there's loads of people living here, you can't know everyone."

"Yeah," thought Laszlo, "do you think we could be friends and then see each other again, and play together sometimes, maybe?"

"That sounds fun," replied Eva, her smile now the biggest it had been.

There was a moment of silence before Eva spoke again.

"We should both be getting home," she said, "It's really dark and late."

In reality it was only half past seven, but that seemed incredibly late to the two children in the alleyway. Laszlo nodded at Eva's suggestion and they parted as friends. The following day was the Sabbath, and Eva and Laszlo were able to smile at each other again from across the street as their families and all the other Jewish families in that area crammed into the Kazinczy Street Synagogue. They smiled at each other every time they saw each other and on the days and evenings when they were not constrained by chores, Eva and Laszlo played with all the other children. These days seemed endless and without worry. All of the children were happy then, and none of them seemed aware of the growing resentment of Jews in Budapest that was increasing all around them. They simply played happily each day and everything seemed endless. The games they invented, the rhymes they sang and the laughter they shared seemed completely endless.

May 1939

Eva sat in the Jewish café on Kazinczy Street, sipping her coffee. Occasionally she stared at the clock on the wall.

"He better be here soon," she thought to herself. She knew she had to be home before dark, and a deep red was already splattered across the sunset, as if the sky was bleeding. Just as she began to think Laszlo wasn't coming, he hurried into the café. Eva smiled.

"I thought for a minute you weren't coming," she said.

Laszlo sat down, out of breath. "I can't stay for long," he replied, "and I'm sorry I'm late, I ran all the way here. It's my dad, he's lost his job at the theatre. Mum's going out of her mind worrying about how we're going to pay the rent"

"It's these new laws, isn't it," said Eva with a sigh, "my uncle's lost his job on the paper as well. I overheard Miklos and his friends talking about war this afternoon. War all across Europe. Do you think…"

But she was prevented from finishing her question by Laszlo taking the opportunity to kiss her.

"Please don't talk about war," he asked, and he kissed her again, although they both knew that Eva's brother had been right about the prospect of war. They had been living in fear for a long time already.

August 1941

It was about this time that people Eva and Laszlo knew started disappearing. War had been raging across Europe for some time now, although the worst was yet to strike Hungary. The worst was already happening for Eva and Laszlo though, and they never got to say goodbye. The residents of Budapest's Jewish Quarter just watched in silence as men, young and old, were marched off to labour camps. Laszlo's eyes frantically searched for Eva as he was marched away by the Hungarian Army on that warm orange evening. But he could not see her. Eva herself was out looking for him, and passed close to where he was. They almost saw each other, but it was not to be. Almost is the saddest of words.

July 1942

Pablo finally prised open the tin of sardines and the men flocked towards him like the hopeful flocked to Christ. In the resulting scramble, men became animals and scratched and clawed at each other.

"I need to eat," came the cry from the back.

"We all do," came the reply.

Laszlo managed to grab half a small sardine, ripped from the hands of a slower man. Tomorrow morning he would be woken at four thirty, the same as every morning, and would carry on the gruelling and pointless grind of hammering a railway into the barren earth. It was relentless and unforgiving work, which would tire out the most able of men, let alone starving men huddled in a makeshift military camp somewhere east of Budapest. The half a sardine was a miracle, useless, but a miracle all the same.

He scoffed it down whole and sat down in a corner near a window, the love-struck pink sunset fought desperately to climb in through the grubby shattered glass. The men had scattered now the sardines had gone. Many had blood and scratches dancing across their hands and fingers from grasping at the tin. Laszlo stared at them as they shuffled back to their business, heads hanging and hair thinning, their cavernous eyes and cheekbones worn into bony ravines over such a short period of time. An older man had once described them as looking like Munch's Scream. Laszlo had never been to an art gallery and revelled in the man's tales of a previous life. A previous life. A previous life.

July 1942

The brick came through Mrs Gerde's front room window at sundown as Nagy Diófa Street was caressed in an unusually cheerful hue of pale pink. It landed on the coffee table and smashed a glass of water with a crash. Shattered glass danced across the room, whilst the water trickled down the table leg like tears. Mr Gerde dived across to the window, but the thrower of the brick was gone.

"They won't leave us alone. They can't leave us alone," he muttered, watching the street outside before his gaze turned to the brick on the floor. "Somebody clean that up".

Eva fetched a broom from the kitchen and began sweeping. Her mother sank into an armchair and carried on shaking. She never ceased shaking, like a lifelong mental patient who feared incarceration and the sunlight in equal measure.

"God only knows what'll happen when Hitler invades Hungary," Eva thought to herself as she swept. The general feeling was that it was a question of when, not if.

November 1944

The first anyone in Budapest's Jewish Quarter heard of it was when the Arrow Cross Party marched along the streets under Hitler's orders, shot the Rabbi and anyone else who stood in their way and declared the beginning of the Budapest Ghetto. Eva watched as people she knew well search for loved ones, for food, for hope, but the fence had already gone up.

***

"Get up!" shouted the guard. Laszlo and other men obeyed and formed into their lines. "You are being removed from your duties here and are being relocated with immediate effect. March!" And so Laszlo marched along through the streets of East Budapest with the other men. And when the sun was at its highest point in the washed out daffodil sky, old Pablo Werkner, one time provider of a sardine tin, slid and fell. His eyes said everything, then nothing as the bullet shot through his head. The rest carried on marching, and Pablo was left behind.

The marching seemed to last 40 days and 40 nights. On the way many more were discarded like cigarette ends whose foul life had burnt out. Only a few dozen remained by the end. They stopped as they reached the edge of the old Jewish Quarter. Laszlo's eyes ricocheted around, trying to identify the buildings. The other men were doing much the same thing, but barbed wire had crept round the architecture like poison ivy and strangled their perceptions of where they were. One of the guards spoke to a man in a strange uniform, before they were guided towards a gate, down a series of familiar streets where Hebrew and graffiti fought for control of the concrete.

The guards left them at a large and decaying house with smashed windows and a Star of David scrawled on the door. A middle aged man with a half shrunken face spoke first.

"Well, gentlemen, welcome to the abattoir."

"Do you think there's any food or water here?" asked Laszlo.

"Somewhere, probably, although there doesn't seem to be any plant life amongst the concrete and wire," replied the man with the shrunken face, "no grass for us cattle."

December 1944

The soldiers in charge of the ghetto would often round up Jews at random to be taken away. Many would end up in Poland or Germany, in places that sickened the Devil. But many didn't go very far away at all. This is what befell Eva and Laszlo.

Early one morning, a group of soldiers broke down the doors of several houses in the ghetto, including Laszlo's. The officers stayed silent, just herded the people out of the houses, jabbing them with their pistols and edging them towards the river. None knew what was happening. Married couples, crying children, trembling grandparents and Laszlo, were pushed and shuffled through the streets. Laszlo watched as they turned a corner and a young woman about his age came into view, foraging for scraps in the gutter. Laszlo recognised her immediately. The officer stopped, approached the woman and hit her with his pistol.

"You should not be outside during the curfew" he whispered. Eva said nothing, the officer just dragged her out of the gutter and pushed her into the rest of the group. "Continue," he ordered, so they did.

Laszlo reached out to Eva and their eyes met. Part joy that they had found each other again after so long, part agony, for both realised that their journey would not end with their happiness.

"Laszlo," said Eva.

"Eva," replied Laszlo.

They reached the River Danube and the soldiers pushed them into line, right on the edge of the promenade. They removed their shoes, as instructed, Eva's brown leather ladies shoes, once delicate and floral, and Laszlo's peeling workman's boots were left behind. Shoes were expensive, it would be a waste if the soldiers simply let them go.

Eva and Laszlo kept their eyes open, and looking down. They could not see each other's faces, only their legs and hands. Occasionally they glanced up at the pale and empty sky above them. Neither felt the bullet through their brain and both were dead before their bodies hit the icy waters of the Danube twelve feet below. And as their bodies were born away and drifted into the nameless mass of history, only their shoes were left behind on the bank of the Danube.

~o~

'Shoes on the Danube' was inspired by a photograph of a memorial sculpture called 'Shoes on the Danube Bank' in Budapest. Conceived by film director Can Togay along with sculptor Gyula Pauer, the memorial takes the form of sixty iron pairs of shoes scattered along the promenade, overlooking the river. They represent the shoes of the 3500 people, 800 of whom were Jews, who were shot dead into the river by fascist militiamen between 1944 and 1945.

Just before they were shot, they were ordered to remove their shoes, shoes being expensive.

The photograph I saw of this memorial showed a pale sky, a grey river and grey promenade and the stark black shoes. It almost looked like a black and white photograph, such was the vividness of the colours and it conveyed an incredibly sorrowful and sombre mood. I began researching the events this memorial commemorates and tried to recreate this mood in my short story. I'm a very visual writer, I like to create strong images in the mind of the reader and so tried to recreate the feelings I'd had upon seeing the photo within the story. One thing that struck me about the photo was the bleakness and the coldness of it, in particular the river and the sky. The image of the sky therefore became very important to me in telling the story; almost every section features a small mention to the sky and in particular the colour of it. As the story progresses chronologically, the sky becomes paler until the final scene in which it is virtually colourless, like I saw it in the photo.

The chronology of the story was also something I spent time on. The opening and closing section are of the same event, the end of Eva and Laszlo's lives and feature this pale sky. I wanted this image, the same image I had seen in the photo, to be the resounding image left with the reader after they'd finished. Opening and closing the story with the image of this event, and the using the main body of the story to show they reached it, was the most effective way to convey the sense of bleak sadness that had been conveyed to me in the photo of the memorial. It is important to me that stories have the right ending and I like stories that finish with a powerful image. This is what I hoped to achieve with this story and much of what I have written since, but I think 'Shoes on the Danube' was the first time it was properly successful.

JESSICA HURSIT
MURDER IN THE MORNING

Jessica Hursit is a 23 year old student who loves reading, movies and chocolate. She spends her time studying with the Open University and working as a learning support assistant in a primary school and plans to start her teacher training next September. Currently studying a module in creative writing and running her own blog, Jessica spends a great deal of time writing and hopes to one day publish her own YA novel.

The church clock struck six, alerting the village that dawn had broken. A cock crowed. A body lay across the entrance to the church, a field mouse curiously nudging against its side, unaware of the coagulating blood it was crawling through. There was a serene momentary quiet after the chimes ceased until the silence was shattered by a baby crying.

Mary awoke at the noise and sleepily made her way into the nursery, her eyes adjusting to the rising summer sun. She cradled the baby against her chest and willed the crying to stop as she resumed her usual position on the nursing chair, her mind foggy from many sleepless nights. As her baby suckled she gazed out of the window, at the village that had become her new home. She saw smoke rising from the bakery and the milk cart in the distance; a familiar sign the village was rising from its slumber. At the top of the hill sat the church, keeping watch over the village and its inhabitants and beyond that, a moor that led to a forest. Mary rose from her chair and blinked, unaware that her sudden movement disturbed her peaceful child. She peered out onto the moor. The familiar tranquillity of the village at dawn was being disturbed as a figure of a man hurried across the fields and into the woodland beyond. Her baby's cries returned her to the nursery and she took up her seat on the chair again, protectively gripping the child. As the cries faltered her mind returned to what she had just witnessed, attempting to decipher what was reality and what was the trick of a weary mind, it had played tricks on her before. Someone crossing the moor seemed so ordinary, yet she couldn't shake the peculiar feeling she had.

Footsteps across the landing signalled that her husband was awake, probably woken by the crying. Her son stopped suckling and Mary covered herself as she left nursery and placed him against her chest.

'Good Morning!' her husband exclaimed from the door of the master bedroom. 'How is my handsome lad this morning?'

'Hungry' Mary replied, exasperated. James took the baby from Mary's fatigued arms and walked towards the stairs.

'Why don't you go and sleep for a while. He won't want feeding for a few hours and you could use a break.'

Mary smiled and turned to walk into the bedroom. She considered herself extremely lucky to have a husband as helpful as James. She collapsed onto the bed and pulled the duvet up to her chin, the warmth surrounding her like a cocoon. It was the most relaxed she had felt in months and she was soon asleep.

Mary rolled over to check her watch on the bedside table. From the noise outside she knew it had to be after nine, when the usual morning commotion began. Realising her watch wasn't there, she began searching her bedroom for it. It was a birthday present from James, but she was always putting it down and forgetting where. She knew it agitated him however he'd never admit it, he wouldn't want to add to the stresses of being a new mother. After a few minutes of unsuccessful rummaging, Mary abandoned her search and went downstairs, this time in search of her husband. She was surprised he hadn't woken her yet to feed the baby.

The hallway at the bottom of the stairs was an eyesore for Mary. They had begun to redecorate when they first moved in to number 12, but hadn't got around to finishing it yet. They had removed the wallpaper, rather hastily, revealing an off-beige paint that looked as though it had been left to discolour for decades; now covered in patches of torn, white paper. The greying white carpet made Mary question why they ever bothered to remove their shoes and increased her jealously at Sarah's brand new cream carpet. Sarah was the only friend Mary had made since they arrived. She was the stereotypical housewife that Mary imagined would live in a small countryside village like Crestfield. She always looked immaculate, like she had managed a solid nine hours sleep, and her two children were perfectly well-behaved, extremely polite and impeccably put together. Sarah's house was just as immaculate as her and recently had a brand-new cream carpet fitted in the hallway.

Mary entered the living room, expecting to find her husband and her baby. Finding the room empty, she continued through to the kitchen, yet that was empty too. Exactly how she had left it last night; unwashed dinner plates in the sink and the bin overflowing. She reminded herself to ask James to empty it, once she had located him. She checked the garden through the kitchen window but still no sign of them. Panic set in. She rushed to the front door and found the buggy still there. James must've left in a hurry. Tragic scenarios played over in her mind, what had happened to her baby? She ran out onto the street, frantic. She didn't care that she was still in her pyjamas. If perfect Sarah could see her now!

'Mary?'

Mary swung round, James stood on the path leading up to the church, with the baby in his arms.

'Oh, thank God,' she exclaimed as she ran up to her husband and snatched the baby away. She cradled him and stroked the back of his head, 'it's alright my darling, I'll keep you safe.'

'Safe from what, Mary?' James asked puzzled.

Mary looked up, she had almost forgotten he was there. She stared at her husband blankly.

'I think we should go inside.' he suggested. James put his hands on Mary's shoulders and led her back into the house.

Whilst he made some tea, Mary nursed the baby and laid him to sleep. When she had finished she returned to her husband in the living room.

'Mary,' James began, 'where were you this morning?'

'Sorry?' Mary enquired.

'I woke up this morning and you weren't in bed.' he continued. 'Where were you?' Mary felt her palms grow sweaty and her hair began to stick to the back of her neck.

'I was nursing the baby,' she replied, 'you know that.'

'Before that.' James pressed.

'What's going on James?'

'A body was found on the steps of the church this morning,' James paused, 'it was Sarah.'

Mary's hand flew to her mouth. She went cold with shock. She couldn't contemplate her friend being gone. Her mind began to spin. Her only friend had died and her husband was questioning her, suspecting her, blaming her.

'I saw a man.' she blurted. James looked up, puzzled. 'I saw a man, running across the fields, away from the church.'

James rose from the sofa, it squeaked as he did. They hadn't brought any furniture with them when they moved, so quickly filled their house with furniture from the charity shop. He walked into the kitchen and towards the bin. Mary followed.

'It must've been him,' she pleaded, 'we should tell someone.'

James remained calm, showing no reaction to Mary's words. He turned to the bin and pulled it into the middle of the kitchen.

'James, this isn't the time to worry about the housework!' Mary cried, confused.

As if he could no longer hear his wife, James opened the bin and plunged his hand inside.

'James, what are you...' Mary paused. Her world began to turn and her mind began to race. James held three items in his hands, two in his right hand, pulled from the bin and one in his left, pulled from his pocket. He held out the pill bottle in his left hand. Mary looked at the bottle, blinked and looked up at her husband.

'I found this in the bathroom cupboard, at least you didn't try to hide it this time.' He shook the bottle and it rattled loudly, full of tablets. 'When did you stop taking them?'

Mary's mouth was dry, her mind blank. She opened her mouth to speak but had nothing to say. She couldn't comprehend what was happening, what her husband was saying. James held out his right hand. Mary noticed the watch first. Her watch. The tan leather strap had a strange stain on it which she had never seen before. Then she noticed the knife. Suddenly her body was shaking, her knees buckled and she grabbed hold of the kitchen counter to steady herself. She felt her breath shorten and her mind became a blur.

'There was a man,' she muttered, 'on the moor.' She looked at her husband, 'running, on the moor' she repeated.

James embraced his wife and rocked her.

'It's ok,' he reassured her. 'I believe you.'

Mary looked up, into her husband's eyes. James stared into Mary's; those piercing blue eyes that he'd fallen for instantly.

'We should move Mary,' he added, 'it's not safe here.'

Mary nodded and nestled herself into his chest. James reprimanded himself for his lapse in judgement, angry at himself for letting this happen again. He said it would be better this time, he would monitor her moods and ensure she took her medication. He'd failed her. He vowed that next time, he would be more cautious.

The church clock struck six, alerting the village that dawn had broken. A red stain lay across the doorstep of the church, surrounded by flowers. There was a mournful silence after the chimes ceased. No baby cried to shatter the stillness. Mary did not enter the nursery. Number 12 stood abandoned. Drawers emptied, furniture left behind. Mary and James drove off past the moor, the village church growing smaller in the distance behind them.

~o~

The inspiration for this story came from an activity that was part of my studies in creative writing in which we were given a paragraph and had to create the next 2 paragraphs. The piece that I wrote was quite dark and mysterious, much different to my usual writing, and I found that I enjoyed writing this genre. I am always the person who can guess the end of the book so my favourite books are ones that catch me by surprise. I wanted to do the same in *Murder in the Morning* and this led me to develop the character that I had already introduced,

Mary. As I had mentioned sleepless nights and weariness from being a new mother I then pursued the idea of a mother with post-partum depression or psychosis. I love all kinds of soaps and TV dramas and feel like this theme would fit well in one of my regularly watched programmes, so I guess I drew my inspiration from there. I researched the symptoms and treatment to keep it believable and tried to keep them subtle so that the reveal at the end was a shock to the reader.

For as long as I can remember I've always loved reading, my childhood is filled with memories from Jacqueline Wilson and J.K. Rowling and now I try to find time to read every day. This love of reading blossomed into a love of writing. I started with stories and diaries as a child and have now added blogging into the mix. Working in a school, I always try to teach children to love books like I do. One day I'd love to finish my own novel and the ultimate dream would to see it line the shelves of bookstores across the country.

DURANKA PERERA
FOR THE FIRST TIME

Duranka Perera is a final year medical student at King's College London with a longstanding interest in creative writing and expression within the South Asian community. With his primary inspirations ranging from those of Jhumpa Lahiri to the teleplays of Avatar: The Last Airbender and Breaking Bad, his writing has been strongly inspired by the patients he has seen on the wards, but is expanding to include a more varied range of characters and settings. In his spare time, he has set up a writing society for healthcare students encouraging them to pursue their aspirations as writers while conducting research into the management of neurological disease, singing and playing the piano, violin and saxophone.

I - Nineteen Years Previously

We had come to Sri Lanka for my husband's nephew's wedding. It was the first time we had taken you there, the first time we had ever taken you on a plane. You didn't cry. After toddling into the pilot's cabin and waving at everyone inside, you spent most of the flight asleep on your father's lap by the window, only waking to exclaim, "Is that England?" as we flew over the island's coastline. I told you it wasn't. You barely turned your head in my direction.

Your father didn't look like you at all, and yet even at this young age, you seemed to take after him. His skin was bronze, his hair straight and gelled tall, walking around the airport with those tinted glasses, that light grey suit and those loafers without socks as if he owned the place. You were olive-skinned, like me, your hair wild and tightly curled. Your eyes glowed amber-gold like his. As you held his hand, walking around the airport baggage carousel, you were always looking at his legs, your right foot coming down when his did, then your left. You were even trying to copy his swagger. I stood a little farther down, straight and stiff like a pencil, waiting for the baggage to come to me. A man with a moustache looked at me, then my hands, then walked away. I heard you ask to jump on the carousel, your bag, the blue one with red flowers, having just gone beyond your reach.

"Kiyoma," your father said, his voice a light through a crack in the ceiling, "you're taller than me, come help her, silly!"

His request felt like being doused with cold water, a shock to the system, a reminder. As I came over, I barely registered how numb I was to the question that had once burned so fiercely on my lips. I didn't love you. I had come to believe that I never could.

The tropical air hit us like a muggy punch as we walked out into the streets. As our driver sat with us, sitting lax without his seatbelt as we squeezed through the Colombo gridlock, you looked curiously at me as my brick of a phone buzzed against my ear, my sister-in-law cackling down the line.

"Did you hear about Aravinda de Silva?" she said. He's a friend of the family. He's meant to be the best man. "My God, the drama."

"What happened?" I asked.

"He's not coming anymore."

Your father heard and turned his head, his lips and eyebrows contorted.

'What the Hell?"

I repeated the sentiment down the phone.

"He's at the hospital," my sister-in-law said. "His wife, we always thought she was a bit odd, the way she complained about everything and hid from everyone, but today she goes completely mad. We went there to pick them up and she starts screaming, throwing plates on the floor, the works."

She was almost laughing in disbelief.

"I've never seen such a scene. I don't think I've seen the poor man look so ashamed."

"Lunacy," I said. The word came lightly from my tongue as I said it, only to stay and congeal into a weight. You didn't know what was going on of course, even after we dropped off our things at the beachside hotel. All you wanted to do was play with your cousins and stuff your cheeks with devilled cashew nuts. How could it have been anything else? At the wedding a week later, the ceremony passed me by in a blur of colour and decadent fruit baskets. I saw mothers dancing with their eldest children, their smiles weary but enduring as they chase after their youngest. I turned away. Your father, after we finished the customary celebrations and the party moved out onto the beach, didn't see through the smile I had stuck to my face.

"I don't know what's worse, having to know your wife is like that all the time, or wanting to leave her," he said. We'd gone up to our room to change, having left you with my sister-in-law and the other children to go swimming in the hotel pool. Your father was readying his Speedos as I changed to a summer dress. He spoke as if his words would make me laugh. "No wonder he never talked about it. Imagine what he'll have to tell his son."

I didn't say much in reply. Your father was used to that. As he dove into the sea with the rest of his family, bobbing in the surf like a herd of sea lions, he didn't look back. Instead, he carried on as if nothing had ever been the matter. That was the way of our culture. To ignore the individual, to appease the many. It was all I'd known. When I left Sri Lanka for University, I clung to it out of comfort, finding every Sri Lankan I could to ease my homesickness. I still did, even as the reality of who they were, who I was, started to hollow me out.

For the next few hours, I sat and read on a deckchair. When left alone with my thoughts, I couldn't be trusted with myself. I needed a distraction. Engaging with some of the older women, we shared small talk, far less insidious gossip. They were pleasant, complimentary of my fair skin and how young I looked. I gave them my opinion on the day's proceedings and they gave me theirs, as was usual at weddings. It was only after a procession of them had gone by that I realised the children had left for their rooms, that my sister-in-law was nowhere to be seen. As were you.

"Thushara?"

Instinct forced me from the chair, the heaving bodies and faceless voices of the tourists and the remaining guests a mess around me. You didn't reply.

"*Thushara?*"

I moved out onto the beach, throwing my book to the poolside. For the first time, isolated on the sand with only the distant shouts of people and the hiss of the wind through the broken boats as company, I was worried for you. Not out of duty to another person, but because there was something in me, a selfish, consuming, unyielding impulse to have you in my arms and nowhere else.

"*Baba...*"

I found you standing where the sea foamed against the sand, the water up to your knees. You were transfixed by the horizon. The sun was setting as if on an Impressionist painting, a light orange dabbed with clouds and soft mauve, a flock of seabirds flying along the beach before veering out and soaring over the endless ocean. I remembered you had never been on a beach. The only times you'd ever seen a sunset were through your bedroom window or between tall, featureless buildings. Standing in the water, you were in your own space, as if in a bubble, people playing at the edges but never breaking the symmetry of the sand that lay either side of you. I stopped calling. Instead, I did something I'd never thought possible.

I tossed aside my slippers, letting the sand envelope my feet. I was silent. Kneeling to your height, I crept up behind you till I was close enough to kiss your little neck. As I buried my face against you, you made a sound between a murmur and a squeal, the kind you only made when you smiled. The water came over my hips. The hem of my dress started to float. You were laughing now, your little hand on my shoulder, clinging to the fabric. I thought that you'd put your thumb in your mouth and look through me, wishing for *Thaththi*, anyone else. Instead, you touched my skin, your fingertips as soft as silk. The water splashed over us, the smell of salt and sea filling our noses, the sand it left behind like a constellation of golden stars in our tangled hair.

The swell rose. If we'd stayed there any longer, your head would have gone under. I took you back a few steps to where the water only covered your feet, my hand at home in the crook of your elbow. I lay down and closed my eyes. I felt as if I could hear the heartbeat of the beach.

"*Ammi,*" you said, touching my arms, lying down next to me, "are you sleepy?"

"*No baba,*" I said. I kissed you again, your skin a little wet against my lips as you blinked and you giggled against a fading pink backdrop. As I looked into your glowing eyes, I felt as if I was really seeing them for the first time. After I carried you back to the hotel room, washing the sticky sand from you in the shower, you started to dance, asking me to join you. After I cleaned you and dressed you in your little white dress, sat down for dinner by the fire-lit lamps that crackled and whipped in the night air, I watched as your eyelids flickered determinedly in the low light, trying to stay awake. For all your energy, for all the sweet *hakuru* and *pol* toffee we shared that night, your flame could only burn for so long. I took you back to your bed and curled up next to you beneath the covers, feeling the blossoming warmth only a dream can bring as it catapults you into a cosmos of impossible things, emotions and experiences you once believed would never become you.

I woke as the sea breeze drifted in through the slightly open window. Your father had gone out for a jog, he'd left the place to air. As my eyes adjusted to the morning light, to your hands resting on mine, so did my mind. Not yet fully aware, abandoned thoughts flooded into my head through the closing gap, swallowing me up and pulling me under like thick heavy oil. Your touch was no longer silken. Instead, your fingertips turned to needles. I backed out and away, confused like a dog hit by a car, my blood thudding in my ears. For hours as you slept and I paced and paced in that small square room I wondered if it had indeed all been a dream, that the cascades of memory we'd built that night had been a taunting mirage of everything I'd ever wanted for you, but the videos, the ones your father had taken while I wasn't looking, didn't lie. Just as I had when you were born, I wanted you gone. What I thought had been washed away still clung to me like a leech.

Dressed in white, silhouetted against the light outside, I must have looked like a ghost to you. You looked at me expectantly with your big eyes, as if yesterday had given you a lifetime of faith, faith that I could be better than who I was. I couldn't come any closer. As you left the bed and came to me, your tiny fingers grasping for affection, I turned and pushed you away.

"No, Thushara."

For the first time on this trip, you started to cry.

II - The Present

You came early into the world, 27 weeks. I was in the garden, attempting to clean out the summer algae that had choked our pond. I never got to finish. As my waters broke and the electric waves of contraction wracked my body, I felt as if somehow you knew something was wrong with me. It was as if you couldn't wait to escape.

After I first conceived you, at the height of love with my husband and painting our future with broad strokes, I slowly realised I'd made a mistake. Your father couldn't know. Having nearly lost both testes to a motorcycle accident just a year before, it would have been the height of cruelty to deny him a child. Everyone would have talked about me. I wouldn't have been able to live it down. I became your home out of duty. Anticipation turned to agony.

As your due date grew closer, I remember sitting motionless on the living room sofa, eyes blackened and dry with my hands held taut on my growing belly. Every fibre of me was willing you to leave, each nerve ending supercharged as if the desperate power of my thoughts could force you out. I never thought they would actually come to pass. Once you were born, my mind became a vacuum. The love cocktail that had possessed my family, the relief, the apparent elixir that my cooing friends promised would change my world never came. Gurgling and grunting as you gasped for air, you became nothing more than a primal nightmare. As you lay fighting for your life in your incubator, I could barely bring myself to watch you sleep.

Your father never got used to waking up in the night, cleaning up after you once we took you home. He never said it, but I could tell he thought that was all on me. He started to spend more and more days in the office, on the cricket pitch, leaving me to sweat on your wellbeing. After three months of exhaustion, I'd become a plaster cast of a person, my identity having flaked off, peeled away. And then, as if things couldn't get any worse, my sister – having come over to relieve the burden - caught me topping up your formula in the kitchen.

"No wonder she looks so skinny," she said, wagging her finger as if she, childless and five years my junior, had the authority of our own mother. "You're not even feeding her properly."

Feeling my skin burn, I told her in no uncertain terms to back off. She didn't know what it was like to have her milk dry up, how it felt to repress the animal bitterness I felt as you spat out everything I gave you, the seething compulsion to silence you for good as you cried. I didn't want any more of that. It...I was wrong. After everything you and I had been through, to know that I couldn't stop failing you was a knife I could no longer bear. I never saw a doctor about this, just as I hadn't for everything that had happened in the years before your birth. After waking up from our night on the beach, cold, as empty as a husk, I came to believe that if even the purest, most beautiful moments couldn't let me be the mother you needed, then nothing could.

You know all this now. You're a twenty-two year old woman with a life and a love of your own. You've had all the time in the world to cut the truth out of me, and as you got older and your father left and you realised the only barrier left between us was my own cowardice, cut through you deservedly did.

But fate was not to be any kinder to you.

I've come home from an appointment, one of what has become many over the years. I see you hunched over by the kitchen sink, a shard of light cutting through what hair you have left, holding onto the worktop the way a person four times your age might do. I could never have known your body would give up on you, not so soon, not so young. It carves me open to remember that I'd ever wished you away.

"Baba, I brought some soup," I say. You turn to me, your eyes ashen. "I'll open it up for you."

You don't say anything. You rarely do. You sit down at the dining table and watch as the old angelfish hangs in the fish tank like a mirror. As the soup heats, the timer on the microwave counting down to zero, I look over at you as you rest your head in your hands. I weep.

It's taken me more than a decade to grind down the diamond walls I'd erected in my mind, to understand how completely I'd been poisoned by a culture that expected every mother to be a saint, that believed depression and mental illness was a lie. I may not have been alone, it may not have been all my fault, but I know now that I made the easy choice by saying nothing. My pride blinded me when you needed me then. As you look up at me, as you did on the beach as I crept up behind you that night, I know I won't let the same thing happen again when you need me now.

~o~

For the First Time was written for two reasons. The first was to determine the most emotionally suitable backstory for two key characters in a novel that I'm working on, and the second was as a piece illustrating an aspect of mental health for the King's Experience Interdisciplinary Award, a University-run scheme to engage healthcare students with the Humanities. Writing it was an illuminating experience, not least because Medicine does not usually offer many Humanities-based projects, but also because of the 3000-word limit and time deadline set by the scheme. It meant that I had to compress imagery and emotion into as few words as possible as quickly as possible. It helped therefore to find a single core image that story could spring from, namely that of the desperate Kiyoma finding Thushara standing in the surf on a Sri Lankan beach. From then on, it became about unpacking the emotions and symbols within that scene and spreading them across the two different time points described in the story. Thanks to the luck of chancing upon that image, I don't think I have ever written a story as quickly as I have this one.

For the First Time examines the pervasive influences culture can have on a first-generation immigrant and her mental health. For her role in the larger novel, the character of Kiyoma was not meant to be the best of mothers to her daughter Thushara. She is a Sri Lankan businesswoman trying to salvage a crumbling empire. Her obsessive desire to keep it afloat – and in doing so silence the psychological demons that have haunted her for years – has pushed a near-insurmountable wedge in between herself and her daughter. It was my intention for Kiyoma – towards the end of the novel - to finally hark back to the time where her demons got the better of her, acknowledge that it wasn't her fault she had those problems, but that she had responsibilities to her daughter regardless and shouldn't have shirked them.

Sri Lanka has absurdly high suicide rates due to endemic negative beliefs about mental health. Moreover, many of my friends and family have commented on a culture of competition there where proof of superiority is king. When moving to another country, it is often hard to leave behind your heritage, for better or worse. Whilst aware that something was wrong, Kiyoma was still hamstrung by these negative beliefs out of a need to remain comfortable and true to the others around her like her husband and extended family. This caused her to shy away from her internal strife, which in turn caused the suffering of her daughter. The story *For the First Time* is part of is called *Emergence*, whose main theme is one of achieving clarity. Through recollecting her past and facing up to her mistakes, Kiyoma at long last achieves that clarity, allowing her to finally give her daughter the love she deserves.

JOHN REID

SINKHOLE

John Reid is a twenty-one year old Glaswegian, currently studying English with Creative Writing at the University of Aberdeen. Steve is his inspiration and his bookmark. No one in the family can explain his passion for writing. He hopes to one day publish a collection of absurdist short stories, and he hopes that that day is in the not too distant future. Steve is his Labrador.

It was bound to happen at some point because there was ample room for the construction of the car park afterwards. And, yes, the visitor's centre too, where people do still find employment.

For the past four years the tourists have enjoyed standing in the sunshine behind the railings and taking pictures of themselves, with it in the background, speculating as to how deep it is. Sometimes they shout down, from behind the railings, and wait for their echo.

Before, the clearing was never traversed by anyone or anything, besides Dirk and Limp who were there the day it happened. There were no *Sudden Drop* signs then. Dirk didn't get too badly injured. He throws sandwiches down for the other one – Limp. Why they'd planned to meet there, God only knows, but four years ago, Limp was swallowed up, by chance.

Dirk's still there. He's a tour guide at the visitor centre. He steadily circles the hole clockwise, with his flock, and finishes the day by commemorating his

125

friend who fell into the ground, four years ago. They were very close, nigh on inseparable, he says. He says that one day just like today, they met in the middle of - what was then - a clearing.

***

They emerged from opposing sides of the clearing and met in the middle. They were followed by their prints in the grass, and the garlic flowers observed, peeking through the blades as if being grated from beneath the ground.

They spoke with their hands and with their feet. Limp produced what seemed to be a small slip of paper and started laughing and speaking and waving it around, like a child on lemonade. Dirk responded without care, his mouth full every time. He didn't check his watch once.

It was difficult to discern what was said. They shared a pair of glasses to examine the slip before Limp put it away again, and then Dirk asked some questions, and Limp provided ripe, sprawling answers. That's what it looked like.

***

After Dirk finishes his speech the tourists applaud politely, and someone like an uncle usually gives him a pat on the back for being a good friend. Then he sits on a chair that he keeps beyond the railings. He doesn't just throw sandwiches down. Dirk sets aside a portion of salary for yoghurts too, and candles and matches and newspapers.

When Limp's mother came to pay her respects, all in black, she insisted that Dirk throw down a blanket and a pillow too. He tossed an inflatable mattress down as well; she liked that.

She questioned Dirk on whether Limp had or hadn't mentioned her in their conversation in the clearing. Dirk told her yes, he had. Dirk told her that Limp had said that if anything were to happen to him - if, God forbid, he should, without warning, be swallowed up by an enormous hole, then would Dirk please be sure to give Limp's mother peace of mind, because, all in all, he was pretty happy with his lot.

She smiled. That was Limp.

***

When the men concluded their conference, the wind intensified, and the trees puffed up like cats. Dirk outstretched his arm, and Limp met his gaze. The men

126

shook hands and embraced.

A noise like a defective flush sounded, and the garlic flowers popped out of the ground and lay there, speechless. An unfamiliar silence draped itself around the men, and then, finally, the ground moved.

With an unholy crack, like from a blimp-sized egg, the clearing started to split.

***

Limp's father also came to visit, though not for a year or so. Dirk found the delay odd but naturally he didn't mention it. Limp once told Dirk that his father was full of himself, and for days afterwards Dirk tried to think of anyone that was full of someone else. Dirk thought it best to simply offer Limp's father the opportunity to throw something down the hole. Limp's father shrugged and said he wasn't interested, though Dirk later saw him throwing down various toiletries when he thought Dirk wasn't looking.

One evening, as Dirk sat on his chair, wondering if he should leave, he thought he heard a voice rising from the hole. He shouted, but his echoes drowned any replies.

After a week of this, Dirk was worried for his health, and his doctor advised that he should take some time off. That being out of the question, he brought a rope into work, and waited for the tourists to go back to where they came from.

Of course the little men were clinging on like burrs. The ground gaped and leered as they tried to crawl away. They were tilted towards the brink without mercy.

Dirk had taken hold of a root and gripped it for dear life. He tried to take his mind off the sinkhole. Failing, he turned his head, and squinted through the dust to see his friend dangling. Limp looked silly when he dangled. It reminded Dirk of something. It would come back to him.

Once Limp was sucked in, the leering stopped and the world composed itself. He could just be heard.

"Give-"

***

The tourists having left, Dirk carefully tied one end of the rope to a tree and one end around his waist. He remembered to strap on his head torch and began to descend, for hours, until the brown sky became just a tiny air hole punctured above his head. The whole way down he kept asking for Limp, but no one pointed him in the right direction. Dirk reckoned that Limp must still be falling, and he prayed that the sandwiches had caught up with him before they'd gone bad.

As it would be morning soon, and the last thing Dirk wanted was to be late for the tourists, he began to haul himself back up. His beam came across an etching on the sinkhole wall. There was an arrow pointing to the sky, and beside it the word: UP. Dirk thought that was obvious.

~o~

'Sinkhole' did not turn out exactly as I had intended; nothing I write ever does. Thankfully, not one sentence from the early drafts has survived. Originally, there were three men, not two, but the third gradually melted into the others. The hole itself was already meant to be present in the clearing when the men first arrived, but Limp was becoming an issue and I wanted to watch him fall. When I first 'finished' the story it was about three times longer, but a slight trim one evening descended into an amputation. These alterations, and many besides, conjured an unrecognisable plot, but the absurdist essence of what I was aiming for endured. I hope.

A bottomless hole seemed an appropriate centrepiece as it opened up numberless possibilities. A story needs a hook, and I felt the hole provided welcome mystery, in the same way as a locked door or drawn curtains might. An enormous hole could potentially mask anything, and with arguably more drama than curtains.

The difficulty of 'Sinkhole' came in placing the narrator. Initially, the voice was purely observational, yet this detachment was too unfeeling, so the narrator was afforded some veiled emotion. This subsequently developed into a restricted insight into Dirk's psyche. There was a conscious desire to maintain a physical distance between the narrator and the two men. After some false starts, I eventually imagined the narrator pinned to a tree at the side of the clearing, and kept him there for the duration of the men's conversation. This proximity allowed the narrator to remain unaffected by the hole, though still in full view of events.

Chance had it that Dirk and Limp planned to meet in the clearing. I always intended for there to be a meeting, then an arrangement for the future, followed by a sweeping, unforeseeable intervention. What they agreed upon in their conversation was irrelevant, as it was never going to come to fruition; their planning was futile. Nothing could immunise them from external circumstance. How can anyone account for chance?

I am intrigued by the absurd genre. 'Sinkhole' explores Dirk's unwavering denial of the ludicrousness of his situation, despite it staring him in the face every day. He manages to make a living by permitting the hole into reality, and simply getting on with it. Dirk's refusal to identify with the absurdity in his life becomes, to me, absurd in itself.

MICHAEL WROBLEWSKI
ROGUE

Michael is a twenty-two-year-old student currently living in Melksham, Wiltshire. He was a medical undergraduate at the University of Liverpool until he decided to follow his passion for English and Creative Writing and enrolled with the Open University. He enjoys the daily challenges that come with studying English and uses the experiences from his medical training to create believable, in depth characters. Outside of his writing, Michael is a keen Badminton and Volleyball player, as well as an amateur tattoo designer. He hopes that as his writing improves, he will be able to publish a set of short stories, leading to an eventual book series.

The alleyway was dark and humid. It was late in the evening and he could feel rats running alongside his boots as he made his way towards the core. Although the alley was almost completely dark, his eyes could still see everything in front of him. Travelling this way was faster, yet these outer city paths were known for being inhibited by bandits, waiting to rob people off their possessions, and lives. The walls were covered in a thick slime, perfect for night shade moss to grow. If he wasn't so tired from the job he had spent the last three days completing, he might have attempted to collect some. On the right markets, in the right cities, the moss was considered a valuable commodity. Regardless, he didn't have the equipment required for the extraction; the moss would wilt as soon as it left the safety of the slime, unless it was suspended in Zerrinian Blue. A liquid equal in price to gold.

As he approached the end of the alley, he felt the bitter cold wind against his back. His leather jacket was terribly worn and needed replacing. It was an expense he had to allow for. The jacket, in combination with the right spells, had saved his life on more than one occasion. It was an essential for his line of work. The core was now just a few feet in front of him; an apparent end of the alley. He decided to scan the area for one last time. Surprisingly, it yielded a result he did not expect. A spy was watching him from about sixty feet away, on top of one of the towers surrounding the area. He touched the wall with one hand, and weaved his other hand into a sign only known to him. It was a mindless task, one performed countless times before. As his hand fell to his side, the brick wall in front of him began transforming. Like snakes, the bricks slithered one across another, forming an arched doorway. The spy no longer made the effort to stay hidden. He knew that he had been spotted. He underestimated the ability of his target to project his aura with such focus and Power. He knew that any movement he now made, would be a waste of time. What he didn't expect was for his target to turn around and with confidence, lock eyes with him. In that moment, the spy jumped off the roof, and vanished into a cloud of black smoke. "*Cheap tricks, meant to scare novices*", thought Rogue, as the brick wall ended its transformation. Where a minute ago was a plain brick wall, now an archway appeared. Not one, but countless archways appeared within the mirror like surface. On closer inspection, the old bricks were engraved with runes of languages long forgotten to man. Each of the archways was slightly different. Some, were made from solid black marble, others from rosewood and ivory. Each belonged to a different place in this world, but he was after only one. He uttered "Vaelisser", a word of the old language, one that had no meaning in this world anymore. The word channelled his Power, and the archway transformed, and became filled with emerald green glass.

It was a portal. A more advanced use of the Power. Not everyone versed in magic was able to conjure one. With practice, multiple portals could be maintained at the same time. Rogue could manage four, and all four were always opened. He had made many enemies, and he had to be able to escape to multiple locations, without the risk of being followed. As an added measure of protection, he had programmed the portals so that they would only let him pass through; anyone else would be transformed into countless pieces of green glass, forever lost in the magic void. Despite hating portals, he knew they were the safest way of travelling. It would take him three days on horse to travel to his safe house, and he would have to travel on roads infested with bandits. He was tired, and wasn't sure that he could face a larger group without suffering injury. As he stepped into the pool of light, he breathed a sigh of relief. Another day was behind him and he knew he was a step closer to achieving his goal. He spent the last three years obsessing over his dream. He would use any means necessary to achieve it. A goal, sacred only to his heart. Nothing else mattered to him.

The damp smell of the underground basement hit him harder than ever, relieving his mind of the thoughts he was having. Stepping into the large basement, he was once again able to be himself. Despite there being no light, he was able to manoeuvre his way through the room without touching anything. His body, moving on its own, simply going through the same motions as always. Despite this, the travel through the portal made him exhausted. With the last of his Power, he cast a spell and ignited all the candles littered across his home. The basement came to life. Despite its modest size, it held more treasures than most people could accrue in a lifetime. The walls, covered in hides of some of the most dangerous animals in the world, animals that normally do not come in contact with people. The ceiling was covered in crests of over a hundred different royal families. Such crests carried enormous favour, and where a part of his plan to achieve his dream. Walking across the room, he unclipped the holster and hung his revolver on a silver hook above the workbench. Then, he carefully reached for his sword and placed it within the wall. With a whisper, he cast a spell and the sword was no longer visible. Only the most adept mages would be able to see through his magic. Without his sword, he was no one. He did all he could to protect his most precious possession.

Wondering through the room, he unbuckled his belt. With a heavy clunk, his trousers hit the wooden floor. He left them behind without taking the care to hang them in their normal place. He felt old. Normally, he would spend some time documenting his last job, but not tonight. Getting rest was his priority. As he got into the bed, he looked at the solid marble inkwell on his desk. It was in a shape of a sparrow, his most beloved bird. "*How I wish to be like you,*" he thought, as his head hit the cold pillows beneath him.

He hated sleeping.

The dreams never left him alone and he wasn't skilled enough to brew the Cytranian potion. Every night he wished that he had been on better terms with the Drams. To them, a Cytranian potion was as easy as child's play. The Drams were a secretive people, and did not make friends with people easily. Especially those trained in the Power. As he lay there, he wondered what he would see tonight. Would it be the soaring skies of Nazir or perhaps the hot sands of Alier? He never complained when he was given a chance to experience flying with the birds of the Great Blue Sky. But he hated the visions of battles fought against the demons in the pits of Rhea.

As his breath deepened, and body relaxed, he began to smell the fresh pines of Azarth.

"*I always loved the wild forest of the North,*" he thought, as his mind began to take him to the land of the never-ending hunt.

***

He was running with the Jet wolves of the North. It was late afternoon and the sun was beginning to set in the blue, cloudless sky. The air was crisp and fresh, and brought comfort to his hard-working lungs. The woodland birds were beginning to sign the songs that marked the end of the day. He grew hungry; neither him nor his brothers had eaten in over a week. They were becoming desperate and could smell the scent of the king elk in the air. Despite his size, he feared the impending meeting with his prey; even the smallest king elks had antlers capable of impaling a bear. Normally, he would stay away from such dangerous prey, but the hunger made him desperate beyond all measures. Suddenly, one of his brothers picked up the smell of king close by. They all soon knew where he was; the tension in the pack grew. Their prey was large, and in its prime. It was going to be a difficult fight. If it was his decision, he would keep moving forwards, knowing that there are other elks in this forest, weaker and more vulnerable than this one. But there was no stopping his brother. He was no longer capable of thought. In that moment, all he could think about what the warm flesh of the slayed beast. The flesh that would sustain his hunger and allow him to survive. And so, the pack began chasing after its prey. Howling, growling and snapping their jaws as they ran.

To his left, two of the youngest members of the pack ran. They had only joined recently and their names were not known to him. The female, despite her young age, was already the size of a strong adult. He knew that in time, she would lead a pack of her own. In comparison, her brother, was nothing more than a pup. His fur was still a mixture of black and grey. It would be sometime until he reached the jet-black colour of his sibling. To his right, ran the leader of the pack, Jazar. He was one of a kind, even for the most ferocious of the jet wolves. After at least two decades of leading his pack, his body was littered with scars from countless battles. The most prominent one, was that which was left by a mountain claw bear; it ran from his ear to his chin and across his mouth. Years of experience combined with his enormous size meant that despite his age, no male in this pack ever dared to question his leadership. His word was the law.

His nose was the first to alert him that they were close. With a single snap of his jaw, Jazar stopped everyone mid-stride. He knew where they were. Hidden by the bushes, he could see what appeared to be a meadow. He knew that the Drams used this place for their rituals, but only during the full moon. With another snap of his jaw, Jazar ordered everybody to move along the meadow, and surround the elk from every angle, other than north. They always used this tactic, if the prey was in a right location. Once they would all get into their positions, they would come out together, growling and spitting at the elk. In a moment of panic, the elk would run towards the only route of escape, where Jazar waited in ambush. One strike to the neck of the elk and the fight would be over. As he took his position, he felt scared. For some reason, something didn't seem right. The air was denser than usual, and for this time of the day, there was an unusual warmth coming from the meadow. He didn't have enough time to think about his worries though, as he soon heard the howl that was their signal to move in on the prey.

He entered the meadow slowly, carefully placing one paw in front of the other. Appearing confident was half of the hunt. If the prey felt any weakness from any of the hunters, it would charge towards them hoping to break the formation. He let out a harsh growl. He heard his brothers and sisters respond. The elk didn't spook. Instead, it continued to graze, unaware of the brutal death that awaited him. He started to feel more scared. Something really wasn't right and this time he was sure that he had felt the sensation before. In that moment, Llyac, the wolf who first picked up the scent of the elk snapped and started blindly charging forward. It was too late by the time he remembered where and when he felt this sensation before.

This was a trap.

Before he was able to get his warning howl out, Llyac was struck by an arrow, then three more, each aimed at one of his legs. He collapsed to the ground right by where the elk had just stood. However, it was no longer an elk, but one of the Shae. This hidden clan of hunters often preyed on Jet wolves. It was a tradition, performed through centuries.

It now all made sense.

The heat in the meadow was coming from a spell cast by one of the hunters. It was supposed to mask their smell. What's more, the spell made it impossible to see the hunters positioned in the trees with their bows and arrows pointed at the open space beneath them. When he was a young pup, he found himself in a similar situation near the southern border of the forest. He was the only one of his pack to survive, and was given a new home by Jazar. There was nothing they could now do for Llylac. With such injuries, he was unable to stand, let alone run.

All hell broke loose.

Arrows were flying everywhere and the air filled with the metallic smell of blood. He felt an arrow strike him in the back, but he considered himself lucky. By then, he had managed to escape into protection of the woods. The shrubs, bushes and low pines bcame his protection from the arrows. As he ran, he knew that he had to reunite with the other members of the pack. His priority was finding Jazar. He ran north, and was joined by the young female of the pack. There were tears in her eyes. He knew that her brother had not made it. As they ran together, more joined. He was surprised by how many had made it out. Just like him, most were injured in some way, but in total they had only lost only five of their three dozen strong pack. They still had the numbers to survive, all they lacked now was their leader.

The smell of blood had filled his nostrils once again.

He didn't want to believe it, but he knew what his eyes were about to show him; the true purpose of the ambush. As he ran into an open space between shrubs, his eyes saw the dead body of Jazar, beheaded and poached of its fur. He howled in frustration. He had been part of the pack for over a decade and Jazar was his closest friend. He didn't want to look at him this way; he wanted to remember him for what he was. The finest Jet wolf to have ever roamed these forests. The hunters were really after their leader, hoping to disband the pack and make easy prey of the remainder. Jet wolves are only a threat when they are led; individually, they cannot hunt and quickly die of starvation. As he turned around, he saw despair in the eyes of the pack. They too knew, that without a leader, they would become easy prey for the Hunters, especially the young, less experienced wolves. He walked away from the pack, and started to head further into the forest. He had lost all hope and simply wanted to live out the reminder of his days in peace. He knew that alone, he didn't stand a chance to survive more than a few weeks.

It was then that he heard the howl. The blood thirsty, angered, agonised howl of the young female. A howl that asked for a response. A response from him, and the other wolves present.

What she suggested knocked the air out of his lungs.

~o~

Rogue is the first piece of extended writing which I attempted to create, and therefore it was a steep learning curve in terms of presentation, styling and plot development.

I started the process by finding out how to present a piece of fiction; double line spacing, indented paragraphs and single quotation marks were all '*foreign*' to my writing and I had to learn how to use them appropriately. As I enjoy writing within the fantasy genre, I decided to create a world influenced by book series such as The Witcher or A Song of Ice And Fire as well as games such as Fallout or ELEX. I picked a male protagonist as recently there has been a real surge in popularity for female characters and I didn't want to be swept by a growing trend. I intended to create a character that fits the world that I am making, and not one which is there simply to please the audience. This is a key lesson which I learnt through writing this story and presenting an extract of it in this anthology. Instead of writing to please a potential audience, I wrote in order to fulfil my expectations, needs and desires. I think this shift in attitude helped me to create a piece which feels authentic and original. It represents a real part of me and this is something that I am keen to work on and develop as a writer. Being a relatively inexperienced writer, I struggled with keeping this piece succinct and cohesive, as it is only a small part of a much larger project. I had to find the right balance between action and background/setting to capture the interest of the reader. The main protagonist of the piece is heavily based on me; something which I really enjoyed experimenting with. For example, I have always experienced incredibly vivid and powerful dreams which often leave me tired and amazed. I think the '*dream*' part of the story was most successful because of my own experience of vivid (lucid) dreams.

There is another aspect of the piece which I am proud of. Many books and authors which inspire my writing use multiple points of view, narrators and settings in their stories. As a result, I was keen to experiment with presenting the story from a different perspective, through a different character. I think this engages the readers more and makes them more likely to be interested in the story. This is something that I want to continue to use in my future writing and develop in the Rogue's story.

However, there were also unsuccessful elements to this story. I experienced a great deal of '*writer's block*' near the start of the piece and almost ended up not developing the idea at all. Using freewriting, as well as thorough editing, I was able to write and present the beginnings of a story which feels authentic and original. A story which I am proud to say I have written.

LOUISE BERGER
THE DREAM CATCHER

Louise Berger is a twenty-year-old writer and illustrator who likes to play guitar in the forest. Studying Creative Writing, Philosophy and Ethics in Chichester, her main interests lie with psycho-philosophical writing and the perception of reality. She frequently sets out to explore the strangeness in near and far places and has a strong affinity for train rides.

Legend said he was the Dream Catcher, an evil spirit that stole the dreams of those who did not care to keep them. But legends sometimes went, this one did not do him justice. He was little more than an ordinary man; he was the gardener of the moon.

His days were spent in the garden, where others came to spend their nights, to play and laugh, to seek adventures that could only be broken by dawn. Days were different, while not much brighter. The garden was dim on its best days, lit up here and there by obscure shimmers that floated, like spirits might, under the leafs of big and violet ferns.

Days were different because they were not spent dreaming. It was the only time he was able to enter the garden and tend to the plants. He would water the flowers that never seemed to wilt and cut the grass that would have regained its length by the same time tomorrow. On some days he would collect dreams that had been left behind.

Lost or forgotten, dreams – when left to their own devices – did the most peculiar things. Flowers suddenly grew ten feet tall, or trees were so small they could fit through the eye of a needle. They turned things purple or blue, or any colour, really. Not to speak of nightmares. Terrors of the dark were rare but could create twisted shows of fright in the otherwise peaceful green. Luckily, however, nightmares proved to be sticky. While their dreamers were eager to leave them behind, they were a dark and tough matter that would cling to their shoes. Most people carried them out with them when they left in the morning.

The Dream Catcher was a good man. A little lost, perhaps, because he himself could not dream, but good nevertheless. He liked the dreams, foreign stories of hearts and souls, for they were as close as he would ever get to dreaming. It was beyond him how they could be left behind, forgotten or even discarded, but there were many things he did not understand. How could one who had never dreamt talk about dreams as if he knew the very first thing about them?

The Dream Catcher was as little a scholar as he was a dreamer. He was a gardener and he was a man with a great appreciation for art. The dreams he rescued became paintings he had not conjured himself, colours he had not chosen and painted. He could admire them nevertheless, and so he did.

When night came, he sometimes watched the garden too, seeing the dreamers play and laugh, so wide-awake and yet fast asleep somewhere down on earth. He did not go out then. He had tried, several times, but how could one that did not dream ever hope to enter this garden at night? It was the Eden of dreams and after dusk only dreamers were permitted.

He had not set out to become who he was today. Many years ago, so many he had lost count, he had hoped to find his dreams. It had been a long and quite impossible journey. Through luck and a lot of coincidence he had found a way to walk on the path of the moon, an invisible and quite fantastic voyage whose existence was greatly debated. On his pursuit he had learned that few people sincerely believed in a link to the moon. Furthermore, the idea that this path was indeed open to ordinary men was little more than a whispered fantasy that lingered in empty streets at night.

His confidence had wavered, but doubt had never outweighed hope, though it was a mystery how he had been successful. On the moon he had found purpose, he had found dreams, but the ability to dream continued to elude him. As the initial excitement about having found the path to the moon wore off, he realized that he was unable to leave this land of the dreaming. There is no escape from the world of dreams if you cannot wake up.

It might have been rage or just fear that had led him to do what he had done the day he had become the gardener of the moon. Back then the garden had been wild and unkempt. Lost so far away from home, so far from a reality he could understand, he had begun picking flowers. He had not picked them the way a boy might pick flowers to present to his mother. He had torn at them, agony, regret, and resentment let loose in a furious attack on the sweet and fragile roses, until the lone man finally collapsed. He had fallen to his knees, crying, dead flowers spread around him. Innocent flowers, a sight of indescribable beauty, had suffered his failure.

He had forced his eyes shut, unable to face what he had done, but the garden had not died. Hours passed where he had not moved, but when he finally looked up he was greeted by a sight of marvel. Soft petals of white roses sprung from the branches. Tiny red flowers grew closer to the ground and the grass shone greener than it ever had before. The garden had regenerated where he had torn the flowers. He promised, partially to himself, partially to the garden, to do whatever he could to help. He wished to take care of the flowers and hoped to one day deserve the second chance he had been given.

Even though he had started out of a sense of obligation, these motives had lost prominence years ago. He no longer tended to the garden to redeem himself. He did it because he cared. Perhaps the lack of other activities on the isolated moon fuelled his efforts too, but only slightly. This was what he had become: the gardener of the moon, the Dream Catcher.

Every morning he got to see the beauty he knew he helped sustain. It was a good life, knowing that everything you loved would be there in the morning. Day after day he kept the garden flawless, night after night he explored the art he distilled from dreams. He did not sleep much; he found it a waste if he could not dream. All remained in order, he knew he would be alone, until one day, he wasn't.

Walking the usual route all looked familiar. Shimmering colours, floating lights, perhaps some signs of exhaustion from the night before. Plants, much like people, needed time to rest. He walked, looking at the ground as he always did. Lost in thought, or rather lost in the serenity of his daily duties it took him an instance to notice her. The Dream Catcher hesitated, caught completely off guard. It had been a long time since he had interacted with anybody. In fact it had been so long that he doubted whether his voice still worked. As he stopped and stared, she too turned her gaze to look at him.

'You are not supposed to be here.' His voice worked just fine.

'Oh, but I am very much supposed to be here.' She smiled. 'Have you not been waiting to find me all this time?'

Her voice had the quality of dawn.

For the first time in years the gardener noticed the morning dew on the grass. It had soaked his shoes.

'I have been waiting for you today.' Her eyes seemed to reflect the colours of the garden.

'I don't see how you could have.' His voice was doing fine, but the damp of his shoes started to feel cold at his toes. 'This place is not for dreamers once the night has passed.'

'So it appears.' She hesitated to look at the sky. 'But not all of us are dreamers, are we? You are no dreamer.'

'No.' He didn't understand why anyone would want to see the sky. It was nothing but blackness. Nothing made sense, and even though it had been years he could recognise a normal conversation.

'Neither am I.'

This was not one.

The gardener, a man who was used to solitude, did not dare to speak. The impossibility of anyone being in the garden after sunrise upset him. He feared that she was not there, that his mind tricked him. One did not speak to flowers.

But as she reached out to him his defences fell. Her hand was timeless, her fingers fluid as if suspended, real. In the garden of dreamers he was no longer alone.

But how? He had seen people try to stay, but the garden had sent them on their way. *How could she have stayed?*

'Who are you?'

It was her turn to remain silent, but only for a moment.

'What if I said I am your dream?'

The Dream Catcher smiled, a rueful smile.

'I would answer that this would be quite charming indeed. Unfortunately for the two of us I do not dream.'

'Will you tell me your name?'

'Vincent.' The taste of his own name lay sour on his tongue, a sweet memory that could never be relived. It had been a part of the past; he had not needed it on the moon. Had he lied to her? He did not know if it really was his name. Could he reclaim it after so many rears?

'Vincent. Can you tell me what happens to dreams that are lost?'

He could and he did. It seemed these were truths she had known all along.

'What would happen if someone wanted to retrieve a lost dream?'

'I don't know. Nobody ever tried.'

'What makes you say that? You know this is not true.'

But it was. They had started to walk through the garden.

'Are you sure no dreamer has ever come back to find a lost dream?'

Looking at her, the thoughts of flowers returned, warm as the sun on earth. He was sure, but she was relentless.

'Why do you believe no one came looking for them?'

'Because I surely would have noticed.'

'But would you?'

The thoughts of flowers and the sun were distorted by her interrogation, a mild stinging appeared somewhere in his body.

'Of course I would.' Now it was him who stared while her eyes were cast to the sky again. The stinging was floating through him, leaving a trail of anxiety. It was in his stomach, his lungs, even in his hands and fingertips. It dismembered him, taking another step suddenly seemed dangerous. He was shaken, his routine broken, doubt returned.

'Vincent?'

He had stopped walking and the woman turned.

'Don't call me that.' He stood still, rigid, trying to hide his falling apart, like a drunkard hoped to hide his drunkenness. Something was not right. Alarm had his mind running in a circle and he yearned for solitude. How could he escape what was on his mind now? He could regain control, he told himself, if only no one was watching.

'I'm just the gardener.' He had to make her understand. 'I don't think I'm the

145

one you need to talk to.' There was nobody else she could talk to. Maybe she would leave. 'I really need to do my work here.' He was rambling and rambling, his words unconvincing.

He was the gardener of the moon, a kind man and a calm man. But even the kindest man has pain that is locked away in his chest. One did not speak to flowers, but he wanted to. He had been so alone; they had been his only company. He wanted to thank them.

She looked at him, her eyes an impossible reflection of a far away sky, blue and radiant.

It occurred to him that he was the one who was not adapted. He felt alien. *A strange thing to say on the moon.*

'I don't mind waiting for you to finish. This is no work to neglect. It's like a promise. Keep it.'

Again, her words were ambiguous but oh so precise.

'It takes longer than you will like. A couple of hours, two at least.'

'That is fine.' She hesitated. 'But I will accompany you. It is intriguing to watch.'

'I don't mind.' He did, but didn't want to. 'Come along all you like.'

Her smile seemed more genuine this time. Not that the others had been misguiding, but they had lacked an exuberance that now unfolded on her lips.

One did not talk to flowers, but maybe this one was an exception.

They walked in silence. The gardener had never been watched while working, but she had the habit to look at the sky instead of him.

She was controlled to a point where every step seemed carefully rehearsed. From time to time she bent down or knelt in the grass to look at a flower, caring for petals and thorns equally. *She does belong here.* Claiming to be a dream had not been absurd after all. She resembled one, just not his own. *Unfortunately.*

They had left the roses and the tulips far behind them. Passing daisies and shrubs, they neared the ferns by the river.

'The moon is a strange place.'

Her eyes met his and he half expected a clear reflection of the violet foliage around them. They remained the colour of a sunlit sky instead. Maybe eyes were mirrors of the soul after all, not of the exterior world.

He nodded. 'You may say so.' They kept walking. 'But what makes you say this now?'

She looked; half turned, and gently lifted a blade of fern with her upturned hand. 'It is purple. This place is filled with strange colours. Blue over there, pink and turquoise here. The colours go from light to dark, all ranges, really, but they all appear somewhat muted.'

She was right. While the colours could be strong, the garden looked dormant, even with the open buds of most flowers.

'It's the garden of dreams.' He had told himself the same thing several times. 'There is no reason for it to look awake.'

She shook her head but remained silent. The same reaction he always had. Something was missing. The garden was not incomplete; it was as complete as gardens should be. It was merely a personal preference. He could not say what it was, but it was there.

In the river the crystalline water rushed over white stones. A dream was caught between two rocks, where it swayed back and forth. He broke the surface of the water with a tall scoop he had been carrying. Waves of colour stirred as the fine net broke through to free the dream that had drowned there. The liquid mirror showed the bottom of the river as well as the stark face of his reflection. Copper hair messed by the labour. It was familiar, of course, although distorted by the water. It was a view into a stranger dimension that probably wasn't supposed to exist. But at the bottom lay a dream.

He caught it, breaking the reflection as he pulled it to the surface.

She looked at the dripping mesh. 'Do you find a lot of dreams in there?'

'I suppose I do.'

Dreams depended on the dreamer that had conjured them and should a dreamer create physical contact, dreams reacted. She reached into the net and lifted the thing that hung between the dripping strings. Nothing happened as she held it close to her face.

'It looks so dull.' Her words might have been disappointed or sad. For him it was the latter.

'They sometimes do.'

She handed it to him with care and he placed in a bag that was slung over his shoulder.

'That doesn't mean it is dull when expressing itself.'

147

'I know.' Her eyes locked on the diamond surface of the river. 'It's a shame they ever do appear this sombre.'

'It is not much of a surprise, really.' He had figured it out long ago. 'They have been cast aside, unwanted and overlooked. Dreams are like people, I think. They wither if they are dismissed.' Some dreams were stronger than others, for not all dreams faded. Maybe those were more independent, if dreams could be independent, or they had been lost but not yet forgotten.

'What do you do with the dreams you find?'

He looked at her summer sky eyes.

'I will show you.' He had never shown anyone, she would be the first. They walked back as the garden grew gloomier. Evening was nearing.

He opened his door and let her enter. Stepping on the creaky wood her feet made no sound, as if the house had not yet realized that someone had stepped inside. Routine. Sometimes even reality seemed to bend around it. The moment he closed the door the dreams closed in around them. She spun in a lazy pirouette, looking around. Paintings framed the room, leaving only the floor. The ground reminded him of the harsh reality that these dreams were not his. He remained the man who could not dream. It was simple. He was the gardener, the Dream Catcher, and perhaps even Vincent. But he was not a dreamer.

Never a dreamer. If what he felt was sadness, he was convinced it was a sadness that would last forever.

'I have never seen this many paintings.' She had started to look at the sky again, only this time the sky was the ceiling that was also fully covered in art.

'A lot of dreams got lost over the years.'

'The Dream Catcher.'

'What?'

She had spoken under her breath.

'I like how you try to display all of them.'

There were stacks of paintings in the corners of the room and a couple of the hanging paintings were overlapping one another. The lack of space was evident, but there were no boxes in which paintings had been hidden away.

'I don't have a choice. They all deserve to be seen. How could I ever chose one over another?'

Both of them remained silent for a long time, looking at the art. Perhaps she was trying to pick a favourite, but it was impossible. One does say for good reason that the best art is that, which is conceived out of the painter's dream. The dream to create, the dream to express, there were at least as many dreams as painters.

'How does it work?' She spoke with a soft voice, humbled and careful not to disturb the strange serenity emitted by the art.

'How does what work?'

Their words carried just above whispers.

'The art. Hoes a dream go from this,' She pulled the dream from the river out of the bag he had put down next to the door, 'to this? What makes such a dull figure become a painting like the others?'

'It melts.' He took the dream from her.

'It what?'

He pulled a canvas from a stack behind his armchair. It was empty and white.

'I'm not really sure how it works either.'

He put the canvas on the low desk and placed the dream on it, checked and centred it a little more.

'It was an accident the first time it happened.'

He told her of that evening he had found his first dream, small but shimmering with bright colours. He had picked it up, wondering where it had come from. Only later had he remembered the thing in his pocket and placed it on some white linen in the otherwise undecorated room. He had left it and the white of the fabric had disappeared. It had been replaced by colour, paint as it appeared, white showing only faintly around the edges. He had searched for the strange object but not found it. With time the white faded even more and the painting had become clearer.

That had been the beginning of his collection, his first companion in a bleak room. Now the walls had grown too small for all the paintings but there were still white canvases for dreams to come.

'How did you know those were dreams?'

'I didn't. Not for a long time, but I think they are. It just seems right.' He gestured at the room. 'What else could they be?' His eyes came to rest on a paining to his left. 'This one, for example.'

She leaned to look past him as he showed it to her.

'Looking at it makes you feel something, doesn't it?'

'A story perhaps? Or a melody?' She hesitated.

'I don't know. I never am able to settle for one. But there is definitely something in these paintings.'

'So you say the stories are the dreams?'

'They might be. I don't know if there are dreams in the art, or if there is art in the dreams, but they go hand in hand. I am sure they do.'

She continued to study his collection in comfortable silence. The dream on the table remained visibly unchanged.

He looked at her, distracted from the art by her weightless steps. Wasn't she floating around the room, her hair swaying ever so slightly?

'Who are you?' He had been wary of her response earlier but it had been replaced by plain curiosity.

She did not answer.

'I can't understand why you came here. Surely not for the art, was it?' Nobody knew about the art. The gallery on the moon was a secret.

'Yes and no. I wanted to see what you had done with them. Still, you are right. This is not why I came.'

'Done with what? The dreams?'

'Naturally.'

'But why did you come then? Tell me.'

She didn't answer.

'Did you ever consider painting anything yourself?'

'I did.'

He had never resorted to brush and paint though. Not up here. He might have painted on earth, he figured, but he could not recall.

'You should.'

The stinging returned.

'I don't think I can.' He had thought about it many times.

'Why not?'

'My eyes are grey and bleak; I could never do justice to scenes of beauty. I couldn't do it, even if I could dream.'

She stared at him. 'That's not true.' There was something in her eyes as they looked into his. Was it knowledge? A memory he did not recall? 'Your eyes are anything but bleak. They are like the river, crystal and marble.'

They were lost in yet another silent moment, the gardener, the woman, and within him the stinging, now bittersweet.

'I came to show you something.'

'Show me something?'

'Something you have been looking for all this time.'

He smiled, but smiles meant many different things. This one was an apology.

'You are talking about my dream.' It was an apology to her.

'I am.'

It was an apology to himself.

'I spent years in pursuit.' The stinging was back. 'But I am afraid this is all in the past.'

'No. Don't cease searching, Vincent. Where would that lead you?'

'Maybe I am lost.'

'Then keep going. Keep going, come what may.'

While he did not believe her he agreed to try. Even outside the garden the moon was quite beautiful. Step after step past flowers and grass, they travelled on a path more alive than you would find on earth. They passed the garden, already full of dreamers.

'The night is alive, much more so than the day. It is strange to see so many people. They make me feel invisible. To them I don't exist. I am such a nobody.'

As he spoke the thing in her eyes returned. Recognition? Something distant.

'You are the one who knows the garden by daylight. There are many things that escape them at night. You put your heart and soul into your work and you get to see it all.'

'I don't do much. I am nothing but the gardener.'

She shook her head again and pointed at the flowers.

'You do something good every day. You sustain all of this; you care for flower after flower. The garden is a series of small things, all brought together. This is your work. Trust me, there will come a day where the dreamers will realize that the value of your work is much greater than the petals of cut roses.'

One did not talk to flowers, but there he was. Over the course of the evening the Dream Catcher had continued to view her as a flower. She had a similar

151

effect on him. She was uplifting company on the lonely moon. For the first time in years he wanted to talk. Maybe she was right. Maybe he had put his heart and soul into his work and maybe he had lost his mind in the process. But right now he didn't mind.

'Why do you always look up there?' While he had looked at the wild flowers, the woman's gaze had drifted upwards again.

'Don't you see it anymore?'

He looked up at the blackness. 'See what?'

'The stars.' She sighed. 'The sky. Don't you see the colours of the night flowing? Swirls and waves like the water in the river?'

He tried to imagine this, tried to paint it up there, on the black canvas. It did not work. 'I don't see anything.'

She kept staring. 'It's up there. All of it.' But after another instance she faced him again.

'You need to remember. It's in your eyes, I know you used to see it.'

Like the river, she had said before, but there was nothing that changed what he could see. They both stared up for a long time, she insisted, but all was black and it was time they continued.

Walking, the Dream Catcher wondered what the sky might look like to her.

They had passed the limit of his furthest explorations long ago, when nature started to change. Here and there white rocks started to emerge from the ocean of violet, blue, and green. The marble of the moon was smooth and edgy at once, he wondered if it would hurt to fall on these rocks. Physical sensations, especially pain, were dulled on the moon. It might seem like a good thing to feel no pain and discomfort, but without them he had forgotten the value of joy. It was better to feel, better to be aware.

'Where are you leading me?'

'To where you lost your dream.'

It was impossible.

'I never had a dream.'

'Yes you did.'

'I came up here to learn how to dream, not to find one.'

Walking over many rocks now, their exchange came to abrupt halts whenever one of them had to climb or find footing on a smooth slab of marble.

'How do you think you were able to walk to the moon without ever having dreamt?'

He had wondered about this too.

'You said no one came back to find their dreams, while you had done just that.' Climbing seemed easier to her. 'You came back without even knowing why.' She skipped while he struggled and stumbled. 'How ironic.'

She stopped several steps ahead of him, not looking back.

'If what you say is true,' he was slowly catching up to her, 'how can I have lost my dream somewhere I have never been before?'

'But you have.'

It was one more step until he finally stood next to her. Prepared to prove her wrong, he looked at what was in front of them.

There was a new colour.

Could it be?

'Don't be shy. If you don't believe me, go and prove me wrong. You know what to do.'

Reaching to feel the petals he was prepared for almost anything, but he had not expected the sky to shift. The moment he touched the gentle flower, the floor was swept from underneath his feet. The moon tumbled, as, with an enormous tug, the black was forced from above. His world was contorted into a most enchanted scene. The night had become alive; yellow, green, light and dark blue.

'You see it now, don't you?' She stepped next to him and together they looked up at the sky, where colours seemed to flow and twist.

He imagined he had seen it before, down on earth. He would have painted it, each swirl a powerful brushstroke, each wave a field of energy. He had not believed her; he had not thought his eyes could perceive such beauty. How could they, for were they not the mirror to his soul?

After a long time of marvelling at this newfound sky, he looked back at the tall flower in front of them. She was smiling again, but this time he was too.

'Do you believe me now?'

'Yes.' His voice was hoarse. The stinging had finally broken free. This was what he had missed in the garden. 'The sunflower,' he stroked the rough centre of the plant, 'it is mine, in a way.'

Surrounded by the marble of the moon and the churning sky, it was just them and the sunflower.

'You know you can go back now, if you want.'

He had not thought of this.

'You can give it another try down on earth.'

Now that he had found his dream, he could wake up into another life.

'I wonder what you name would be this time around, Vincent.'

'Me too.' They sat thinking. 'It might be nice to try again, but at the moment I am as happy as I can imagine myself being. I would not ask for more.'

She smiled; again there was the thing in her eyes.

'I think I will plant the sunflower in the garden.'

'The one thing it still needed.'

Dawn slowly crawled over the horizon. When he got home he would paint. After all he had found his dream.

~o~

The Dream Catcher was an opportunity to explore the dynamic of a past filled with forgotten tragedy and the remainder of identity, which has become alien to the protagonist.

Drawing inspiration from the artist Vincent Van Gogh, his idea of death as a means of travelling among stars brought forth an idea for the setting.

> '[L]ooking at the stars always makes me dream [...]. Why, I ask myself, shouldn't the shining dots of the sky be as accessible as the black dots on the map of france? Just as we take the train to get to Tarascon or Rouen, we take death to reach a star'.

With the freedom of writing a piece of fiction, the moon lend itself as location for an ostracised dreamer, juxtaposing external harmony with his mental instability.

It was insufficient to simply create a character, who bore resemblance to the painter and shared his name. Instead, I found it crucial to create a plot that could lead the reader away from the tragic realities of the painter's life, while remaining faithful to who the character of Vincent Van Gogh might have been.

Throughout the story there is a consistent descriptive quality to the narrative tone, relating the piece to the medium of the artist, where words imitate the brushstrokes used to paint Vincent Van Gogh's passion. Contrasting this, the protagonist's speech alternates between kindness and defiance, representing the individual's internal struggle.

As the story proceeds and the Dream Catcher gradually remembers his identity, references to the artist become more prominent. His reflection in the river alludes to Van Gogh's *Self Portrait*, while the river itself refers to his eyes, the mirrors of his soul, crystalline with a drowned dream at its bottom.

Furthermore, while the protagonist begins to speak in reference to quotes from Vincent Van Gogh as the link to his identity strengthens, the most comprehensive references are to sunflowers, as well as to Van Gogh's *The Starry Night*. Even though the artist's prominent qualities such as his bold vision and expressive brushstrokes remained unappreciated during his lifetime, they are pivotal to this story.

Ultimately, while it was pleasant to resolve the tragedy of the tortured painter, it remains an exercise that is reserved to fiction. Having found his dream, the Dream Catcher is given another chance in reality. To accept this, however, he would have to abandon his previous identity. Vincent Van Gogh can never wake up.

HARRIET JACHEC
SICKENING SWEETNESS

Enchanted by all things literary, Harriet takes inspiration from history, humanity, and the world around her. A recent graduate from the Literature with Creative Writing BA at the University of Greenwich, she is determined to keep writing as she embarks further on her teaching and academic career. She currently lives in Oxford, where she spends her time walking, reading, laughing, and studying for her PGCE.

The farmland was sodden from the previous night. A gradient of clouds stretched beyond the expanse of the pale horizon, the stained sky reflected in puddles and streams below. Fresh air seeped in soundlessly through the kitchen window, left ajar, just how she preferred it in the mornings. The lavender scent visited now and then.

Bittersweet coffee in her blue mug. She poured the remnants of the drink down the plughole, and washed it under the tap. The tea towel scratched at her malleable skin as she dried the porcelain. She placed the cup deliberately inside a cupboard.

'Jenny, the clumsy one,' she could hear him growl in his smoker's voice, like he was still sat in the living room, his feet propped up on the sofa, the big toe of his left foot discernible through his shabby slippers.

The news would blare out from the flickering television set, 'there has been a backlash from unionists —'

She'd always implore him to switch it off, to minimise his own misery. He would simply tap his pipe into the ashtray, engrossed in the images on the screen.

Thirty years of marriage – it was hard to believe that they stuck together for that long. She found herself clutching the dishcloth to her chest, and set it down. Beyond the fence, Bessie, with her dirtied legs, grazed wearily. Others snoozed in the far distance. If only she could be as dumb as a cow. Then she wouldn't have to deal with the rascal that relentlessly invaded her farm.

That bloody scoundrel, at her chickens again yesterday. It was tough, though, to be so unforgiving to something that was merely surviving. Nevertheless, she had to trap the damned animal to maintain her own survival.

Three pairs of thick wool socks padded her already tired feet, and in the hallway, her steps were soft against the worn floorboards. She pulled on the green rubber wellingtons. They were his best pair until he gave them to her, and the smell of old, dried dirt was comforting. The soil that stuck to them served as evidence of times gone by. She was careful to tread on the newspaper pages when she wore them – no use muddying the house up, making more work for herself. A sturdy, blue mackintosh, to battle out the day with. An elastic band kept her wiry hair back. She would be fifty-five years old the next day. But this morning, she was still fifty-four. Keys – already in the coat pocket.

The door opened with a squeal, and Manus was already there, panting at her feet, sniffing at his master's boots. He barked once, and she bent down to quiet him.

'There, boy.'

His black and white fur was flecked with brown. She patted him gently, and pulled her fingers back and forth through his matted coat.

'You've been at the puddles again, haven't you? It makes you look like a proper worker.'

He smelt of damp. She stood up, her back aching, and her eyes instinctively squinted. The green of the land was fresh, and the wild flowers swayed together. They speckled the landscape, with blue, red, yellow, and white. The distant hills undulated and swam like strange water.

The gravel beneath her rubber soles crunched as she turned around and shut the door.

'Come on boy, come!'

Manus leapt away from her towards the fields. Droplets flew in the air as his paws met the ground violently. He shook himself off as he continued to run.

'No, you daft creature,' she yelled after him. The keys jangled as she unlocked the Rover. 'Come back here, Manus.'

He did so, and jumped onto the backseat, panting ferociously.

The scent of leather mixed with dog smell and cut grass met her, the pungency making her head throb dully. She shut the door behind him, opened the driver's, and got behind the wheel. She started the engine. It chattered to life, and she set off.

The car tore through the landscape. Her hands were dry against the coriaceous steering wheel, like they would be after handling resin. She could not forget its heady smell. She was much younger the last time she had used it: the amber stone that, when smoothed against the strings of her bow, would coat it with a balmy protection. Her flesh was softer then, apart from after rehearsing her pieces, as the strings would bite into her fingertips. The scent of polished wood filled her senses, and the melodies of times gone by reverberated through her memory.

A strange jolt in her stomach made her heart leap, as she realised that she could have made it as national Fiddle Champion if it weren't for the accident. After that, all her parents were concerned with was securing her future. What could be better, more rounding for an Irish girl, than to become a farmer's wife?

It was a good thing she had met him, otherwise it would have been a long, lonely road in running the farm. She could envision his younger face now, turning towards her in Killay town hall. His grin lit up his face, his blue eyes shone once more, and his hand took hers in their first jive. As they sat on the terrace afterwards, drinks in hands, she was fascinated by his stories of his family, his dreams, and the war.

But that was a time long past.

Driving along the dirt track propelled her back into the present; she gasped loudly, and pushed down hard on the brakes so as to avoid collision with a small, grey animal. A dart, a leap, and the rabbit jumped into the hedge on the left, safely out of reach of the car. Driven wild by the action, Manus barked and yelped.

She breathed fast, and grit her teeth, her pulse intensifying. Why was it out of the hutch? She switched the engine off, and got out of the car to inspect the wire fence. Bent upwards, with loose parts jutting away from it, the turf underneath was messily carved out. Dry, crumbly earth was scattered all around. She frowned, her hands placed on her hips.

One daybreak, years ago, Pa had taken her to a similar scene on the farm. He pointed towards the small trench, and made her stoop down with him, poring over the scooped-out ground. 'Remember this rhyme, Jennifer,' he had told her, '"a hole in the ground, there's a fox to be found."'

That was the third time she had glimpsed such a hole within the space of a week. A fox to be found. She locked the car, so that Manus would not run away. Mad dog.

The old oak tree grew beside the area where the rabbits were kept, its bark mottled and knotted with age. The light that broke through the leaves licked over the wooden hutches.

She entered their grazing area, and closed the fence with a metallic sound as the lock clanked into place. The air was dank, musky.

Clumps of rabbit fur were strewn across the glistening, neatly clipped grass. She crouched down and picked up a piece, immediately dropping it as her fingers became slightly bloodied. The attack was recent. She wiped her left hand on her jeans, and stood up. The salty smell of urine became apparent. The confirmation of the fox's presence made a lump appear in her throat.

She checked the hutches. When she poked her head in, one rabbit looked up at her with its watchful eyes and twitching whiskers. There were still enough left for breeding. She stepped away, and the smell of hay and rabbit faeces lingered momentarily.

This time, she would trap the damned thing.

***

As a child, she adored animals – they were prevalent in the fields dotted throughout the town. She had always wanted a pet horse, and would dream of owning one almost nightly. By day, she would plead with her parents to get one.

In a momentary lapse of his typically austere nature, Pa bought her two hamsters. He must have sensed Jennifer warming to him, and – despite this glimpse of compassion – stated, 'I don't believe you have what it takes, young lady, to handle a horse by yourself. Let's see what you make of these little pets, shall we?'

She fondly named them Percy and Olive. Determined to prove that she could handle the responsibility, she helped out more than usual to earn money for their upkeep, and cleaned their cage and fed them by herself.

Some months passed, and with them came a plan to appeal for the horse once more. After all, she had proved herself to be a highly meticulous owner.

She dragged her parents by their hands to her bedroom, and turned to them as soon as they had passed through the door.

'Ma, Pa, listen to me. I can do it – I've looked after them well, don't you see?'

Ma moved silently past her. Gravely, she picked up the cage, and held it so her father could see.

He shook his head, checked his pocket watch, and went downstairs.

Placing the hamsters on the floor, her mother crouched down so her face was level with Jennifer's. 'Oh, love,' she consoled her, 'you tried your best. Not to worry.' Ma followed Pa out the door.

In the cage, Percy drank fiercely out of the water bottle. Olive lay on her back, her pelt sullied with blood, her eyes wide open in horror.

***

She had to be tough, now: some animals must be held accountable for their actions.

She sought out the fox's hiding hole, trudging through the pulpy leaves in the woods beyond the farm. The outer woodlands had smelt comforting, warm; these inner parts were repugnant, compost-like, and unwelcoming. Manus was not by her side – best to leave him at home to not pester her in this time of concentration. Two treecreepers flitted through the foliage above her, their brown stomachs pumping up and down when they landed on a branch nearby.

Droppings – paw prints – here is good. Ensuring that her set was well placed by its lair, she lathered the opening in beeswax to lure the creature to its capture. Then she could free it, far away from her land, to be bothersome somewhere else.

Her work done, she stood back, and swiped her hands firmly against each other to rid them of the wax.

Jennifer's subsequent seven days were filled with various duties: mucking out the pens, milking the cows, sowing seeds for the new harvest, and collecting the eggs from the hens. All the while, the fox was present at the back of her mind, lingering there, taunting her.

The time arrived for her to address the problem-child.

Another car ride, but the daydream was missing this time. The interior of the vehicle was cold, but she did not turn the heating on, and her body shivered along with the jittering of the engine as she passed a distortion of fields and sheep. This sort of task was usually left for him to take care of, the nitty-gritty parts. When they worked together, he had tried to preserve as many of her ladylike qualities as possible – an odd sort of chivalry. It was the first time she would have to do it in the half-decade since his passing. She shook her head, a slip of grief passing over her eyes as she drove.

The car quaked when she slammed the door behind her. She was on the border of the woods, garden gloves to hand to wrestle anything that would attempt to escape her grasp.

The mulch gave way to the sinking force of her wellington boots as she approached the spot. The dusk was gloomy, and it was almost as if her dearly departed husband had exhaled pipe smoke down from above, half concealing the woods in curling smog. Streaming roots clasped desperately to the ground, and lined the way to her prey.

There it was, the creature – but something was awry in that small, metal trap, half buried amongst the web of undergrowth.

A sickening sweetness filled her lungs, and she pressed the back of her hand to her mouth, suppressing a gag.

~o~

'Sickening Sweetness' is about grief and loss, and how individuals deal with these strange, unwelcome emotions. In this piece, the fox is symbolic of this – its decaying body is hinted at, but it is still obscured from the reader. This imitates our dislike for confronting what might happen after we stop existing.

'Sickening' is also about national conflict. I've always been interested in history; my dissertation research – how the Northern Irish Troubles are represented in feminist poetry – inspired me to write this piece. I mirrored militaristic 'duties' with Jenny's internal narrative, her occupational responsibilities prevailing over her personal morals. Further, women throughout history are typically shrouded from more 'masculine' roles and ideals, such as war. This is subverted through her husband's absence, resulting in Jenny having to take on traditionally masculine, messy duties, mainly conveyed through sensory techniques.

Great ideas tend to arrive in the dead of night, which was certainly the case for this story. I was falling asleep one night, when the concept of a sensory piece about farming sprung into my mind. Originally, the story was going to be written from the farmer's point of view. Somehow, Jenny's voice took over, and I decided to write her standalone narrative. I felt that it was important for her to be grieving the loss of her husband, as many lost loved ones during the Troubles. This added a new dimension to her character, humanising her.

Daily, I try and aim to write at least 250-500 words, but given that my life is presently dedicated to becoming a teacher, that number is a little shorter for the time being. Despite this, threads and fibres are beginning to weave themselves into the form of a new story.

NYANNA BENTHAM
TWO HALVES OF A POMEGRANATE

Born and bred Londoner, Nyanna Bentham-Prince is a daughter of Caribbean immigrants (coincidently named William and Catherine) who has been captivated by the stories from Caribbean folklore and Greek mythology from an early age. After working for the National Trust and Southbank Centre, she is now reigniting her love for story-writing and currently studying Creative Writing and Classical Studies at the Open University.

You would never see the village of Sadler's Hollow on any map of England. It was a Tardis of a village, home to five hundred thousand Lionheart Elves (a group of werelions discovered by Richard the Lionheart who eventually evolved into chimerical elves five hundred years after) and situated between London and Hertfordshire, it was home to Stephanie Noble. The seventh child of the seventh child, Miss Noble lived with her parents and her younger brother in a medium sized cottage, located near the village centre.

The rest of her siblings had moved on to other places; three were married, three had children and two were trotting the globe in their separate routes, while Stephanie or Stevie as she was commonly known in town, had her own florist stall in her mother's fruit and veg shop. "Stevie's Flower Power Boutique" can be instinctively recognised with her crazy and fantastical paintings, sculptures and flower pots, the gigantic flower crowns and kitschy fruit-hats and of course the abundance of various flowers ranging from the humble yet magnificent sunflower to the carnivorous and compelling Venus flycatcher.

You name it, she had it! Everyone brought a flower every time they would visit; even Mrs Pennycliffe the other day who only wanted some tinned tomatoes! But there was something that was yearning her heart. Love. She always had love; love for and from her family, the love for nature and even the love for Morticia Addams, but now she wanted the love from her Gomez.

"It's so cliché," she thought to herself while trimming the tulips for Jodie Winston, "but there is no use in pretending when "it" strikes your heart. It happens when you watch the lovers walking down the street holding hands, silently wishing it was your hand being lovingly held. Or when you're on the Tube, wishing you had someone with you, who would whisk you away from the couple opposite who are either re-enacting a fight scene from an overdramatic soap opera or enthusiastically sharing saliva through a game of tonsil tennis!"

For Stevie, "it" had struck her heart during her epiphany, when she was wrapping the roses for Mr Hollingsworth to present his wife on their thirtieth wedding anniversary and realised how often she has been helping her customers with their love life but has never until this day thought of her own.

"It's not that easy to live in a town full of pretty King Arthurs and eccentric Merlins!" she said aloud,

"Pardon me, love?!" a manly, cockney voice interrupted Stephanie's attention, she looked straight at the short man with long, grey hair and lengthy, grizzly beard to match, he wore a well-worn denim jacket that heavily smelt of musk and petrol oil. Stephanie laughed at her foolish outburst and smiled at him,

"Oh, I'm so sorry Mr Hollingsworth," Stephanie handed him the vivacious bunch of roses, "Thirty-two pounds, please!"

On one wintry evening, where a murky fog framed a scene of dead, twisted trees and the lawn caked with thick frost. Stephanie walked from the cottage to the local care home where she volunteered through the local women's group.

"What a joy!" Stephanie said to herself, "Reading to a bunch of cranky old patients while they ogle at girlie Britney Taylor and her bursting watermelons! Honestly!"

Finally reaching the red brick building, Stephanie swiftly went through the entrance and into the reception area where she was greeted by Felicity, the manager.

"Why hello, Steph! How are you? I always see you in black."

"It's Wednesday. I always wear black on Wednesday." Stephanie justified as she placed her coat on the rail.

"Well, we have a new resident today on respite care." Felicity walked her through to the dark stained oak-panelled study that reeked of mothballs and hyacinth, striding towards a fiery red-headed man with porcelain skin and sharp cheekbones, dressed in oxblood red, sitting near the fireplace, clutching a thick, ebony cane while leaning on a mahogany table with his head in his hand.

"Mr Jasper, this is Stephanie," Felicity said slowly "She's going to read to you."

He didn't respond; his pale blue eyes just stared up and down at the girl in black. He remarked her short and plump stature, her aubergine hair tied in her loose bun, and that she had two medium sized amethyst stones for eyes and her chocolate toned skin was clinquant and glowing. The man just stared at her for ten seconds then abruptly turned his attention to the fire.

"Best of luck!" Felicity whispered to Stephanie as she sat down opposite him, "In his late 30s or early 40s, I see." Stephanie thought to herself. Taking out a magazine out of her bag, she observed the two halves of a pomegranate on the table and its seeds blazing and sparkling like rubies.

"Oh, so you like pomegranate?" Stephanie inquired politely, "My favourite also! Very nutritious!" Again, Mr Jasper did not answer, "Okay then!" Stephanie muttered. She began to read an article from her magazine,

"Drip...drip...drip. These were the only sounds filled the sour, acidic air of the vacant factory. There was hardly any light except for the fluorescent, fetid-green viscous fluid from the cylinder tanks which my marble-like body was contained in one of them. Its bleak walls caked the gooey, noxious grime like beads of sweat. At the time, none of these details matters to me then but as I speak now I can smell the reeking scent of acidity and hear the sounds!"

"I remember I was being lifted, floating in a balloon filled with the liquid until it hits the ground and I burst out it. Breathing in the stale air thick with chemicals that animated my body, making me strong enough to stand and view my surroundings. I slowly step forward to the metal signage I noticed going across the cylinder "BHP 264: Human Manticore", The phrase "Human Manticore" rings in my head, putting me in a confused stupor until I look down, and see the monstrous hind legs that appeared to be my own, then instinctively, my tail is lifted to eye level and I stare at the shiny stinger dripping with venom. I screamed in horror while its echoes drown monotonous sounds of weeping fluids."

She sighed heavily and looked for Mr Jasper's reaction, it was then she noticed that Mr Jasper's attention was elsewhere, his eyes were was still on the fire as he yawned theatrically, feeling very irritated, she slapped the magazine hard on the desk and blurted out,

"So after spit-roasting Hansel for 45 minutes, the witch devoured the entire body within minutes!" Mr Jasper slowly turned his head and looked at Stephanie with a vacant expression,

"You're deaf, aren't you Mr Jasper?!" He responded by nodding, "Wonderful, everybody loves Bouncing Britney and I…wait a minute!" She gave Mr Jasper a long, hard stare till his expressionless face burst into a Cheshire cat grin,

"You have such a beautiful voice!" he said softly in a deep voice, a speechless Stephanie sat frozen in amazement. He then pushed one of the pomegranate halves towards her, "Care for some pomegranate, my love?"

~o~

"Two halves of the pomegranate" is an extract of an ongoing project of mine, "The Harding Wolfpack", a dark comedy novel about supernatural beings, particularly werewolves living in the present world. The extract, in particular, is based on one of the most well-known stories of Greek mythology, the myth of Hades and Persephone.

Although there are many adaptations of the myth, my version has many differences; firstly the characters are supernatural beings living within the human world, in this case, a small English village rather than being deities living in a godly realm. I hope that this will create some familiarity for the readers especially those who are living in a close-knit community or small villages but still retaining the feeling of entering a fantastical world.

Many versions portray Persephone as innocent and girlish and falling in love with or kidnapped by Hades and subsequently acquires a gothic image whereas in "Two halves of the pomegranate", Stephanie is a self-confessed afro-goth- a bit like myself- who is looking for love from someone with similar interests and the story is set when Hades and Persephone i.e. Stephanie and Jasper have just met, realising their attraction.

They are also a biracial couple, not just because I personally know many friends who are either are in or children of biracial couples but it correlates with the theme of light and dark which I have observed is one of the aspects of the myth that still intrigues us.

I have been writing stories since the age of nine and mostly in the fantasy genre but stopped until my internship at National Trust in a property called Sutton House where I wrote a number of children stories based on the house and the newly opened garden. When it comes to characterisation, I like to research name meanings as it not only help to develop the characters' personality but also their roles in the plot lines.

In terms of literary influences, I have always admired works from Zora Neal Hurston, Anne Rice, Agatha Christie and Mary Shelley and I hope in "The Harding Wolfpack" to portray different perspectives of supernatural creatures, influences by different cultural folklores including African and West Indian.

JENNIE BYRNE
DEATH WORE A RED DRESS

Jennie Byrne is a poet and short story writer from Wirral, Merseyside. She obtained a first class Creative Writing degree and is now finishing her master's at Edge Hill University. Her work has appeared in Defenestration, MIR Online, Ghostwoods Books and The Black Market Review. She has interviewed established writers such as author and historian Kate Williams, novelist Rodge Glass, poet Robert Hampson and short story writer Nicholas Royle. Recently, she was shortlisted for Jane Martin Poetry Prize 2017 and currently works for Edge Hill University Press in association with Arc Publications. If she isn't writing, you can most likely find her painting and binge watching TV shows.

So this is how I wake up Saturday mornin'. Expectin' to be face deep in the toilet with my guts feeling like they've been given a Chinese burn. But instead, I wake up on the fuckin' beach with a mouth full of sand and water cruisin' up my arse. And I'm only wearin' one shoe.

First thing I think when I look up is that me and Kee jumped a plane last night and ended up in the fuckin' Caribbean or somethin'. It wouldn't be the first time one of our nights out took us far from the Wirral. Woke up on a park bench once with this tiny sausage dog starin' at me. Took me an hour to realise we were in fuckin' Newcastle. The dog should've tipped me off. The smallest dogs people have in Wirral are Rottweilers. That's the danger with tequila I'm tellin' ya. Beer's great. Gin's usually fine. But never tequila. If you ever wanna be blackout drunk, then tequila it is, and be prepared to wake up in a different city.

But I swear, this ain't like no Caribbean I ever seen. The entire island is the size of two footie fields, with a beach house smack bang in the middle. And fuckin' sand everywhere. How do you even build a house on top of sand? It's fuckin' nuts. I stand up and my jeans are squelchin' like I've pissed myself. That's when I notice it ain't just me here. Tons of people are around, drinkin' and partyin' around a huge bonfire.

"Hey mate, where am I?" I ask this guy and girl walkin' past.

"Babylon man," the guy says and raises a red paper cup towards me and salutes with his other hand. Figures the first guy I meet is also a scouser.

I just stare like he's a fuckin' alien, then he looks from me to the girl and mouths a dramatic 'oh'.

"Sorry to be the one to tell ya, but this is purgatory man. You're dead. Washed up on the shore of Death's island."

"Fuck off," I scoff, but the dudes just starin' with pity in his eyes.

He ain't lyin'. I really am dead.

So get this, that guy who told me I'm dead, his name's Joey, right? And the girl, she's Crystal. Joey tells me that purgatory is where every dead soul goes while God and Satan can have their little cosy business meetin's. And us poor dead bastards are stuck at this never endin' beach party. Waitin' for the moment those celestial bastards decide if we belong in heaven or hell.

You wanna know what purgatory really is? It's a fuckin' waitin' room.

And the whole time you're here you've got the end of a barrel pointed to your temple. Ain't no party about it the way I see it. Could be hours, days or even years before they decide what to do with us. But you'd never know it, because there is no time. The sun never rises. You spend every moment under the stars. But apparently there's this list and Joey tells me to report to the offices in the beach house so I can get my name put down. He hands me his cup of whiskey.

"Dutch courage man," he says and slaps me on the back.

"Cheers mate. I feel like death warmed up." Oh the irony.

"You look like it too Bradley," Crystal says.

So there I am, a little buzzed from that whiskey, walkin' into a beach house to sign away my soul on God's fuckin' list. Who could've guessed this was how I'd be spendin' my Saturday mornin'? Kee must be goin' out of his mind by now. I wonder if he's the one who found me body. I can tell ya now he'd be shittin' bricks. Probably thinkin' I'm fakin' it or somethin'. Kee freaks out if he has to have a serious conversation, never mind findin' the corpse of his best mate after gettin' trolleyed.

Me Ma's gonna kill him.

'He's bloody trouble that one, all them who live on the Nocky estate are. I don't know why you're friends with someone like that,' she always used to say.

As if livin' in New Ferry like we did was any better. Fuckin' shithole if I ever did see one. Screw foxes, you'll find some homeless guy rootin' through your bins in the mornin'. Don't know why Ma ever thought that way, but it could also have somethin' to do with the fact Kee once watered her plants with his piss. He was only fourteen. Didn't exactly make a good first impression with me Ma. Never stopped him though. It's been over a decade since, but Kee always tries to win me Ma around.

That's the great thing about Kee, he's so laid back he makes it seem like you have no problems in the world expect the next drink to buy or pussy to find.

'Life's a simple as that', he would say.

It was easier just to believe him. Saves worryin' all the time.

So anyway I go inside the house. It's just one huge room with rows of tables all the way to the back. And typin' away on computers are demons. Just sittin' there like it's a fuckin' call centre.

This demon right in front of me has skin like a lizards, all scaly lookin' and a puke green colour too. His cheeks are hollow, held together by a few strands of slimy skin. Every tooth looks like a vampires fangs and this long assed pink tongue like a snakes he's usin' to lick his lips. He has no ears, just giant holes in the side of his head. And his eye sockets are sunken in, but the eye itself is normal. A sky blue colour. Just like a humans. Even worse he's wearin' glasses. A thin clear pair, the kind your dad wears 'cause he thinks it makes them invisible, like he doesn't really need glasses. What a con. Even this demons body is like a fuckin' reptiles, you can see a massive green tail from behind his chair.

"Are you recently deceased?" The demon asks me. His voice is bored, like a cashier who's suicidal.

"Either that, or I'm havin' a fuckin' nightmare," I say back.

The demon sighs and begins rufflin' through some papers. You can tell he says the same three sentences day in day out. Don't blame the guy for bein' so miserable. His name tag says 'Clive'. Clive the demon. Fuck me man. He's not even wearin' clothes, it's just pinned straight through his lizardy skin.

"Please fill out these forms so we can get your information on record." Clive shoves some papers towards me and goes back to typin'. I wonder if he's writin' his autobiography.

Could this be any more bizarre? Nobody ever said death was like this. In all those cases of people dyin' for a few minutes, they all say they saw a bright light and felt overwhelming peace.

Not one fuckin' person said anythin' about a call centre full of demons. What the hell is that about? That's how you know it's all bullshit. You have to die and stay dead to find out what's really goin' on. 'Cause anythin' else is just a fuckin' fantasy.

I take the papers from Clive. It's a questionnaire. And it's ten pages long. How detailed do they need to be? Don't they already know how good or bad we've been in our lives?

'Question 1: How did you die?' Hell if I fuckin' know.

'Question 4: Circle which of the Ten Commandments you've broken:' This should be interestin'.

'Thou shalt not take the Lords name in vain.' Well I broke that one at two.

'Honour thy mother and father.' Fuck me if I ever listen to a word me Dad says. Waste of fuckin' space. Anyway, I ain't seen him in five years.

'Thou shalt not kill.' Does my hamster count? He only died 'cause I forgot to feed him. I mean, give me a break, I was only six.

'Thou shalt not commit adultery.' I've never had an honest relationship in my life, so that's out too.

'Thou shalt not steal.' Dammit. I'm seriously fucked here.

But it's only a questionnaire, not a lie detector, so how would they know?

"It is an anti-lie pen, I wouldn't test it if I were you," Clive says to me, without lookin' up.

Can these demons read our minds?

"What is this? Harry Potter? An anti-cheating spell or some shit?" I snap back.

Clive ignores me. This fuckin' world's crazy.

Takes me a lifetime to fill out that questionnaire. Goes into so much depth I doubt I left out anythin' bad I've ever done in my life. No doubt I'm goin' to hell. Joey and Crystal are waitin' for me when I walk out to join the party. Joey hands me a beer and I take a huge gulp.

"God I need this. What in the hell is that questionnaire? Felt like I was in school again." I complain.

Joey snorts. "Worse than school mate. It's like takin' confession, but for every year of your life."

"Every bad move, every sick little thought you've ever had permanently written down and filed away to be judged," Crystal says.

Joey gives her a look. "Are you tryin' to make the kid feel worse? He's only just died, have some respect."

I chuckle. Some things I don't think I'll ever get used to. Being dead is one of them. Before Crystal can even respond this fuckin' voice comes out of nowhere.

"Amy Roach, please report to the elevators. That's Amy Roach to the elevators."

You can hear it everywhere. As if there were speakers all over. You just know it's one of those demons. Probably Clive, it sounded just like that miserable shit. This Amy girl's not far away from where we're standin'. She's blowin' kisses to her friends, like she's just goin' home to sleep off a hangover.

"What's the elevator?" I ask Joey and he gags on his drink.

"Fuck Brad, keep up. The elevator's our ride out of here."

"So, you mean it-"

"It either takes you up to heaven or down to hell," says a voice behind me.

I spin round to see this bird standin' there. A long haired brunette in a bright red dress that hugs every inch of her. She's somethin' straight out of a porno. Fuckin' smokin'. The way Kee saw it, if you spot a bird in a club and she's wearin' a red dress, it's a sign from the gods that she's filthy in the sack. If her nails are painted red too, then she's full on psycho.

"I haven't met you yet, you must be new," she says and holds out a hand to me.

175

She's wearin' blood red nail polish. I swear, I start droolin'. I lean down to kiss her knuckles and give her my best smile. It works 'cause she smiles back.

"What a doll you are," she coos.

You just know you've scored when a bird coos.

"Bradley Murphy at your service."

"Oh Bradley dear, you misunderstand. It's me who is at your service. So tell me, what is it you desire?"

Right now? "You," I say and wonder why the hell that just came out my mouth. I never meant to tell her that.

"Of course you do. Tell you what; I'll see you over in the hut in five. And all your desires will come true. I suggest you bring a bottle with you," she points towards the bar and struts away, disappearing into the trees.

I think I jizz my pants. You know I might of gotten this place all wrong, 'cause it's turnin' out pretty good so far. I look behind myself to see the bar is actually a tree with various bottles of alcohol hangin' from the branches. Booze really does grow on trees. I think I could get used to this place. And just as I'm about to grab a bottle, Joey and Crystal grab me by the shoulders.

"I wouldn't do that if I were you mate," he says.

"Are you crazy? The hottest bird I've ever seen has just told me she'll fulfil all my desires. No offense, but I'd rather be over there than here lookin' at you." I go towards the tree again, but Crystal steps in front of me, placin' her hands on my shoulders.

"Do you even know who that is?" She spits.

She's defo lost the plot.

"'Course not. I've only just died. I know shit all about this place. If you let go of me, I might be able to find out." I try to side-step her but she's havin' none of it. Even Joey blocks my path.

"Man, that's Death. In all her temptin', sexy glory," Joey tells me.

Fuck me. The Grim Reaper is actually a chick.

"She's got one form, but she appears to the darkness in all of us. It's why she's here. All of this is just a test to see if we give into temptation or not," Crystal says.

"And if we do?" I ask.

"Then you've just signed your own hell warrant. Ain't nobody give a shit how

176

you lived. That's what they want you to think. What matters is how you act here. And Death? She's just the forbidden fruit."

"Ain't nothing sexier than forbidden fruit," I whisper to myself and look towards the trees.

"Exactly," Joey replies.

"So go on, tell me this then, how did you two figure all of this out 'ey?"

Joey just points to Crystal. Figures. I doubt the guy even passed one subject in school. Of course it had to be her who figured it all out. The way Crystal saw it, pretty much everyone here had done somethin' in their lives to earn a place in hell. Except this one guy. Real squeaky clean he was. Devoted Christian. Went to church every Sunday, sometimes in the week too. Did school and university, became a doctor and spent his life savin' others. Married this nice Christian woman, had a few kids. Never put a foot wrong. Always generous. Always selfless. I mean, a real swot if ask me.

"Well nobody asked you, did they?" She fires back.

Anyway, this guy dies a completely natural death at eighty-eight. And while he waited for the inevitable news he was goin' to heaven, Death kept him company. Death kept a drink in his hand at all times. Death was the temptress in a red dress. And boy was that uptight bastard tempted. And eventually he cracked. Took a bottle from the forbidden tree, followed her back to the hut and ravished her to his little hearts content. Next thing this guy knows his name's bein' called. And he thinks there's no doubt where he's gonna end up. But when he steps into that elevator, there's flashin' red lights everywhere, and the destination reads: HELL.

"Not once did this guy put a foot wrong, until he washed up here. And he still got sent to hell. That's when I figured all this out. Your sentence can't have anything to with your life choices. It has to do with ability to resist temptation down here. Otherwise Death would have no reason to stick around. She could be on Earth stealing souls, but she's not."

I gotta say, Crystal has a point. I almost feel sorry for that poor bastard. Spent his whole life doin' good, thinkin' if he believed in God and followed the bible he'd have eternal peace. And one mistake down here, he's sentenced to eternity in the fire.

Before I know it Joey slaps me. "You can have your fill of anything you want here. Except her. You give into her; you're one step away from becoming a ritual sacrifice."

"Does that really happen?" I ask, worried.

"No it's just a metaphor. Anyway, this is why you need to stick with us, so you don't end up selling your soul to the Devil." Crystal says.

"You mean Death. The Devil is a dude," Joey corrects her.

"What's wrong with havin' a drink with her? What is the worst that could happen?" I say.

Crystal frowns. "Have you ever had a drink with a woman and not slept with her?"

"Don't be ridiculous, of course not. But there's a first time for everythin'," I grin.

Crystal don't look impressed. She says the alcohol tree is forbidden. Like the tree of knowledge in the garden of Eden story. Death's the serpent temptin' me and I'm Eve about to be seduced. Sounds real weird, I know. But I figure, if any bible story is true, then it's bound to be true in purgatory, isn't it? This is just a floatin' oblivion. Joey's right. If we were all judged on our sins from life, then every single one of us would be ridin' that elevator down to hell. And there'd be no reason for God and Satan to have those meetin's. What matters is what we do now. Accordin' to Crystal, that's stayin' far away from Death. Accordin' to Joey, that's partyin' (the legal way of course).

So Joey shows me the buffet and drinks table and tells me to stay far away from the food and drink trees, no matter how temptin' they look. Crystal starts introducin' me to everyone. It's chillin' how many young people are in purgatory. I've only met two old people. And I swear I saw one of them nick a ham from the buffet tree earlier. Yeah, a whole ham. We all know she's goin' to hell for gluttony. Doesn't take long for me to feel like I'm fittin' in. I guess bein' dead agrees with me.

Here, there's a kid playin' peekaboo with me. You wouldn't get any of this at home. A kid's first word in Wirral is either 'fuck' or 'cunt'. Ain't no other way about it. You're likely to be punched in the tits before you're ever smiled at. Judgin' by his accent, he must be a Londoner. And he's nice so clearly not a Northerner. The kid seems less freaked about bein' dead than I do. I ask him how long he's been here. He says maybe six months or two years. Hard to tell in a place with no time, I guess. I don't know how he's stayed sane. I ask how he died.

"Bad tissues," he says and starts pullin' on my bracelet.

I take that to mean cancer or somethin'. Bet the doctors didn't even tell the kid anythin'. Tryin' to protect him or some shit. Never mind the fact he was probably bein' poked, prodded and pumped full of drugs that made him feel worse than the cancer did. Poor kid. Probably washed up on Death's beach scared as shit and cryin' for his mum. I give him my bracelet. Least I can do.

Kee would probably tell me I've got a soft head and if I'm not careful this kid will start treatin' me like his Dad. I can just hear him now. Guys like us don't settle down. Ditch the kid and go get laid. But that's Kee for ya. He's about as sensitive as a spiked javelin down your throat. He'd never feel sorry for the kid. I, at least, have some morals.

I watch the kid as he puts my bracelet on. When I say bracelet, I just mean a black rubber band with 'METALLICA' printed in white capitals. I wish I had my phone on me when I died. I could've let the kid listen to some songs. He looks depressed. But I'd be worried if he didn't. Kee once told me the antidote to depression is just to stay depressed. Nothin' can go wrong if you already feel like shit. Worst thing is thinkin' you're happy 'cause sooner or later you'll get pushed off the emotional cliff. It's better to stay miserable. Least you know where you stand there. Most of the things that come out of Kee's mouth are a load of shit, but that one I always got. Especially now. See, I always said I never wanted to turn thirty and I figure this is Death's sick joke to me. Let's kill him off at twenty-seven and he'll get his lifelong wish. Well let me tell you now, I meant something like the fountain of youth, not this fuckin' shit.

Crystal drags us onto the dance floor, which is basically just a really worn part of grass. She takes both of the kid's hands and starts dancin' in circles. The kid laughs. I laugh. And for the time since I've been here, I'm actually havin' fun.

I can feel her watchin' me from the shadows. Her presence like thunder, except everywhere I look there's no sign of that red dress. She's like Predator, invisible, blends into the trees, just acquirin' the right knowledge to take me down. Well on an island full of Billy's and Blain's and Dillon's. I'm gonna be the only Dutch.

The last survivor. The guy on the plane at the end of the film, exhausted as fuck, but thinkin':

'I fuckin' did it'.

Well, I'm not 100% sure how this happened. I mean, I was a little wasted. Things got blurry in me left eye and in my defence, I was only supposed to look out for a brunette in a red dress.

So okay, technically she was wearin' red, but it was an oversized Liverpool footie shirt over a pair of those skinny jeans. How was I supposed to know she could change her clothes? Joey said she'd worn the same thing the whole time he's been dead. And well, as a red blooded male, presented with a hot bird in a Liverpool tee…how can I resist that? She put on this fake, sexy scouse accent as well. What's a man to do? You know, I was tricked.

God'll understand…right?

~o~

'Death Wore A Red Dress' began after reading Chuck Palahniuk's *Damned*. As a reader, I connect most with stories that are quick paced, use repetition and in Palahniuk's case: very dry and sarcastic narrators. Palahniuk isn't afraid to describe the obscene, often his novels contain subject matter deemed too controversial, this was the reason so many publishers initially rejected his idea for *Fight Club*. It is a quality I strongly admire and what I believe makes his work so transfixing. In general I like reading stories that can shock, disgust and make me laugh all at the same time. For example: Josh Kilmer-Purcell's *I Am Not Myself These Days*, Nicci Cloke's *Close Your Eyes* and Claire North's *The First Fifteen Lives of Harry August* to name a few.

Mark Twain said: "Write what you know." For me, this meant using my culture to my advantage. I have lived in Wirral my entire life. I know the accent, colloquialisms, the setting and people better than most. Therefore having my protagonist from the same place was important for me to construct a fully rounded character. However, I chose to set my piece in purgatory because it is a world that hasn't been described in many stories before. I felt it gave me the freedom to create an entirely new realm, with inspiration drawn from *Damned* and the 'Garden of Eden' from the book of Genesis. I wanted to merge two completely different worlds: Purgatory and Wirral. How somebody who has lived in one place his entire life suddenly finds himself forever disassociated with it.

The premise of Palahniuk's *Damned* is an innocent thirteen year old girl supposedly dies of a marijuana overdose and wakes up in hell. Inspired by Dante's epic poem 'Inferno' and Judy Blume's *Are You There God? It's Me Margaret* which also follows a young girl but in her religious journey and self-discovery as she goes through puberty. Despite using *Damned* as a basis for my story, I wanted my protagonist to be the complete opposite. I wanted my narrator to be an adult male, who's already been through his journey of self-discovery only to be pulled back into that frame of mind. To the point he is forced to remember his past, his relationships and ultimately, his failures.

It was my aim to suggest that introspection doesn't end when physical maturity is reached, but continues throughout adult life. Bradley was very self-centred and emotionally inept when he was alive, but having been forced to confront his crimes and failures he is able to recognise what he needs to change. This, therefore, helps him to connect with the likes of Joey and Crystal and even to feel compassion for this small boy who's been all alone for so long.

Writing short stories has allowed me to experiment with story, character and place. It is my aim over the next few years to use the knowledge and skills I've acquired to begin developing my novel idea and a poetry collection.

REECE A. J. CHAMBERS
THE COAST

Born in Northamptonshire in 1993, Reece became interested in writing as a junior school student, thanks in part to the success of the *Harry Potter* series. He's been writing on and off ever since, and studied Creative Writing at the University of Northampton between 2011 and 2014. It was during this time he began producing poetry, with prose taking a slight backseat. He began an MFA, specialising in poetry through Manchester Met in 2017. He has also blogged for several years about topics such as the Eurovision Song Contest, and almost all his work is available online. Further interests include movies, and he has a varied, eclectic taste in music.

'A girlfriend?' she says, emphasising the second syllable. And now comes the part where I have to explain, except this time I decide not to, not in full anyway. I rue myself for even mentioning it.

'Yes, a girlfriend. We sort of lived together but things fell apart I guess. I don't know where she is now.'

'Did you love her?'

'Yes.' The word gallops out from my mouth so quickly I shock myself.

'Do you want her back?'

'Well, it's doubtful, but… look, why are you asking these questions. I thought you knew who I was?'

Her smile evaporates for a moment and I realise I raised my voice a notch above what I planned.

'I do, but I didn't know you had a *girl*friend or anything. Like I said, it's been years.'

I sigh and the idea to turn around and head back in the opposite direction away from her becomes very appealing indeed. I don't need some woman who apparently knows me asking questions about Robin. They don't know a thing, and they shouldn't know a thing.

'I always knew though.'

'So you did know I had a girlfriend?'

'No, not that you nonce. I always knew you liked girls. Never knew you to have a boyfriend.'

'What?'

'I mean, I must say I'm very surprised you don't recognise me. After all, we've kissed before.'

That last sentence flashes up as a lurid neon sign in my head. I walk slower, begin thinking again. She's always known. And I've kissed her. When did that happen? Was I drunk? What a terrific day this is turning out to be. Surely there can only be one explanation.

'Was it a drunken kiss?'

'No, we were sober. We were young so I forgive you if you don't remember, but ooh, you always had strawberry lip-balm,' she peers out to the sea for a second, 'which reminds me, I never did give you it back.'

'How old was I?'

'Just turned seventeen.'

'And you were seventeen as well I presume?'

'Almost, but not quite.'

So she is approximately my age, and there I was, believing she was pushing twenty-five. She looks younger by far. She could put on a chessboard-style tie, a pair of Vans and an Evanescence patch on her jacket and pass for a mid-2000s teen. Turn the blonde hair black and that's almost all the boxes ticked.

'And we kissed?'

'Many times.' I swear she grins as she turns her head to stare at the sea again.

'But I don't know who you are.'

'Sure you do.' At this point she stops, removes her hat from her head and places it onto mine.

'Always liked a girl in a hat.'

'What's that supposed to mean?'

'It means that I've always liked a girl in a hat. Do keep up.'

I don't know what else to say, so I just keep trudging along next to her. I don't give her the hat back because she'd probably toss it straight to me again anyway. She returns to smiling and looking over every few seconds with those candyfloss lips and wide blue eyes. She also appears to be walking in a slight zig-zag motion over the pavement for some unknown reason, as if excitement is flowing through her veins at the prospect of what will come next. She clearly loves this… I suppose she would title it an 'adventure.' Then it slaps me like a wet mackerel across my cheek.

'We went to school together didn't we?'

'Hear that? It's the penny dropping.'

'Where are we going?'

'I'm surprised it's taken you so long to ask. Did you never learn about Stranger Danger?'

'But you're not really a stranger are you?' Don't know her name though, still.

'I'm an illegal immigrant putting on this accent and I'm going to swipe all your cash when your back's turned actually, but no, I'm not really a stranger.' She giggles at her own joke and shoves me playfully on the shoulder, just like Robin used to do whenever she'd roll out a lukewarm-funny line.

'Are we going to the school?'

'We're a bit old aren't we?'

'Were you in my form group?' The questions are coming quickly now and if I don't pause before I speak I'll be asking what colour her knickers are in a minute. I'm still not sure why I'm even doing this; my headache hasn't faded one jot in the past hour and I'm pretty sure the cider didn't help matters. I proceed to do the usual trick of working my way down the alphabet. I've kissed this girl. Many times. So I trawl through the names of yesteryear, fleeting images of each girl popping up like whack-a-moles. Alex, Beth, Charlie… I only kissed one of them though…

'Maybe, maybe not.'

'I think you should tell me who you are.'

'I will. But it's so much more fun this way.'

'Is it though?'

'I'd say so. Come on, Casey. Live a little. It's either this or Monopoly, and that never ends well.'

'Have you been watching me?'

She tuts. 'I'm not a creep. But I've seen you sitting on the steps of the Empire a few times. Daydreaming. Probably waiting for this ex-girlfriend to walk on by and say she regrets how it ended, wah bloody wah. Look, I've decided it's time to make you less lost. Think of me as Blair Waldorf and you as, I guess, Little J.'

We've moved past a bus stop when I become almost certain we're going to the school. As it's a Tuesday morning in early October, kids will be going to the same place in less than an hour. I spend a minute reflecting back on the days of navy skirts, the boys playing football on a pitch choked with mud in the rain, curse words swirling through the air like autumn leaves. I remember the girls in their red PE shirts talking about how they knew when a period was on the cards and the park just over the road where I spent a lot of time with the few friends I had, trying to sing 'How You Remind Me' in our best Chad Kroeger voices. Given everything that's been said in the past fifteen minutes, one of those friends was probably this fedora-wearing tongue-pierced girl, who continues to glance at me and beam as if this sort of thing happens every day and I'm the one who is acting bizarre. Good point. What am I doing?

The nostalgia dwindles as soon as it came, as if photographs leaking their colour when I realise I didn't enjoy school all that much and vowed never to return, walking away from the place with a can of Sprite and an envelope containing my so-so grades. I remember that I have a Snickers bar to eat so I reach into my back pocket, unwrap it and take a bite. The other girl, who I ought to just refer to as OG from now on, doesn't notice this. I take her hat off my head and put it back on her own.

'Had enough have you?'

'It's not my hat.'

'True. But you suit it more.'

Five minutes later, my watch informing me the time is now quarter past eight, the brickwork of my old school materialises in the distance. A friend of mine, Toni, used to live down this road, and probably still does. You fall out of touch with people and years later their names float back into your head and for some reason you have a sudden and powerful itch to want to know exactly what they're up to and how their lives have been since you last spoke. If I actually knew who OG was, maybe I'd think the same about her.

Not much has changed since I used to go to the school over a decade ago, and despite being closer to middle-age than a teenager I feel an unusual twinge of wistfulness and loathing gurgle over me as a tepid wave. Over half a decade spent at this place trying to work out the sort of person I was, and I still don't know. You don't get an identity when you're barely sixteen. You drift as if suspended between two things; the child you were, and the adult you assume at that time you'd really like to become, torn between more education or taking a shoddy job. But these days, or rather these years, I thought I would be clued-up on the person I am, the job I work at, the friendships I cradle but easily shove to one side, the relationships that come and go more quickly than Usain Bolt on a great day. I was clearly jolted aside when the right direction presented itself to me like a glittering yellow-brick road. I'm guessing OG was already at the Emerald City by that point.

She's cheerful as we stand outside the entrance.

'Ah, this is where it all began.'

'And ended.'

'You're such a sourpuss.'

'I'm not a sourpuss; I just don't know why we're here.'

'Did you listen at all when I said I've got to jog your memory? This is where it all began? This is where we met, Casey.'

'And why is where we met so important?'

'It's not. But while we're here, let's make the most of it.'

As OG finishes saying this, a man in a brown suit and skinny tie approaches the front door carrying a small box full of dark red exercise books. Thinning hair. Slight paunch thanks to a sedentary lifestyle. Glasses. Given the drab colour of his outfit, I'm going for history teacher.

'Hello, erm, excuse me?'

'Yes, hello?'

'Hi, I was just wondering if it's at all possible to maybe have a look around the school? You see, me and my friend here are former students, and we're on a bit of a stroll down memory lane, you know how it is.'

I can't quite believe that OG has even said this, and when she turns her head my way, I can only mouth a 'what the hell are you doing.' She sticks her tongue out in response. Meanwhile, the (possible) history teacher appears as though he's been told he has a life-threatening illness and will be carted off to hospital shortly.

'I'm not sure if that's possible. I'm the wrong man to asking I'm afraid, I only teach geography. You'd better wait a while and see if you can grab the secretary, she'll be better informed on whether you'd be allowed back. Are you giving a talk or something?'

'No, it's simply a one-off little glimpse around.' OG flutters her eyelashes.

'I see. Well, Yvonne should be around somewhere. Pop through the doors, she might be about.' I glance forwards enough to see that his name is Mr. Hamilton.

'Thanks so much.' OG spins round. 'We're so in.'

'What are you playing at?'

'Don't you want to wander about, reminisce?' Her face is riddled with glee.

'Not really, no.'

'Rubbish. This is far more interesting than just sitting on the steps of the Empire. Am I right?'

Yes, she's right. But our old school? Couldn't she have chosen somewhere, anywhere, better than this place? I don't want to be reminded of the stench of the changing rooms, watching the girls share their under-arm deodorants, making sure packs of fags were well stashed away. Nor do I don't want to be reminded of the classrooms, and the hours spent answering questions from ancient textbooks when you'd rather be reading Smash Hits. And yet, part of me does want to be doused in those memories again for a second of a second, if only because it's a part of my life that happened. But, as I never think about it, it feels like it never did happen. Friendships buried under a stack of clothes. Perhaps they are irretrievable. Do they even need to be revived?

We walk inside the school. I'm immediately slapped by the smell. It sounds strange to say that, because you'd presume the first thing you'd notice would be the walls, the displays, the groups of kids wondering who the hell you are.

But there are no kids yet, and no displays that I can see. Instead there's only gloominess everywhere I look. My mind rolls back and I briefly recall the décor being the same. At least there is a fleeting splash of colour, most of which appears to emanate from the school office directly in front of us. OG leans forwards and taps on the little window, at which point a short brown-haired woman scuttles over, pushing her glasses back up her nose.

'Can I help you?'

OG clears her throat and adopts a more uppity tone to her voice.

'Yes, hello, I'm a former student of the school. I was in the area and wondering if I could maybe spend an hour or so taking a look around. I know it's a strange suggestion, but I have good memories of this place and would love to peruse the premises.' She glances at me and flashes another smile my way, her tongue piercing on full display. The secretary eyes us both up, especially OG. Girls in high-waisted denim shorts, black tights and a fedora clearly don't waltz onto school premises every day.

'Well, I'm not sure today is a good day. It's more something you'd have to discuss with the head teacher and he's got an important meeting starting very soon. I can take your name down though and inform him when I see him. Your phone number too, dear. Is your friend interested in as well?'

I realise I have to open my mouth now.

'Er, yes, sure.'

Oh great. There I go again, not quite thinking it through.

'OK, can I just write down your details? We've had former students come back from time to time to assist and whatnot, I don't see any harm in you two coming in. What's your name?'

'Casey Blake.'

'Casey Blake' OG repeats in a soft voice so only I can really hear it.

'And yours dear?'

'Jessie. Jessie Stanley.'

As soon as the 'ley' in Stanley is said, I immediately recall who this girl is, and I can't believe I didn't know her right off the bat.

We give our mobile numbers ('I have your digits now' says Jessie, no longer an OG), and make our way back out the school entrance, the time still not even nine in the morning. I take the Snickers out my back pocket, which has now melted a little into a gloopy mud-like slush, and take a large bite.

'I promised you a drink.'

My head has gone a little frazzled, in a shaken-up bottle of pop way. I tell her the truth.

'I've done more in the past hour than I have done in the past month.'

'Then why stop now?'

'You're Jessie Stanley.'

'Oh that? A pseudonym. I'm really Jennifer Lawrence.'

'And I kissed you?'

'Yes. Quite a lot actually. You certainly seemed to know what you were doing. We never bumped teeth and you never wriggled your tongue down my throat. I've never been kissed the same way since.'

'But you're straight?'

She ponders this question for a moment. 'You know, I don't know. And what does it matter? Either we'll have to put a ruler against me or I'll have to check my last CV. Regardless, maybe you'll answer your own question before the morning's out. '

~o~

'The Coast' began in early 2016 after I came up with the idea of three short pieces linked together by location, each part focusing on somebody at a different age. As somebody who has holidayed on the east coast multiple times in the past, I felt it would be a good place to set a story, particularly as there is something drearier and perhaps a tad eerie about coastal towns outside of the summer. What is included here is an extract; more has been written, and hopefully the story will be completed in the not too distant future.

The aim, at first, was to just produce something that wasn't poetry for a change. I worked in stages, writing 500 words here and there. I knew I wanted to write from a female perspective, as I don't often do that, and I also wanted a fair dollop of dialogue as I often use little. The character of Jessie came to me almost fully formed, with her sarcastic humour and fedora hat (she didn't have a name for a very long time), while Casey was harder to visualise.

The Empire is an old theatre in Great Yarmouth, and I knew from the start that my story would begin there. I had a vague idea where it would go, and I found myself thinking more about what hadn't been written than what was in front of me. My work is generally quite thin on lots of action, but I'm sure more will come before long.

I'm interested in the way people interact with each other (parent to child, teenager to teacher etc.), especially as you get older, and so the main focus of this story is two old friends who reconnect in a rather unconventional way after years apart. One is more confident, more outgoing, the other rather reserved and nervous about the future. The specificities of how people behave and react are important to me as I write. Casey is confused, but goes along for the ride anyway without thinking much about it. Jessie hasn't quite matured yet. The feeling of nostalgia is a topic I also tend to address in my prose and the notion of whether it is a pleasant emotion or not.

Certainly, I aim to keep on writing and produce a novel within the next few years. While the main focus is on poetry, I enjoy reading and being inspired by others. It might take a while, but I will do what I can to reach my goals.

SARAH GONNET
TILDA

Sarah is a writer, artist and autodidact from the North-East of England. She makes work in a variety of forms, predominately theatre but also poetry, arts journalism, prose, painting, artist books and moving image. She trained as a playwright with Graeae Theatre Company and as a director with the Regional Theatre Young Directors Scheme. She talks publically about mental health and disability and runs a mental health support group. She spoke at the 2017 NAWE conference about access to Creative Writing education. In February 2017 she received a grant from DadaFest to develop a novel based on the life of Louise Bourgeois. She is on the Board of Directors of The Writing Squad and reviews policy in a role for Rethink Mental Illness. Sarah is also the editor of The Female Gaze film magazine, and is currently under commission by Random Acts to make a short film about the beautiful structures to be found in the homes of compulsive hoarders.

I'm not here.

There's blue paper over my stomach. I should have shaved my legs, they're thick with stubble. The doctor is standing rubbing Vaseline onto his plastic device. His fingers slip over it a bit and knock it open. I'm not here. I didn't just see how wide that thing can go.

I count my pain on my fingers as he slowly pushes it inwards.

"One, two, three, four."

The counting is something my mother taught me. She always claimed she got through childbirth without painkillers; but one day, when The Problem was just beginning to raise its head, my dad took me aside and told me otherwise. Told me she had had an epidural. Since then when too much wine at family dinners have made her tell the story again, I have never let on that I know. Her pride is irrevocably linked to that pain.

He makes one last push and I almost shout the numbers aloud.

"One

Two

Three

Four."

I inhale the clinical air deeply. Over my knees I can just make out his metal tray of objects. He picks something long and thin. I hear the pop of a packet opening. Then I feel a scratching inside me. I think he's put a cotton bud up there. One of those with a really long stem. A second cotton bud follows. Then he pulls the plastic out of me, making my eyes water.

"Thanks." I cough, thinking that he's done.

"Just one last pull. It's got a bit stuck."

He yanks at the speculum again and it feels like he is taking my insides with it.

"Fuck." I mutter and then "Sorry." Are you supposed to swear in front of doctors?

I sit up gently. My insides throb with bruised flesh.

"We'll have the results back in a week or so. Ten days at the most." He says and doesn't look up at me again as he begins to label the parts of me that he has taken.

I squeeze my knees back together and then the length of my legs. When I slide myself off the bed my feet plop back into my ballerina pumps.

Once the doctor indicates I am free to escape, I walk back down the corridor to the waiting room; then beyond to outside, with a distinct lack of grace.

Our house stinks of coffee. I make mine black; even though David frowns at me. It's the usual: a frown that says I need to put some weight on. He tinkles the blue capped milk carton at me but I turn away from him, towards the TV. He doesn't ask me about the appointment. I can't blame him entirely; we both thought it was only a rash. He still could have asked though.

"Toast?"

I hate that he's become my monitor.

The TV tells me there been a murder, an earthquake, three sexual assaults on underage...

"Cereal?"

Shaking my head I leave the room, go upstairs and sit on the toilet. I stay in there for an abnormally long time because I want him to think I'm throwing up. Whilst I'm there I have a look in my pants. There is a light spotting of blood but nothing worth putting a sanitary towel on for.

Eventually I carefully creep out and downstairs. I try to gently pull my bag down from the peg on the cupboard, but the door creaks and he's on me.

"I'm going to college."

"You got money for lunch?"

"I'm not a kid."

He tries to give me a cereal bar. I leave without it.

"I know you're not a kid!" he shouts after me.

I don't turn around.

I'm sitting in college with my feet flat against the fake whitewashed wall that marks out the boundaries of my tiny studio space; I draw something but nothing that could be construed as work. It's some kind of creature from a weird corner of my brain. My battered oil pastels scratch away at the paper and end up satisfying an itch from inside. I sketch out a wide anime eye with scrawny, towering legs. I work around it too; quickly making a mountainous landscape and twisted orchids emerging from the ground. Before I'm done I realise the eye is staring me out and I turn the page on it. I like beginning again anyway.

Everyone else is in the workshop room for registration. I've missed it and I don't care. They're all kids anyway- straight from school. Being a mature student makes me seem elderly to them. And their fucking giggling...

It takes a determined mind-set to enter the dingy toilets that service the entire art department. Once inside I head for the first cubicle I see. I'm hit by a new, fishy, smell and sure enough there is a throbbing red tampon in the toilet bowl. I try to sit down and ignore it, but I can't. So I back out again, and look around, but I'm forced to realise it's the only cubicle free.

I really need to go.

I enter again, sneaking up on it, as if that will make a difference. I give the flush button a hefty push but it bobs up to the top again.

The movement of the water dilutes some of the blood from the main mass.

I should pick it up and put it in the bin.

Remember that time dad pulled a decapitated mouse out of a trap and it bled everywhere, all down his arm?

I back out again, deciding I'll pee on the floor if I have to.

Just in time a girl in full cosplay (cat ears, Alice in Wonderland dress) backs out of another cubicle and I make a run for it.

I'm back home on our battered sofa. The TV blinks to offer me soaps or soaps or the Mystery Channel. There was no money for Sky Atlantic this year and my usual torrent sites are down. I need to see Game of Thrones, I'm months behind (and Penny Dreadful but I don't as freely admit I like that one. Secretly I wish I was a witch drawing pentacles in salt).

Instead I'm sat here watching ancient episodes of The Bill.

They're not even in chronological order.

Some of the ad-breaks dissect lines of the script down the middle.

TV off and music on. First up on the playlist is Courtney Barnett. The sound makes me limp along instead of dancing, like a cowboy in a western who's been shot in the leg: I have bursts of energy but ultimately I trip myself up.

I should be drawing. My sketchbook is gaping wide and white on the sofa behind me. The sofa isn't as clean as the pages. It's covered in paint and tactless throws of varying shades of orange.

The tampon.

I keep seeing the tampon like a horror-film flash.

I need a wee but I don't dare go. I'm going to see it, and then the blood and then the blood will bubble up out of the bowl and then...

The garden?

It would be an option, except there are those loose planks in the fence and I'm fairly sure Mia, the neighbour, can see through it. It's certainly big enough for me to collect all the tab butts up and drop them through when Mother visits.

David will be home soon.

I should be drawing.

I should cook him a meal. Or order in.

Order in. I'll just have a couple of his chips and claim I already ate.

I should be drawing.

I really should be drawing.

He comes home and switches the music off. It had shifted to Laura Marling and he hates Laura Marling.

I haven't cooked dinner.

I haven't ordered in.

I try to suggest this to him with my eyes; but he insists on looking in the oven anyway.

"It's not even on." I say and then go upstairs to sit on my own again. He shouts something after me, that I pretend so hard to ignore I forget to actually listen.

I try to go back to the TV but it's the time of day when quiz shows take over and I can't handle them. They always get to me because of their intense music. Music that is always counting down to something. Counting down whilst the viewers waste their lives. Not something I have anything against, but there is no point in emphasizing it. I just can't do all that so I go to bed instead. It's only five in the afternoon but I drop off straightaway.

I wake up with one of the mattress springs driven hard into the small of my back. In my half-conscious state it makes me think of a penis. An old memory of a hard penis from when I was in high school. David is so stressed by the whole training to be a doctor thing that he can't quite get there. Not that I particularly care. I'm not as driven as I used to be either.

I go back to sleep.

I wake to him snoring.

I get up, get my notebook and try to write.

My brain spits out two paragraphs, then leaves my pen wavering over the rest of the blank page. I get Robin Thicke lyrics in my head, maybe because of the mattress spring; maybe because I want to be a feminist but my brain thinks I'm an idiot.

I write out Blurred Lines for the rest of the page. Then I cross it out, blurring the lines with thick pen.

I should tear the page out, but I don't want to ruin the sacrament of the notebook. Every word is sacred.

Shit. Just like that Every Sperm is Sacred is in my head.

I spend the rest of the night watching Monty Python sketches on Youtube. My mother used to love Monty Python. She could do all the voices and memorised whole scenes of the films. Then she'd just come out with them when we were sat in a café or something. Locally they got used to the Spam song being sung at every opportunity; but when we went to Paris one summer she got spat at. It made her start smoking again. Over there they have multi-coloured Ladies' cigarettes. I begged for a puff because I thought they were fruit flavoured. Eventually she gave in and let me hungrily suck the smoke up. I almost choked.

I wake up again. He must have come and gone during the night. I gently fondle the indent in the mattress where he was. It's easier to love him when he isn't there. I'll give him some credit though- he didn't wake me up when he got up this morning. I hold this thought until I go into the kitchen and find ten thousand pans in the sink from the hefty breakfast he evidently cooked for himself. Then I open the locked cupboard (where he insists we keep household products: because that's how his mother did it at home) to get the washing up liquid, and find a prominently placed ClearBlue test. Is he poking holes into our condoms?

I walk away from the cupboard and leave the kitchen a mess.

A new morning. Not particularly bright. Not the apocalypse either. Should I go into college today?

It's become a regular question now. I used to love art. I used the word "passionate" six times in the personal statement I attached to my UCAS application.

But today to get in I'd have to: have a shower, get dressed whilst wet, put some make-up on, rub make-up off, re-do make-up, re-do make-up again, pack my bag, find my fucking keys, walk up to the bus stop, wait up to an hour for the bus…

Sitting beneath the narrow set of shelves and drawers David once built for my make-up, I paint my nails; all the time trying to focus on the middles and not perfecting the edges. Perfectionism in nail painting only leads to bumpy slips of polish.

I've chosen teal for one hand and sparkly blue for the other (odd hands, odd socks, odd Converse). I don't think that reflects anything about what I'm feeling, but you never know.

The doorbell rings and its Mia. I can tell from the prim perfection of her push.

I open the door and say "Sorry I'm just in the middle of something." and let her make her own way in.

Mia sits down and then I sit down.

I nervously blow on my nails because I wish I could do my cardigan up to hide my stomach flab.

"Hello Tilda. I was wondering how you were getting on."

"With what?"

"College. You're still at college aren't you?"

"Yeah. I started again, got fed up with English Lit half-way through second year. It's uni really. They just call it college because it's an art school."

"So they call it school?"

"No. They call it college. You were right."

She looks impressed with herself.

"Whatever. I never claimed to know all about these things."

"Well it's a university course but…"

I stop. Mia is looking at her watch; she isn't listening to me.

"I would stay and have a chat, but to be honest I came here to ask a favour."

"Really?"

"Yes. Just a small one and I'll pay you of course. Give you some extra money for paintbrushes or something…"

I want to throw her out, but money is money.

"Ok."

"Could you watch Jason for a few hours? His Au Pair is sick and I need to go out."

I pause. His "Au Pair"?

"Business dinner." She clarifies.

I nod, try to get over…His "Au Pair"?

"Yeah sure."

I never knew she even had a kid. Where does she keep it? I've never seen it.

"Thanks. I'll send him round in half an hour. I'll pack something for his dinner, he's very fussy."

"I'm doing pizza…"

"He really is very fussy."

I lead her out of the door, touching my nails against her pale M&S coat and staining it with teal strands. She won't notice straightaway, but it's the kind of thing her bitchy friends will probably point out when she meets up with them.

The kid comes round with a Tupperware box full of salad.

"Hey I'm Tilda." I say and bend down to shake his sticky hand.

"You like pizza?" I ask and he nods violently.

"Good."

I haven't got any toys so I give him one of the boxes we shoved in the spare room when we moved in, telling him it's a ship.

Then I go and smoke in the next room. Something about the sight of a kid apparently makes me want to smoke. Plus I'll need all the hunger-suppressing effects possible to deny myself a full pizza later. When I was a kid we'd have it as a takeaway all the time. I'd finish mine dead quick then guzzle down any left-overs as well. I was disgusting.

Cigarette finished I check on the kid again and then order a pizza. I'll just sneak a couple of slices from his. David won't be home until after we're done. Most kids eat at about five yeah?

He likes the box, which is good because it means I can watch TV. I shove on a boxset of The Following then remember that he's only seven and stick on Mad Men instead. If a kid was going to drink they'd probably go for alcopops not bourbon so I'm probably safe…

…I wake up to next door's cat mewing.

In a panic I check the kid, but he's fine- asleep on the other sofa.

David opens the door. Evidently the mewing had been because he had been approaching.

"Something smells nice. Who's the kid?"

"It's Mia's."

At some point the pizza must have arrived.

David opens the box.

"You didn't get me anything?"

"The kid ate it all."

"For fuck's sake Tilda! I'm hungry."

"So are the hippos."

"What?"

"Hungry, hungry hippos."

"What the fuck does that mean?"

I bite the air next to his face, just like a hungry hippo.

He walks off back into the kitchen and starts to heat up a tin of curry.

"Do you really think…" he starts to say as it comes to boil.

"What?"

"Nothing."

"What?"

"How many times have I suggested we…and you say…"

"What?"

"You say you're not ready…and then you take in someone else's…"

"Yeah, for one night. That's not the same thing."

"Yesterday you wouldn't even let me talk about kids."

"So?"

"Nothing. Stir this. I'll check on him."

I stir the curry but I don't touch the bottom with the spoon so that there'll be a burnt layer for him to wash up.

I almost knock it off the hob and all over myself when David wails from the next room.

"Fuck! Tilda! Fuck!"

"What now?"

"Call an ambulance."

"Why?"

"The kid. The fucking kid Tilda. He's barely breathing!"

"What?" I refuse to move, so he comes in and drags me through to the other room.

"Look!"

Clutched in one of Jason's hands are the innards of a pill-packet.

That's right. I took some sleeping pills.

I gave him the packet. He was popping it like bubble-wrap.

Was the packet empty?

I'm sure the packet was empty.

"It was empty. We were playing a game."

"Phone a sodding ambulance."

David is right there clearing Jason's throat and checking his pulse.

"Call. The. Ambulance."

"It was empty."

I dial.

~o~

I am a feminist and I am angry. So a bit of a cliché really; but a cliché forced upon me by the ridiculous state of the current world.

Although my novella has big themes- feminism, mental health, fertility- it has a very specific focus. Ma/Tilda looks at the lives of three women: only two of the women are actually versions of the same person, so I suppose you could say it looks at the lives of two women. If that's a bit confusing, for now it's ok. The extract included in this anthology looks at only one of the 2/(3?) women- Tilda.

In the full length piece, Tilda's story is to be considered alongside the parallel life of Matilda, and the third character of Mother. I chose to write the book like this to examine in detail various roles which are assigned to women. I wanted to look at both being a carer, and being cared for. I wanted to look at fertility and infertility. I wanted to look at being mentally ill in a relationship, and being in a relationship with someone who is mentally ill. I wanted to see how these things would affect the same character. So I create a world where two versions of the same person exist.

The Mother character is also essential. Throughout the text it is ambiguous as to whether Mother is the parent of Tilda or Matilda or versions of both, so her narration highlights aspects of both of the daughter(s) lives.

This novella fits in with my larger body of work. I am active in the feminist community as the founder/editor of The Female Gaze film magazine, which is written entirely by women, and people who identify as non-binary. My work as a playwright and filmmaker frequently returns to the same themes considered in this piece. I am currently working on projects which look at Schizophrenia, feminism, disability rights, and compulsive hoarding.

My next extended prose piece will be a historical novel based on the life of artist Louise Bourgeois. I am fascinated (read: obsessive) about Bourgeois' work and her links to psychoanalysis. I am also interested in the way that her life spans the breadth of the twentieth century (and a little into the twenty-first). I want to look at the roles of women throughout this period. I received a grant to develop this piece earlier this year. I will apply the lessons learnt in writing Ma/Tilda to this new piece.

I am currently approaching agents and publishers who might be interested in taking Ma/Tilda on.

IEUAN BRIERS
THORAN TUNNEL

Originally wanting to be an actor, Ieuan Briers began taking a strong interest in fictional writing, when he started creating scripts for short sketches as part of his Drama Bachelors Degree; this branched out into him writing plays and other pieces of drama, it was when he enrolled into MA in Creative Writing at the University of Swansea he tried other outlets including short stories, radio dramas and nature writing. He now hopes to become a professional actor and writer, with plans to combine the two worlds of drama and creative writing.

The story I'm about tell, is one I have carried around for many years. As an engine driver one expects a long, hard and sometimes demanding career. I was a driver for the *Sittington and Coalfield Railway Company*; this event took place long before that. At the time the story takes place I'd been working for the railway for nearly five years, working on tank engines and tender engines and with duties that included passenger trains, freight trains and shunting trucks around the yard.

It was on 18th October 1921, I was sitting at a heavy wooden table in a small pub located not far from the station, called *The Railwaymen's Arms* it was often used by railway staff coming off duty to spend a few coins and have a pint to celebrate the end of a hard working day. It was already half past ten and the weather had turned for the worst; there was no rain or wind, just heavy fog and an icy sense that even a heavy overcoat was unable to keep out. I had just finished a pint of ale, when suddenly the heavy wooden door flew inwards as though someone had forced a shoulder against it and attempted to break it clean off its hinges.

Standing there, framed in the doorway, was one of my colleagues, Charlie Higgins. He normally worked the express passenger service to Coalfield, which connected the main line that ran to Shrewsbury. Charlie looked in a right state, his hands were clenched into fists his face was pale and his eyes looked like they were bulging clean out of their sockets. "Charlie" I exclaimed, standing up and walking over to him. With the aid of a plate-layer and a signalman, we were able to get the stricken Charlie Higgins into a chair. And started pouring brandy down his throat to counteract the shock, soon he had managed enough strength to start talking. "Cheers lads," he gasped "I needed that."

"What happened Charlie?" asked Harry Simkins, the signalman "I thought you were taking the late-night express?"

"Aye, I was," replied Charlie gasping deeply "we were doing all right, making good time and the engine was working well. Then we had to wait at a red signal by Thoran tunnel." So far there was nothing odd with his story, Thoran Tunnel was a long structure located about ten miles away from the pub, nearly forty meters long, it burrowed though the heart of a large hill. As the hill is made of hard stone, the tunnel was only built to encase a single track and trains had to take it in turns when travelling through it, hence why Charlie Higgins had been waiting at the signal.

"Well, we'd been waiting there for a few minutes, when we heard the whistle from the other train heading towards us, when that passed us, the signal turned green and we were allowed to carry on. We entered the tunnel and that was when we heard it."

"Heard what?" asked Harry Simkins

"The screaming, blood-curdling it was, as though a poor soul was being tortured. The fireman and I looked at each other and we realised that there was something sinister going on. I reached out, opened the regulator to full capacity and thrashed the engine forward. I look through the window of the cab and saw her."

"Her?" I asked "There was a woman there?"

"Aye," agreed Charlie "Young woman, standing there on the track in front of the locomotive, I shut off steam and put the brakes on hard, but it was too late."

"You knocked her down?" gasped one of the plate-layers, Fred Jackson.

"That's the thing" explained the distraught driver, we felt no impact. The engine passed right through her; there was no sound other than another blood-curdling scream. I didn't stay to find out. We opened up the regulator again and we ran at full speed until we reached the next station." The last part of the story clearly distressed him. Fellow driver John McLaren had grabbed another brandy from the landlord and forced it into Charlie's hand, who poured it back down his neck.

"So there is a strange, demented woman, walking around in Thoran Tunnel?" suggested Fred Jackson, breaking the silence, however Charlie Higgins shook his head vigorously.

"I don't know what is going on," He replied "but I'm not going back through that tunnel at night again."

Charlie Higgins was defiant in what he said, the following day he went straight to Mr. Bailey, the Director of the Railway and said that he would not be doing the late night passenger run. Mr. Bailey was surprised, but said that he accepted and respected Charlie's decision, sending him to work in the yard, marshalling trucks ready for the various goods trains.

For a few weeks life carried on as normal, then one day it happened. I was aboard my own engine and was waiting in the siding to take a slow goods train down the line to Coalfield, when I noticed John McLaren walking across the yard; he spotted me and came over, climbed up the ladder and joined me in my cab.

He told me that Mr. Bailey had asked him to take the late night express train to Coalfield. However I could tell in his voice that he was a little nervous. Clearly Charlie Higgins' experience had worried him. I had known John McLaren for years and he was not a man to be easily scared, though there was something about him that seems a little nervous. I reassured him and as I was finishing in the afternoon I would also travel on the train as a passenger to see if there was any truth in the screams coming out of Thoran tunnel. McLaren agreed though he admitted he would have felt a bit more at ease if I was actually on the footplate, but the regulations stated that only on duty crew were allowed in the cab; the most I could be was a passenger in one of the carriages. However I could travel with McLaren and is fireman when they returned back after the train had reached its destination and this seemed to reassure him tremendously.

That night the train was ready to leave Sittington, the platform was crowded. Passengers and station staff trying to get aboard. Porters were loading luggage, people were saying goodbye, tickets were stamped and doors were closed. Soon came the familiar chimes of the station clock indicating that it was half-past nine. McLaren, who was on the footplate, looked out and saw that the signal had turned to green, all that was left was for the guard to blows whistle, wave his green lamp and they would be away. I had decided to find myself a place in the third class carriage, the first one behind the locomotive itself. The train was full, though my compartment was actually empty. As I sat in the seat looking out of the window I wondered if there was any truth in what Charlie Higgins said. Like McLaren, Charlie Higgins had been a personal friend for a number of years, he had never told a story like this before and wasn't in the habit of fabricating events. I tried to put it out of my mind, I laid-back, folding my arms and pretty soon the cold wave of sleep began to wash over me.

Outside the guard finally waved his green lamp and blew hard on his whistle, acknowledging the signal McLaren opened the regulator and the train began to slowly creep forward. The sounds of screaming steam, creaking metal and the slow rumbling of the wheels along the rails soon echoed through the cold, October night air.

Puffing, hissing, wheezing, chuffing, blaring the whistle, roar of the engine, screech of the brakes; the sensation of being held forward, the sense of being hit by a flat object and a blinding woman scream. My eyes snapped open and I found myself lying flat on the carriage floor, I'd clearly been thrown from my seat probably due to the sudden force of the stopping train. The sounds I had heard had whirled around inside my head like the fog that hung heavily beyond the carriage window. I headed out into the corridor, found the nearest door and let the window down, I took a deep breath and forced my head out into the cold night air. The train had indeed stopped and looking out I saw the face of McLaren his fireman looking back at me; the locomotives tender was the only thing that parted us. The fireman gasped and said quickly to me "Did you see it?"

Still feeling half asleep I muttered "Did I see what?"

"That woman," cried the fireman, "that strange woman standing in the middle of the track!" like Charlie Higgins, he was in a state of great excitement and his eyes appeared to be bulging from his head.

"Where's McLaren?" I asked trying to get the conversation away from the topic of ghosts

"He's here, have a look"

I open the door and slowly let myself down, jumping the last foot and a half to the ground, by now the trains' lack of progress had aroused the attention of several of the passengers who, like me, had opened the windows and were staring out and calling out asking why the train was not moving. I walked around the tender and using the fireman's assistance managed to climb up into the cab. What I saw made the hairs on the back of my neck stand-up, John McLaren was in one corner, cowering with his hands and arms over his head and a look of terror on his face. I instantly went over to him, "Are you alright?"

McLaren looked up "I saw it Tom" he cried, reaching out and grabbed the front of my jacket, "She was there, the screaming woman Charlie talked about." I looked at his face, now contoured in a look of terror and reassured him that he was safe. Looking at the fireman, who was more confused than scared, I asked him if he could still work and that I would take over the driving. The engine wasn't that different from my own and I was able to get the train moving again.

The rest of the journey was uninterrupted and when we reached Coalfield, we were only a few minutes late, I decided to inform Mr. Bailey of what had happened and asked to use the phone in the stationmaster's office. The fireman and a member of staff helped McLaren out of the engine. His eyes were still wide and kept mumbling about the woman he had seen. As they lowered him onto a nearby bench I was reminded of Charlie Higgins when he came into the pub and felt so sorry for him.

I phoned Mr. Bailey and told him, partially the truth, saying that due to fatigue John McLaren had been taken ill and was unfit to drive the locomotive back to Sittington. He commended me for my quick actions and instructed that I take the train back. Having no other choice I had to agree and informed him that I would see him in his office first thing in the morning, it was a journey and visit that I didn't want to make.

I repeated my story to Mr. Bailey. The Railway Director sat quietly and listened carefully; occasionally he took a pen from the rack on the desk in front of him and made notes. Once I'd finished he paused and puckered his lips, showing a face of concentration and concern. "These reports are happening more and more. First Charlie Higgins and now John McLaren. I've approved his application for leave but if this carries on, we won't have a railway left to run."

"You have any ideas sir?" I asked

Mr. Bailey shook his head "Not at the moment Carter, I suggest the best thing we can do at the moment is for you to return to work and try and keep this railway running." I paused for a moment; surely Mr. Bailey had more planned than just pretend nothing was happening. Yet he was still my employer and I didn't want to give a reason to dismiss me so I gave a nod of understanding and left the office.

Over the next week, more and more drivers and engine crews reported seeing the strange woman of Thoran Tunnel. As my duties were normally done during the day, I never saw the figure. I did get a sense of unease when I went through the tunnel though. Eventually I received a message that Mr. Bailey wanted to see me in his office. When I went there he was engaged in conversation with a rather strange looking man. Dressed in a dark suit, white shirt and black tie, he had a large round head and was completely bald. Surprisingly he had no eyebrows though he had quite a thick looking moustache underneath his pointed nose. He reached out and grabbed my hand. I'd forgotten to wipe it and when he pulled his palm away, he found it covered in grease and oil. I apologised and offered him a clean handkerchief, which all railwaymen carry for such occasions. After we had shook hands again Mr. Bailey introduced the newcomer to me. "Carter, this is Doctor Zander from the University of Vienna, he is an expert in the paranormal and unexplained."

"Good afternoon," greeted Doctor Zander "I understand strange things have been going on, on zis railvay." He had an accent, though it wasn't thick and he appeared to speak fluent English.

"Are you German?" I asked

"Austrian," came the simple reply "perhaps you can tell me Mr. Carter, of the events that have been happening."

He sat down in a chair to the side of Mr Bailey's desk. The Railway Director remained in his usual position, sat directly opposite me and I had been given no invitation to sit down. I stood there and told the entire story from first hearing it from Charlie Higgins, to the strange events involving John McLaren. Doctor Zander listened. Occasionally nodding in agreement and looking fully engaged with my story. Once I'd finished he reached into his bag and pulled out a large book which appeared to be a recorded history of the local area. Mr Bailey opened a drawer and pulled out a map which he laid out. Flattening it out, he traced the layout of the line with his finger finally coming to a small point where the line broke up for a couple of centimetres, showing the location of the tunnel.

It was now Doctor Zander's turn to speak "You are probably vondering, why Herr Bailey asked for my help, as a academic in ze paranormal, vell it seems zat the area vere that tunnel was built, used to be land where the souls of the departed were laid to rest."

"You mean a bit like a graveyard?" I asked.

The Austrian scholar nodded before asking "when was the tunnel built?"

"The original construction," replied Mr Bailey "began in 1908, but these reports only started about a week ago. If the railway disturbed something then surely we would have heard about it long before now."

Doctor Zander paused for a moment, clearly wondering what the Railway Director had said "maybe maintenance work disturbed something?" Both Mr Bailey and I knew that routine repair work on the tunnel had taken place nearly three months ago. The workmen hadn't reported anything unusual and the work was completed on schedule. Doctor Zander slowly turned over the leaves of the book on his lap. Eventually he paused and looked up at me. He said "This book mentions a story that happened near where the tunnel is now built. Before the railway came, the only way to get through the hills was on a small path to run over the top. Towards the end of the last century the land was owned by the famous Halford family who had two sons and a young daughter, Nancy. Many men came from miles around to ask her father they could have Nancy's hand in marriage; however she rejected all of them. Them one day a young soldier, fresh from the fighting in Africa came and asked her father for her hand in marriage. This soldier was not an officer but nothing more than a humble private. Nancy wanted to, but her father did not approve. He was furious, he discovered that Nancy had plans to run away and elope with the soldier and he took a road to the hill where the tunnel is now and shot her."

"So you think that this strange woman that all the railway crews have been seeing," began Mr. Bailey "is the manifestation of Nancy Halford?"

"Remember what Mr. Shakespeare said in Hamlet Mr. Bailey" corrected Doctor Zander, "That 'there are more things in heaven and earth than are dreamt of in your philosophy' it is purely reasonable to say is that it is the spirit of Nancy Halford that is haunting Thoran Tunnel."

"What do you suggest we do now?" I asked, though the hairs on the back of my neck were already standing up. I had a nasty feeling that I was not going to enjoy the answer.

"Tomorrow night" explained Mr. Bailey "we will cancel the late night express to Coalfield; instead you will drive a train consisting of your engine and an inspection coach and re-trace the journey made by both Higgins and McLaren. We'll see if Doctor Zander can make contact with the spirits and if so what they want?" Once again I had no choice and nodding, I braced myself for the long night I had ahead of me.

Regulations stated that any railwaymen working late into the night had part of the day off. I arrived for work at around seven o'clock; I was feeling nervous and would have given everything I owned, to go back to that night in the pub and leave, just before Charlie Higgins turned up. As I climbed up into the cab of my locomotive I was surprised to discover that my fireman was the same man who had been with John McLaren that fateful night. I decided not to let my nervousness show, remembering that McLaren had been physically uneasy and he'd become a jabbering wreck.

The late express to Coalfield, left Sittington station at twenty-five minutes to eleven and in the time between me arriving for work and taking the train, was mostly spent in the yard, shunting trucks into their correct sidings and aligning carriages for the forthcoming trains. At ten o'clock we collected the inspection coach and filled the engine's bunker and tanks with coal and water. We set off for the station.

Doctor Zander and Mr. Bailey were waiting on the platform. The paranormal expert was attired in a long coat and black hat; he was carrying a black leather bag and greeted us in Austrian. "How do you feel?" asked the Railway Director

"I'd be lying if I said I was comfortable" I murmured

"I understand your concern Carter. Just do what Doctor Zander says; I'm sure he knows what he is doing." With that the two men climbed into the carriage and when the station clock chimed half-past ten, the signal turned from red to green. Slowly I gripped the regulator and moved it. There came the hiss of steam entering the pistons and steadily the wheels began to turn.

Our trip to the tunnel was uninterrupted and soon we found ourselves at the points where the double track narrowed into one and the signal which thankfully was at red. That wait must have been one of the longest moments I have ever experienced; I looked over at the fireman, who busied himself keeping the fire stoked. "Do you believe in ghosts?" I asked, in a feeble attempt to make conversation. The Fireman, who had just thrown a generous shovel-load of coal onto the fire, looked up at me with a blank expression, but I could tell that he was feeling the unease too and I said no more.

The whistle of the approaching train coming the opposite way broke the eerie silence. So still was the air that the sound actually made me jump. Looking ahead I could see the white orb of the engine's lamp, shining from within the dark abyss of the tunnel and soon with a hissing roar the train raced passed, like some ferocious beast, released from its cage. Once the last wagon had clattered passed, I saw the signal move up and light change to green. As if by some psychic force I heard Doctor Zander say "Go on Herr Carter."

Heaving a sigh and gripped the regulator once again we moved forward, Doctor Zander told me that I was to move slowly through the tunnel, that myself and the fireman were too keep our eyes fixed ahead all the time and despite what we might want to do, not to speed up at all.

The passage through the tunnel was long and my fear grew even more. At one point I looked down to check one of the pressure gauges, I noticed my hand was shaking so violently, that I was worried it would slip off the regulator handle. As with all steam engines, the clouds of black smoke from the funnel soon filled the cab, making us both cough and splutter. With the inky blackness all around us and our sight reduced by the haze, looking ahead was almost impossible. Yet with tears rolling down my cheeks, I saw her, a dark shape standing in the between the rails ahead of us. She didn't move a muscle, but I could clearly see her, silhouetted against the tunnel arch.

Taking my hand of the regulator and instantly slammed on the brakes, so forceful was the braking, that I was mentally picturing both the academic and Mr. Bailey, being thrown to the floor, much like I was. With my eyes still stinging I looked out, the woman was still there, I reached out and feeling the Fireman's shoulder, I grabbed hard and asked "Can you see her?" whether because of the smoky interior of the cab or fear, the words came out as nothing more than a gasping croak. The fireman said nothing; I briefly looked over and saw him rooted to the spot, his face a mask of complete terror. I heard one of the carriage windows being lowered and Doctor Zander's voice calling out "Have you seen anything?"

Before I could reply the clump of wood against wood, signalled that one of the doors had been opened and the crunch of the ballast under feet. Something reached out and grabbed my hand, causing me to cry out in shock. "It's me dummkopf." Hissed Doctor Zander, who was scrambling up the steps and into the cab.

In the tight confines of the cab he tossed his bag over to me and threw open the catches, reaching into it; he pulled out a piece of wood I recognised a crucifix, before descending back down the steps and onto the track. The crunching of the ballast beneath his feet echoed chillingly off the darkened walls of the tunnel. I looked out through the window. In front of me was the same woman standing there, completely still on the track, visibility was getting harder, smoke and steam from the engine was beginning to fill the space, I was finding it hard to breath as in the smoke-filled environment, my throat felt as though it was closed tight.

Just then there came a loud hiss of escaping steam and the sensation of the floor moving beneath my feet. I looked down and saw that the fire man had reached over and pulled the engine gear lever into reverse and had opened the regulator. It was sending us backwards. "What are you doing, you bloody fool!" I shouted, but my voice was no louder than a whisper against the roaring snort of the engine, I reached over and tried to stop the train, however my hand was knocked away. Without thinking of what I was doing, I headed out of the cab and perched precariously on the steps, I was aware of the solid texture of the tunnel wall against my back. Closing my liquid eyes and I jumped off and hit the ground hard, no sooner did my boots make contact with the ballast than I forced myself against the tunnel wall and watched as the locomotive heading back and was soon out of sight. Now all alone apart from Doctor Zander and the apparition that he was talking to.

I walked towards the opening and could see two figures there, both clearly in front of me. I drew nearer but I decided not to get too close as I had no means of a quick escape. The figures were now only a few meters away and I could hear the loud booming voice of Doctor Zander say "What manner of being are you?"

Then I heard a voice, an eerily, quivering sound that carried on the wind and echoed in my ears, it said "I'm Nancy Halford, I want to go home."

"We can take you home," replied Doctor Zander "show us where you are."

Nancy didn't say anything instead she pointed into the tunnel, the academic looked back and spotted me. "Herr Carter, come please" he beckoned me forward. Steadily I walked forward and joined them, Nancy Halford, was a woman of youth and slight beauty, which I could see even at this time of night. She was wearing an old-fashioned dress, with a low-cut front and a large, wide-brimmed hat. Doctor Zander broke the silence "You are still in the tunnel." Nancy nodded and then she completely vanished and it was as though she had never existed.

I looked at Doctor Zander who, placing a hand on my shoulder said "Tomorrow, we shall close the tunnel, get a priest and locate Nancy's remains. I think once she has been laid to rest, these incidents will stop. Come." The last point he said with a beckoning gesture. However rather than turning towards the tunnel he headed towards the grassy bank that ran at the side of the track. I followed him. "You are probably wondering where we are going?" he said after a while

"It had crossed my mind" I admitted

"We have no way of getting back and I'm not walking back through the tunnel at night."

"Because of the supernatural events?" I asked.

"Because it's dangerous" he corrected sternly

The next day the tunnel was closed, buses and lorries ran passengers and goods from Sittington towards Coalfield and only a handful of engines were steamed up to do nothing else but run about in the shunting yards. I was still in a daze after the previous night. I had walked with Doctor Zander until we had come across The Railwaymen's Arms. I went in but the academic carried on and walked towards the station. I, on the other hand, ordered drinks and sat at a plain wooden table. I don't know whether it was a delayed reaction to what I had seen or a more supernatural reason, but the next thing I remember was waking up in my bed and I quickly dismissed the events of the previous night as a dream. I washed, dressed and headed for work. Only to be told that the tunnel was shut and no trains would be running.

I saw no-one from the night before, no sign of Mr. Bailey, Doctor Zander or even the fireman who was with me. The few engine crews that were on duty didn't talk much and the strangest part was that I was unable to locate my engine. I looked around the yard, but was unable to find it, nor the inspection coach that was coupled with it. I went to Mr. Bailey's office but there was no sign of him. His secretary said she hadn't seen him all morning. As I sat on the station bench, wondering about what to do, it came to me, I got up and decided to walk toward Thoran Tunnel. I headed along the country road and found myself looking down at the track and the opening mouth of the tunnel, as I watched I noticed a group of figures were ambling along the track towards the end of tunnel. I crouched down and from my vantage point I could see them, including the raven black figure of a priest. Behind him there were a number of railways workers, one of whom was carrying a large box. The rest appeared to be railways workers carrying picks and shovels. Slowly they headed up the line and were soon out of sight. I was still confused. I realised that I had no-idea what was going on and no work, I simply stood up and walked home.

Life after that seemed to slow down, the tunnel was re-opened, but things were never the same. Work dried up and steadily road transport began to prosper, meaning that only a few years later the board of directors decided to close the line. We were laid off and the track was ripped up. I never saw Doctor

Zander or Mr. Bailey again and don't know what became of them. I went off and worked for another railway, though sometimes I do go back to Thoran tunnel, stand at the mouth and look in and yet at the very end, I can see the faint figure walking across the opening, only for it to leave before my very eyes.

~o~

Thoran Tunnel combines two of my personal interests, creative writing and railways. I've been a steam enthusiast since I was a child. I had returned from a steam exhibition at Barrow Hill Roundhouse in Derbyshire when I prepared for the competition. It was the lead up to Halloween, when things start turning spooky and I decided to write a horror or ghost story and decided to create a ghost story and set it on a railway.

I'm not too sure where the idea for a haunted railway tunnel came from. I had read stories of haunted railway stations and other places. Though a tunnel is a better setting for a ghost story, maybe it's the chlostraphoic atmosphere, the fact that inside of a tunnel is always dark and you can't even see the side walls, allowing your mind to wonder what lurks inside, also tunnels are normally situated in the middle of nowhere, adding to the feeling of isolation.

I've written ghost stories in the first person narrative before, simply for the reason that it makes the emotions and the sense of being alone more believable. It also works in this case, as the protagonist (Tom Carter) doesn't actually see the ghost, until he has to drive his own engine through the tunnel, thus keeping the element of mystery as he doesn't know if what is happening is real or not? It's also unique when the train stops in the tunnel and with the heat and smoke making it hard to breathe and see.

Amongst the lists of playwrights and authors that have influence my writing one of the most unique, in terms of language use and style is Dylan Thomas, I've studied his radio play *Under Milkwood* in depth. In particular the creative and wafting way he describes things, I see a similarity in comparing the numerous sounds an engine makes.

I wanted to create the general feeling of past tense, as though Tom Carter was re-telling this story many years later. Rather than focus on the current events in his life, I've concentrated more on the story. The mysterious ending and the

217

lack of reasons of what happened to the other characters was influenced by the twist endings found in the works of M.R. James and J.B. Priestley. James would frequently tell ghost stories to his family in the cold winter months and in Priestley's famous play *An Inspector Calls*, there is the mysterious character Inspector Goole appears as though from no-where, with little back story. This can be likened to the character of Doctor Zander. Writing in a first person narrative also helps with this literacy ploy as, like the narrator, Tom Carter doesn't know anything about Doctor Zander apart from his physical appearance.

I've really enjoyed writing this entry and I intend to carry on writing, whilst I've written a ghost story, I hope to expand into other genres, go into other media and achieve my ambition of becoming a professional Writer and Actor.

STEPHANIE HICKMAN
UNPREPARED

Stephanie Hickman is twenty-one year old student, studying a Masters in Creative Writing with the Open University. She began writing when she was around 13 and decided she wanted to become a professional author. After graduating from her BA in Philosophy, Ethics and Religion, she worked in a crematorium for four months which had a profound affect on her writing. She enjoys spending her time crocheting, doing jigsaws and writing, all with a mug of tea.

The silence of the fading night was interrupted by the jangle of Debra's keys as she locked her front door and walked to her car, her high heels click-clacking against the paving stones. She held her handbag in the crook of her elbow and she was glad she had decided to wear a thick, woollen cardigan as there was a distinctive chill in the air.

She climbed into her car and turned on the engine. The radio came on but only static came through the car speakers. She scowled and tried to tune the radio but all she could get was the static. A bit of a disappointing start to the day; she really enjoyed listening to BBC Radio 2 on the way to work. She switched to a CD but turned the volume down low. The Monday blues weighed on her mind, affecting the positive energy that she needed to radiate through her to help her cope with the stressful day ahead.

The drive to the Crematorium didn't take too long, especially since the roads were deserted. She had set off to arrive at work over an hour and a half early but still, there should be other commuters. Everyone must be sick. Or scared. Debra twisted her mouth in disgust, why would people be scared of a little cough?

Approaching the Crematorium gates, a sharp pain on the left side of her abdomen caused her to gasp. She let go of the steering wheel with her left hand and clutched the area. The pain quickly faded, leaving Debra feeling more annoyed than worried. This was related to the particularly bad bout of IBS she had experienced earlier in anticipation of the stressful day ahead. She was not going to ever let it affect her day. Ever.

As she drove into the dimly lit staff car park, she saw that only Brian's 4x4 was parked there, he must have been on the night shift. Where was everyone else, though? Shouldn't there be other staff finishing on the night shift? She parked in the space nearest reception and checked her appearance in the car's mirror. Her make-up was still decent, concealing the lines that had begun to form around her eyes and lips. She pulled out her comb and combed through her straightened, blonde bob to make sure it was still completely neat. Leaning forward, she examined her roots in the mirror, deciding that she should dye them again this weekend, her dark hair was beginning to show through. Sighing, she put her comb back in her bag. She didn't feel ready for a Monday morning yet but she got out of the car regardless.

A siren wailed in the distance as she walked up to the reception. The doors slid open automatically but the room was dark; no-one was at the reception desk. She turned the lights on before letting herself into the admin office beside reception, where Kevin and Tracey usually worked, and then walked through to the reception desk. There was a massive stack of cremation forms waiting to be put on the computer system and the computer was off. Had no-one been in?

She made herself a cup of coffee and then set about putting the medical forms onto the computer. However, the forms had been changed because of the sheer quantity of people dying from the flu. The doctors no longer needed to have attended the person and they were using a stamp to indicate the body was safe for cremation. Debra scowled at the form in her hand, struggling to comprehend the information before her. She vaguely remembered that her boss, Melissa, explaining that there had been a change with the forms but Debra couldn't remember well what Melissa had said.

The reception doors slid open and Brian, the crematory technician, walked in with a stack of polytainers in cardboard boxes in his arms. He wore a baggy sweatshirt with a coffee stain down the front and Debra thought he needed to shave the stubble forming across his face.

'Morning.' He said, putting them down on the reception desk. 'Just you then?'

'Seems so. Are Kevin and Tracey sick?'

'I don't know. It's just me over there.' He gestured to the crematory, a separate building to the left of the reception, behind the chapel.

'Really? Haven't you just been on the night shift?'

'Yes.'

'Shouldn't you go home? Aren't any gardeners here? They can cremate, can't they?'

'No gardeners here, it's just me. And I'm not leaving until someone comes to take my place.'

A small, blue car drove into the staff car park, parking in the space next to Debra's car.

'Ah good, Gary's here.' Debra said. 'At least we have a chapel attendant now.'

'They're not doing full funerals.'

'Oh?'

'Public gatherings have been banned. Only immediate family can come and they only get ten minutes. They just ditch the coffin and go.'

'Wow.' Debra said, feeling very behind. She had only taken Friday and the weekend off work, yet so much seemed to have changed already. The Pandemic must be peaking.

'I need to go and get the rest of them.' Brian said.

'I'll sign these in.'

Brian left and she signed the ashes in on a form, placing them in the cupboard. The cupboard was already pretty full so Debra ended up having to pile most of them up in the admin office. Brian returned with more polytainers but had to leave again to fetch others. He made two more trips back, each time carrying as many of the boxes as he could. Debra had never known Brian bring so many over.

'That was all from yesterday?' She said as he put the last pile on the reception desk.

'Yes.'

'How many cremations were there yesterday?'

'Twenty-three.'

'Twenty-three? We don't usually cremate on Sundays, either.'

'Record number today, twenty-eight.'

'Wow...'

'I should be getting back.' He said, turning to leave.

'See you in a bit.'

A hearse rolled up outside the chapel and Debra frowned as there were no flowers inside it. When pallbearers took the coffin into the chapel, there were no mourners entering behind them. She looked on the system, this was a 44 year old man's funeral, usually it would be packed with mourners.

She checked her emails, there was one from David, who ran the cemeteries, saying that he was sick and unable to make it in. Debra sent him a get well soon message before carefully reading through her daily horoscope email. It calmed her to know what her future would be. Today, she would be faced with new challenges and it would reveal a new part of herself, which she liked the sound of very much indeed. It meant a day filled with positive energy and personal growth.

She went back to putting forms onto the computer, trying desperately to get through the gigantic pile. The pink forms with the details of the funerals were different as well. As people were no longer allowed a full funeral, they could only pick one song to be played and often the forms stated the funeral would be unattended. This was so bizarre.

A funeral director popped in to drop off at least seven more forms but he was in such a rush that Debra couldn't ask him about what was going on on his end of the Pandemic. She put a few more forms onto the computer. The phone regularly rang with funeral directors booking funerals, explaining why their paperwork would be late due to sickness, or members of the public wanting to know if they could attend a relatives' funeral.

'Hang on...' She muttered, looking through the paperwork for a 23 year old's funeral. There was no registrar certificate. She called up the funeral director but there was no answer so she called the registrar's office.

'All the registrars are off sick.' The receptionist said after Debra had explained the situation to her.

'I need the registry of death for this person. Will the registrars be back soon?'

'I don't know, sorry. It's the flu.'

'Oh...I'm going to have to cancel the funeral, the medical referee won't sign off the form until there's the green certificate.'

'There isn't anything I can do. The whole country's in mayhem.'

'Oh...well, thanks anyway.'

She put the phone down and glanced up at the clock, it was now eleven am. Wow, the time had passed really quickly.

She called up the funeral director but there was no answer again so she left a message that the funeral next week couldn't take place without the registry of death form.

Just as she was going back to the paperwork, the phone rang. It was Brian at the crematory.

'I've got a bit of a problem.' He said. 'You need to come over to see it. I'll be by the cremator doors.'

She walked over to the crematory, going through the side door and stepping into the warmth. She walked under the giant environmental, air filters and passed the three cremators. Even though she knew she shouldn't look inside through the small peepholes, she always did. It was like whenever she drove passed a car crash, she had to look no matter how shocking. The decomposition of a person in the flames fascinated her and she was disgusted by that aspect of herself. She walked around the side of the cremators and behind them, where the doors into the cremators were, the exit of the catafalque and the steps into the music rooms.

'Oh...' She said, pausing before she went to stand beside Brian. There at least ten coffins on the floor, in piles of two.

'With a body being dropped off once every ten minutes...' He muttered, rubbing under his eyes where huge bags had started to form.

'And it takes an hour and a half to cremate...I thought we were supposed to have insulated lorries?' She said.

'They haven't arrived.'

'Oh God...'

'Neither have the body suits.'

'Yeah, you're supposed to be wearing protective gear to stop you from catching it.'

'Mmm.' He said.

'With a back log this big already...Oh dear.' Debra put her hand to her face, tapping her index finger against her cheek. 'They estimated 15,000 people in this county would die from the flu.'

'Let's hope other crems are doing their fair share of this.'

'Is there anyone we can call?' She asked

'I've tried the delivery company, no answer...'

'I've only been here for four months. I still don't know what I'm doing...The council sent out pandemic information when the disease was first found in India but... You know what? I'm going to call Claire, the big boss at the Town Hall. She'll know what to do.'

'Good idea.'

Debra went back to the office and phoned Claire, the head of Environmental Services, which was the department that ran the Crematorium. There was no answer. She tried her colleagues on their mobiles or home numbers but there was also no answer.

She opened up her email where there was the Pandemic information attachment. She reread the information, explaining what the Crematorium should do if the flu hit Britain. However, the report estimated that the pandemic had morality rate of 2-2.5%, like the Spanish Flu. But this pandemic must be closer to 4%, if not more. And there were procedures in place to follow but it didn't explain what to do if certain aspects of the procedures fell apart, like the refrigerated lorry not turning up.

'We are so unprepared.' Debra muttered to herself.

Her throat felt tight and dry, she pulled her water bottle out from her bag and had a drink, wishing that it was actually vodka. She looked around the office, it felt weird that she was the only one there. Usually, there was Tracey and Kevin in the office on the left, the admin team. Melissa, the head of the crematorium, and David, the head of the cemeteries, in the office at the back and Patricia, the boss of the entire crem and cemeteries, in the hidden office behind that. Now it was just Debra, a bereavement services assistant who still didn't understand parts of the job, such as the cemetery's legal aspects.

Debra's eyes widened and she whispered, 'Oh God,' before picking up the phone and calling Brian.

'Yeah?' Brian said.

'I've just had a horrible thought.' She said.

'Is that so?'

'Yes, you know David is off sick.'

'Yes?'

'He runs the cemeteries, which means he witnesses all the burials that take place and sends the Registrar forms back to the Register office. But, if he's off sick, no-one can witness the burials so no-one can be buried either. And with the registrars all off sick, no deaths can be registered so no-one can be cremated that has died in like the last few days. People are still dying left, right and centre.'

'So, a massive back log of dead bodies. Let's hope the funeral directors' fridges are big enough.'

'The Hospital's mortuary must be full by now.'

'It's a mess, Debra. It's a mess.'

'What should we do?'

'Keep working, what else can we do?'

'True, true. How's Gary getting on?'

'A little stressed, nothing too bad though. Call me if you need me.'

'Okay.'

He hung up and she went back to typing up forms onto the system and answering calls. She ate her lunch at her desk, too busy to take a break. Every ten minutes a hearse would pull up outside the chapel and drop off the coffin. A pallbearer would bring in more paperwork but they couldn't stay, often because they had another two or more funerals to do that day.

The phone rang and Debra answered it without glancing at the number first.

'Hello, Bereavement Services.' She said, maintaining a cheerful voice.

'Hey...Debbie, it's me.'

'Adam.' Debra straightened up, her hand tightening around the phone.

'It's just...Karen's dead.'

'Oh.' She said. 'I'm...I'm sorry to hear that.' But she didn't feel that way, her dislike of Karen clouded all sympathy for her.

'I just don't know what to do. They won't let me see her body and I'm in the house all alone. And...I've been thinking. Things weren't great between me and Karen, we fought a lot and said stuff. And I've realised. I miss you. I just really, really miss you. And with this flu going round and people dying, I just really need you back in my life.'

'Well, you left me.' Debra said.

'I know I did and I really regretted it. Being with you was amazing and I was stupid for not seeing that. Remember all of those amazing holidays we used to go on? To Greece and Spain and Turkey? And you were always up for a night out. You were such good fun.'

'Yeah, so?'

'I just really want you back.'

'You're grieving, Adam.'

'I know but I'm not too. I'm glad. I'm really glad Karen is dead because it means we can get back together. We can start where we left off.'

'I don't have time for this, Adam.' Debra slammed the phone down and then let out a long breath. She breathed in slowly, trying to control the palpitations of her heart. She hadn't heard from Adam in three years, his voice was still so familiar and welcoming. But, no. Even if Karen was dead, there was no way Debra was willing to have Adam back in her life. Her stomach churned, threatening to send her to the bathroom with a bout of IBS. No, she was not going to let Adam affect her. Not now, not ever.

She went back to uploading forms onto the computer when a pickup truck screeched into the staff car park, narrowly missing Brian's 4x4 and parking up outside reception. A man stood on the back and he tossed what looked like a mannequin over the edge of the truck. It slammed against the tarmac and the car reversed out, turning around to go back the way it came.

Debra climbed over the reception desk and rushed out the doors.

'She's infectious!' The man on the back shouted, before the truck raced away.

'Oh my God.' Debra put a hand over her mouth.

The corpse of a woman lay face down on the tarmac, her black curls strayed out around her. She wore pink pajamas and her skin was a waxy, whitish-grey colour. The tips of her fingers had turned blue, the skin around the nails retracting.

Debra rushed inside and called Brian up. The phone rang for a few minutes before he picked it up.

'Brian, you need to come to the staff car park. Right away.'

'I'm a little busy right now.'

'It's urgent.'

'Right, okay, give me a minute.'

Debra went back outside and stood over the body.

Brian walked out of the crematory, beginning to rush over to her when he saw the body

'Has there been an accident?' He shouted to her.

'No, someone has dumped her.'

'Oh.' He slowed, walking to stand next to her. 'Flu?'

'Probably.'

He frowned at the body. 'We need to do something about this.'

'Should I call the police?'

'They're probably too busy setting up blockades around infected areas.'

'Then, what?'

'I don't know. This is your job more than mine.'

'I am a Bereavement Services Assistant. My job is to put cremation forms onto the computer and do grave or cremation searches and mark up grave plans and sort out memorials. This is not my job and I have no idea what I'm doing. I don't think a body has ever been dumped at the crem like this before. Why would someone just dump a body at the crem anyway? Why would someone do this to a relative?'

'Hmm...' He said, looking at the body.

'Is that all you can say?'

'We can't cremate her.'

'...yeah...' Debra nodded. 'The woman could have been murdered, look at the marks on her legs. Dumping someone here is a bit suspicious."

'That might just be from the blood settling.'

'We're no experts though...We can't cremate someone without the correct paperwork; three doctors' signatures and a registrar certificate. We don't even know her name. We cannot cremate her. I think I need to call the police. They can get an ambulance to pick her up.'

'If you think that's the best idea.' He said. 'We can't leave the body out here for a mourner to see...Even if there are very few of them today.'

'It would not make the crem look good at all if there's a body in the staff car park.'

'Where should we put her?' He asked.

'Um...It's too warm in the offices at the crematory, she'll just rot faster...The back office, for now. She'll be tucked away and I'll turn the heating down.'

'Okay then...We'll carry her in then, you get her feet.'

Brian pulled the woman up under her arms, turning her over so she was face up. Her head flopped, her shrunken eyes unseeing.

'The body's not stiff.' Brian said. 'Gives us an idea of when she died.'

'Eww.' Debra grabbed her ankles, feeling how cold they were and she hoped that the legs wouldn't come out or something. When they lifted her, Debra was surprised how heavy the corpse was. She had expected it to be light, like a doll.

'She looked like she's seen better days.' Brian said and they walked up the steps to reception.

'Disgusting.' Debra muttered. The reception doors slid over and they carried her inside. They laid her down on the floor in front of the printer in the admin office.

'Well...she kinda looks like she's having a nap on the job...or a mental breakdown.' Debra said.

'Mmm.... Are you working at reception?'

'Yes?'

'Are you not worried about getting sick? They say you can catch the flu off the dead bodies.'

'I'm not going to get sick.'

'How?'

'Well, it's all in your mental process, isn't it? If you think you're going to get sick, you'll get sick. If you're scared of sickness, you'll get sick, if you know what I mean? Like when I was in Thailand, I thought I was going to get sick, so I did. I had that tummy bug that lasted two weeks, you know. But when I went to Egypt or Tanzania, I thought that I would not get sick. I was not going to let myself go down with something. And, I didn't. It's all in the mind, right?'

'I'm not sure but if it works for you.'

'Yeah, it really does work.'

'Hmm...' He said, looking at the body with a scowl on his face. Debra scowled at him, not understanding why he would not agree with her beliefs. She had evidence, right? Enough to prove it.

'I just took a call from my ex-husband.' Debra said, desperate to break the silence that had formed between them.

'Oh, really.' He said it as a statement rather than a question, but Debra still took it as an invitation to continue.

'Yeah. That whore Karen is dead. He wanted to get back with me and stuff. No way, ever. Would never work, what did I expect when I married an Aries? Our signs were just incompatible.'

'Yeah.' He said, though he seemed to only be vaguely paying attention to what she was saying.

Debra waited to see if he would say anything else and then she said, 'We better get back to work then. I need to call the police.'

Brian left while Debra turned the heating off. She also went over to the reception doors and fiddled with the control pad for them so they stayed open. Then she sat down at reception and phoned the police. Thankfully, someone answered the phone and said that a police officer and an ambulance were on their way, reassuring Debra that she had done the right thing calling the police and was not wasting their time.

Debra put down the phone and sat at the desk, unsure what to do. The hairs on the back of her neck began to raise as she felt the strange sensation that she was being watched. No, there were no ghosts at the crem, she was sure of that. It wouldn't make sense for them to come here as they have no emotional attachment to it. They would stay at home, right? Still, she felt the urgent need to check on the body.

She stood up and moved to the doorway of the admin office. The body still lay there, unmoved and discoloured. She stepped slowly forward, realising that in front of her was something with no spiritual life force anymore, the very essence of all Debra valued. No energy. Just emptiness, a void. A concept she feared.

Putting a hand over her chest, she felt herself begin to hyperventilate from both fear and revulsion. She had just carried a corpse into the admin office with Brian and it scared her how okay she had been with it. She felt like she had been dragged into a dystopian future or a horror movie. This was not her job, she was an admin assistant, not a...a...there was no job that involved having a corpse lying on the office floor. Pathologist or funeral director was the closest job she could come up with, two jobs she began to feel disgusted about. Yes, she worked in a crematorium, that wasn't for the faint hearted. She was okay with what came out of the cremators; ash and bone to be ground up. She just realised she was really not okay with what goes into the cremators.

A pain erupted in her stomach followed by a gurgle. She needed to get to a bathroom, now. She rushed into the staff bathroom and managed to get to the toilet in time, where she had explosive diarrhea. She had experienced IBS at work before but never this bad. After cleaning herself and the toilet up, she sat down on the bathroom floor, her knees drawn up to her chest. Her hair was messy with knots and her side parting had become wonky. She felt like crying, feeling a need to drink an entire bottle of red wine. All her positive energy had been drained out of her, she felt like an empty void was growing inside her. A darkness enveloping her spirit. She leaned back against the toilet wall and closed her eyes, wishing she was elsewhere. Anywhere was better than here.

She remembered her horoscope from the morning; new challenges today would reveal a new part of herself. That had to be referring to this, mustn't it? Yes, definitely. But what new part of herself? She swallowed, rubbing her nose on the back of her hand. Her determination to keep going? Yes, that was the new part of herself. She would keep going, no matter what. She would complete the job and she would do it properly.

Standing up, she washed her hands again and then went back to her desk, walking confidently with her head held high. She sat down, reapplied her lipstick and brushed her hair through with a comb. Then she set about putting more forms onto the computer, waiting for the police to arrive. She desperately wanted another cup of coffee but she was too scared to leave the office, as if the body might somehow mystically not be there when she got back.

Around half an hour later, a police officer arrived, followed a few minutes later by an ambulance. Debra described to the officer as best as she could remember the man who ditched the body and what the pickup truck looked like. The paramedics, wearing full body suits, zipped the lady into a body bag before loading it onto the stretcher. Debra and the police officer followed the paramedics out of the office and watched the stretcher be loaded into the ambulance.

The officer informed Debra that she might be contacted in the future about this before getting into their car. Debra watched the paramedics climb into ambulance before they all drove away. She sat down on the concrete steps into reception, resting her elbow on her knee and her chin on her hand.

She heard the crematory door close and turned to see Brian walking over.

He sat down next to her. 'I just needed some air.'

'I couldn't agree more. An ambulance has taken away the body.'

'Good.'

'Looks like it's going to rain.' Debra said, looking at the sky.

A hearse drove up to the chapel and they watched as the pallbearers took the coffin out of the car. The coffin didn't look like it was made of wood. Debra squinted at it, it looked like a makeshift coffin made from cardboard boxes put together. With the flu, ordering coffins must be a bit of a nightmare.

'Three children today.' Brian said.

'Three? Oh my God. I've never know that happen.'

'Me neither...the whole country was so unprepared for this flu.' Brian said before lighting up a cigarette. He exhaled, the smoke swirling around him. 'It really makes you wonder whether all this is worth it. Maybe we should just go home and wait it out. Let someone else clear up the mess.'

'There might not be someone else.' Debra said. 'We have to keep working.'

'Hmm...'

'Well, I'm determined to keep working, no matter what. I'm not sick, I'm not going to let myself get sick and I'm going to prove to everyone that I can keep this crem running. I have to keep working. There are still forms that need putting on the system. And I need double check the details for the funerals tomorrow, then do the daily run off so you know who you're cremating tomorrow. At least I don't have to sort out flower cards, there's no point with ten minute services where most are unattended.'

'You're right...I'll stay. There is still a backlog of coffins.'

'You should go home and sleep, come back tomorrow. You stayed up all last night, you're probably tired.'

'I'll catch up with naps. I can't leave, not now. Like you said, we have to stay.'

'We do.' Debra smiled slightly, she hadn't realised Brian could be so easily persuaded before.

'Gary can help me out, he's always been interested in cremating. Maybe this will motivate him to get his qualification.'

They watched the hearse drive away, the smell of smoke causing Debra to feel slightly nostalgic about Adam. They stayed there for a few minutes, silently trying to motivate themselves to stand up and go back to work. When Brian's cigarette burned out, he returned to the crematory while Debra brushed herself off and went back to her reception desk. She continued working into the night, her motivation fluctuating as her naïvety of the situation faded and the realisation of the horror became clearer.

~o~

What I wanted to explore when writing this was that no matter how many guidelines there are, a crematorium might still be reasonably unprepared for a pandemic. If the key people, such as doctors, go off sick during a pandemic then the cremation paperwork cannot be filled in correctly so a dead body cannot be disposed of legally. If the pandemic staff were to go off sick then the paperwork couldn't be processed which would also mean that the dead body couldn't be disposed of.

I based the crematorium and it's system off the crematorium I used to work at. However, I was still working there when I wrote this which meant it would not have been appropriate to reveal which crematorium it was or to discuss the local area. I researched writing this by talking to my colleagues at the crematorium and reading pandemic guidance about how the crematorium would deal with a pandemic. What I learned was fascinating, such as using refrigerated lorries to store bodies until cremation and keeping the crem open 24/7, including the admin team. I have always found pandemics interesting to write about. The first novel I wrote was about a pandemic (It's unpublished - I wrote it when I was 14 and I cannot read it back without cringing at my bad writing.).

My original idea for the plot was that once the dead body was dumped at the crem, Debra wasn't able to get anyone to move the body until the evening but the body was already decomposing. Debra would end up putting the body in the staffroom fridge but I decided that this idea was too grim and changed it to her calling the police. I took inspiration from Christopher Vogler's *The Writer's Journey* in terms of what I should do with the plot in relation to the concept of 'The Hero's Journey'. This helped guide me on what to do once Debra had contacted the police about the dead body dumped at the crematorium.

Debra was an interesting character to write, her viewpoint of the world was so different to my own. She believed in horoscopes and spiritual energy, her ideas about disease was vastly different to my own. I enjoyed being able to use these beliefs to shape the plot and her dialogue.

Writing this was a different experience for me as I don't usually write short stories but prefer novels. I find novels more enjoyable because I can really explore the characters and their conflicts more, as well as navigating a much larger plot. This was still a very enjoyable short story to write though.

ALEXANDRA RIDGWAY
VAIL

Having studied Oceanography for the past four years, Alexandra writes to escape the world of science and enter the world of her imagination. Alexandra's writing often combines her passion for animals and nature with the sense of a great adventure and the unknown. When she isn't writing, she loves to go for long walks with her cocker spaniel Bella, as well as to swim at her University club. In the future, Alex would love to be able to write more fiction, and experiment with other styles of writing such as theatre or even radio and broadcasting. Her dream is to one day write a story good enough to be adapted as either a play, a film or a computer game.

Imagination is its own form of courage; at least that's what my father used to tell me on nights like this. October storms are always the hardest to survive. Even the most adept of rune makers struggle to survive them without adequate shelter. I used to find it beautiful; the beauty of the green leaves turning into the most spectacular shades of red and gold against storm winds and the grey sky, forever crying with rain. Amidst this chaos of beauty and anger is where I found her. My most loyal companion. It is here, at her deathbed that I remember how we met.

I would often travel across the Unyielding Woods in search of rare ingredients. The people of Hearth City relied on us, the rune makers to protect them from the outside world. As long as we perform our duty, we are welcomed in their sacred city. Of course, there are still those who hate us. Heretics leading crusade to purge this holy land of magic. In their eyes, we wield a power that no man should ever have. And perhaps they are right, as the price that we pay for our power is more than most people would be willing to give. As I approached the Tree of Sacrifice, I found her. The barbaric custom of killing to appease something that may not even exist is still deeply rooted within the people of Hearth City. I made my way towards her with the feeling of guilt and anger spreading through my body. My hands, shaking, their hairs standing, knowing what I was about to do. Knowing I was going to have to help her die. I could never understand the innate prejudice found in humans. How quickly we are able to bring the axe down on the head of that which we don't understand. How we are able to destroy something which is of equal value to our lives on a chance that it might buy us forgiveness for our sins. Her body was half broken; the fur soaked in the violet blood of her people. She had broken ribs and her tail was almost completely ripped off. And as the rain washed away her blood, nourishing the earth surrounding her dying body, she looked up and stared straight into my eyes. In that moment, it felt as if God himself had peaked into the deepest corners of my being. Her eyes, like liquid silver, inspected every aspect of my soul. With a single look, this magnificent being had stopped me in my tracks, leaving me paralysed. Unable to move. I slowly lost all control over my body. In this silence, we stood. Time froze around us as it often does when magic is present. It was her choice. She wanted to die in dignity, alone, without help. But she was too weak, too close to the death's door. Her scream pierced the tranquil sound made by the rain hitting the soft soil beneath us. Any magic that had taken control over my body dispersed. I was once again able to move according to my own will. I quickly made my way towards her, already chanting the words of the rune I was about to cast. With what little knowledge I had of her species, I cast the most basic of healing runes in an attempt to save her live. In the time that is takes for the heart to produce a single beat, what most men would call a beast had become the single most important thing in my life. Even if I did not realise it at the time, it was in this moment that a bond between us came into existence. A bond that cannot be broken. A bond conquered only by death. As I prepared the teleportation runes, I heard something. A faint whisper, a ghost amidst the falling rain. "Vail" she whispered, "my name is Vail".

~o~

Whilst writing *Vail*, I wasn't entirely sure where the piece was going to take me. I didn't want to write a story; I was simply letting my mind wonder and do as it pleases. After a while, I noticed that certain ideas kept repeating and coming back to the table; the season of Autumn, loneliness, sadness. As I was beginning to write this piece in early October, my mind was preoccupied with the sight and smell of Liverpool changing. Becoming more colourful, beautiful. But there were more dramatic changes too. The temperature had dropped, the winds picked up and the rain once again became a permanent feature of the city. And this leaked into my writing; we find the main character reminiscing of how he met his companion, amidst a stormy October day. Furthermore, other aspects of my life influenced the writing. Recently, my long-term boyfriend had to move away from the city and live with his parents; I experienced a great sense of loneliness and loss. For the first time in years, I was alone at University, facing my Masters course. And this too seeped into the story of *Vail*. Vail, the dying, wounded creature saved by the narrator is in some way a reflection of myself. I felt that I needed a companion, a friend for these tough times ahead. I wanted to create a piece of writing which is emotionally charged, and which has a hint of depth to it. Despite being a short introduction to a greater story, I feel that it really does capture the audience's attention. I feel that there is a good balance in terms of description of the environment and character development. However, I wish that maybe I had written more about what happens after and included it in this submission. However, I decided against that as I wanted to create a single image, showing the difficult relationship between the need to save someone and the need to be saved. Furthermore, I wanted to start to create a world in which conflict is apparent and which reflects our own world. Vail is found almost dead having been sacrificed in hopes of people achieving atonement. This sort of behaviour is increasing in the real world. We abuse nature and the environment hoping to better ourselves with no regards to the world in which we live. I want to develop this idea further in the book and question whether or not it is the right thing to do. Through my writing, I want to be able to explore a world where people live hand in hand with nature and care for it. I know that I can use my passion to drive future stories and plotlines however I must be careful so that I create a balanced world which is interesting for the reader to explore and learn about. No world is perfect, and I have learnt that conflict is a good way of capturing the audience and it's interest.

IONA MACCALL
ONE NIGHT

Iona MacCall is a twenty-three-year-old English teacher from Fraserburgh, Aberdeenshire. Iona has always loved reading and writing fiction and developed her skills during her time at the University of Aberdeen where she attained her Master of Arts in English Literature with Creative Writing. She currently teaches full-time at Banff Academy but hopes one day to see her published work on the shelves in book stores across the world.

I go to sleep contented.
He wakes frustrated.

He lays the shiny piece of card on the kitchen bench. His mother barely acknowledges him, focused on wiping at pizza crumbs with a sponge. The air, bitter and heavy, is tinged with the taste of charcoal from the scorched crust.

"Mum?"

She looks up then, seemingly surprised that he's even in the room. Her hand is cupped underneath the edge of the counter, mopping specks of food into her palm.

"What is it, Charlie?" she asks. There's a weary tone to her voice but it's most likely not because of him. It could be because of work, or because of her back pains, or because she burnt the pizza.

"I want to talk to you about something." He gets the words out, feels them dry his mouth. "I want to tell you something."

His mother brushes the crumbs from her hand and deposits the sponge into suds. "Tell me what?" It's a reflex, honed from seventeen years of being a mother. She says the words but he knows her heart isn't in it. She has to ask but she doesn't really want to.

He picks the card up again and rubs his fingertips across the edges. He presses fleshy pads against the corners. He smooths what is already pristine. "It's about Prom."

"Prom? What about it?" She turns her head to give him a quick, sympathetic glance. "Charlie, there's still time for you to ask someone. I'm sure someone will go with you."

"No, it's not that. Clara is going with me, remember?"

"Oh, of course." She smiles to herself. She likes Clara, she often tells him. She thinks Clara would make a good girlfriend for him.

"Mum, this is about me."

She slips a plate into the soapy water and jostles the bubbles. "I told you Charlie, we'll look into hiring you a kilt this weekend. There's still plenty time."

"I don't want a kilt."

She purses her lips. "I don't think a lot of boys will be wearing suits." She shakes her head. "You'll just stand out and have people laughing at you."

He rubs the edge of the card harder, faster. "I don't want a suit either."

His mother dunks another plate into the sink. "For God's sake, Charlie, what else can you wear? It's a big event, you have to dress formally."

The card bites into the flesh under his nail. He remembers when he was four and his cousin Elisa was five. His mother had let them dress up in costumes; Elisa as a pirate and he as a geisha. She had painted their faces and taken photos. He remembers when he was eight and he wanted to dress as Cinderella for Halloween. He remembers begging his mother to let him try the dress on in the Disney store and her scolding him because he was too old for that sort of thing. He remembers being fourteen and watching the girls in his class gaze into their compact mirrors and slick lip gloss onto their mouths. He remembers the moment when he was sixteen, watching the boys in the changing room, seeing them differently. He remembers feeling something he'd never experienced before. He remembers the longing, the yearning for what he wasn't. He remembers the moment he just knew.

"Mum, I want to wear a dress."

He hears the instant his mother loses her grip on the plate and it hits the bottom of the basin. He sees the second her body freezes. The distance between them, from the sink to the table, seems to grow with each passing beat; further and further away until she disappears. He loses her to the soapy water and life before.

He always thought she had been happier when his father was around. His childhood memories were blissful – sandy toes, perfect snowmen; barbeques at dusk and kisses before bed. His father had been one half of everything. Then he had left, found someone better and that was that. His mother met David and said he made her happier than she had ever been. His parents were in two different worlds whilst he still wanted to live in the one before; the one where the three of them had picnics in the garden and autumnal walks through the park and evenings playing board games.

"Say something, Mum. Don't just stand there in silence." Minutes, hours, a lifetime pass by and she can't even look at him. He has no idea how long she's been frozen with her hands plunged in water or how long he's been clutching the prom ticket like a life-line.

"Mum-"

"Why would you want to wear a dress?" Her voice is a crackling whisper and her lips barely twitch. She's a ventriloquist doll without a puppeteer. A marionette caught in string.

"Because I want to go to prom as myself. Because I'm sick pretending to be something I'm not supposed to be." He pauses, readies himself for dealing her the final blow. "Because I'm a girl, Mum."

Her body trembles then. He thinks he hears her whisper something he can't make out. He wants to cross the distance and hold her but he's afraid she'll break if he touches her and crumble into nothing.

He knows now his body betrayed him. For a while he thought it was his mind, that there was something in his brain that was all wrong. He knows now that it's the body. It's like fighting a losing battle, trying to change the unchangeable and move the unmoveable. It's something isolating, between him and his body and no one else.

"Mum, please, I just want you to understand. I just want you to try and see things from my point of view."

"You're a boy, Charlie. I gave birth to you. You are a boy."

"This shouldn't have been my body, Mum. I shouldn't be in here." He gestures to himself but she isn't looking at him. She doesn't want to see him.

He wants her to see how the fingers are too stocky, the arms are too hairy, and the jawline is too square. More than anything he wants her to see past the body. He wants her to know that Charlie's body is all wrong.

"If you just let me explain, I think you'll feel better."

The front door opens and he hears it the second she does. His mother breaks down at the sound of David's voice calling to her and a violent sob erupts from her chest.

He stomps into the kitchen. "What's wrong, Di?" David's hands and eyes work over her looking for physical injury where there is none. "Is it your folks? Has something happened?"

She shakes her head and looks up, her nose swollen and red. There's accusation in her eyes.

"What have you been saying to her?" David asks.

"I was simply discussing some things with Mum."

"What's wrong with Diane?"

Tyler and Grant walk into the kitchen, covered with sweat. They dump half drained water bottles on the table. The studs on their football boots clatter against the linoleum.

"Well I don't know" David answers. "Apparently Charlie has upset her."

The two boys turn to face him, looking at him with as much interest as they do every day. He's a wallflower to them; there in the background but not worth noticing. It's a common thing, at home and at school. No one notices him with his mousy hair and non-descript face. He's a plain, ordinary, unremarkable boy.

"What's he said to you?" David asks his mother. He locks her in a grip, scours the skin of her shoulders with his hand.

She'd been so hopeful when David had moved in. He was going to be a new father figure, more reliable than the first model. He was going to unite them as a family. She hadn't expected David's sons to loathe her child. She didn't know that Tyler and Grant would see her son as weak and boring and would torment him at any chance they got.

She should have known that David would favour the views of his sons and see him the way Tyler and Grant did. His birthdays weren't celebrated the way theirs were. His school photos were always hidden behind their grinning faces. He was expected to do more chores because they were always out playing football or with their friends. His mother, desperate to cling onto her second chance at happiness, let him live in the shadows of his step-brothers.

"I was telling Mum that I don't want to wear a kilt to prom because I'm going to be going as a girl. I'll be going as myself."

In his head, he's brave and fearless. He's standing up and stepping out. He's shed his old skin and now stands before them, shiny and new. To his step-family he's completely other. He sees it happen before his eyes. He has changed from different to separate. A transformation from boring to strange.

"You're going as a what?"

"A girl?"

"You want to wear a dress?"

"How the hell are you a girl?"

"Freak."

"You'll be a joke."

"Freak."

"You're an embarrassment to this family."

"Freak."

Freak. Freak. Freak.

His mother doesn't say anything. She's too mortified for bringing such an abomination into their lives. She lets them tear him apart, she lets them rip him to pieces and fight over the scraps.

"You won't be going to the prom" David says, his finger jabbing into the air. "I forbid you from stepping out this house if you're going to be dressed like some drag queen."

The words, and the implications behind them, hurt. He doesn't want to dress as a girl because he likes the way the clothes feel on his skin. He doesn't do it because he has predilection for make-up. He doesn't want to stand up at the front of a bar and sing Celine Dion. He only wants the person he is on the inside to be reflected on the outside. He only wants everyone to see him as he is, as he knows he can be.

"You can't forbid me to do anything."

"He can if it stops you from humiliating us at school" Tyler says. "I mean, can you imagine, what the other kids will say when they see you?"

"And then what they'll say to us?" Grant adds. He's horrified at the thought of being associated with the boy in the dress. He's horrified at the thought that anyone might know they live in the same house.

"Get this ridiculous idea out of your head right now, Charlie." David takes a step toward him. "I mean it; you better not say another word about this. You're banned from speaking about it and you're banned from going to that stupid prom."

"You can't do that!"

"Yes I can. I will not have you dragging this family through the dirt."

She still doesn't speak; it's as if his mother isn't even there. She remains silent and motionless, a pale imitation of the woman he once knew. She's not the woman who played the prince when he wanted to be the princess. She's different from the mother who had tucked him in at night with a story and promise of unconditional love.

He grabs the prom ticket off the kitchen table and crushes it in his fist. It digs into his palm, the sparkles scratching his skin. He brushes past his step-brothers and tries to ignore the fact they take a leap away from him, as if he carries an infectious disease.

As he hurries to his bedroom he thinks he hears words followed by muttered profanities, vulgar curses at his expense. He definitely hears laughter.

He waits out the rest of the evening, for them all to go to bed.

Under the cover of darkness he pulls the box of gifts from Clara out from the depths of his wardrobe. He lifts out the plastic containers and shiny trinkets and lays the glossy hair across his bedroom floor. He smooths and buffs the ivory cream into his skin. A blend of brown and gold across his eyelids is lined with a flick of black. He combs mascara through his eyelashes. He paints on his favourite lipstick. He tucks his hair into the wig and lets the dark- blonde curls drape over his shoulders. He revels in the feeling.

He steps into Clara's old dress—the one she wore to her sixteenth birthday.

She knew how much he liked it, wanted him to have it. He lifts it up over his torso and slides his arms through. The mirror reflects what he wants to see.

I reach behind and pull the zip up to the nape of my neck. The dress doesn't hug my body in the way it did for Clara but it's beautiful regardless. It's all scarlet satin pleats and lace capped sleeves and dramatic taffeta hems. I slide my palms down the material and twist my body back and forth in the mirror. It's strange, the feeling of completeness that comes from simply changing. It's wonderful to see myself looking back at me, rather than Charlie. I know he's still there but it's easier to forget. It's easier to forget how wrong things are when I see myself in the mirror. It's me and not him.

I go to sleep contented.
He wakes every day frustrated.

~o~

Through basing the story on 'Cinderella' my goal was to keep the skeleton of the original version visible when reading but to flesh it out with modern twists and relevant issues. In my mind, it was an interesting concept to portray the Cinderella character as an oppressed male who was being tormented by his male step-family. This idea then spiralled into a story about transgender acceptance and I wanted to redefine gender in fairy-tales through examining how a male protagonist would deal with the issues that are placed predominantly on female characters. The struggle with this piece stemmed from personal worry and fear—I wanted to make sure that I was giving Charlie a voice rather than claiming I knew what he was going through. It was complicated trying to portray something I myself cannot begin to fathom and I agonised over how to phrase certain thoughts without seeming as if I was stigmatising what it means to be transgender. I decided to add what I believed to be stereotypes into the piece in the hope they would make the reader aware of them and of my aim to avoid portraying Charlie in that way. In the end, I do believe that I have given a voice rather than dictated what it means to be transgender and the result of that is a heartbreaking, beautiful story about personal acceptance. I did want to add something different to the narration and I am very happy with the effectiveness of shifting from third person into first person when Charlie transforms into a female. I give a teaser of the dual narration at the very start and open the piece in a way that is as intriguing as it is baffling:

I go to sleep contented.
He wakes frustrated.

By repeating this phrase at the end I hoped to tie every thought and feeling Charlie experienced in that one night together, as well as highlighting the struggle. I also hoped to convey the absence of a mother figure, an important aspect of the original 'Cinderella' story. I did not want Charlie to have a deceased mother whom he missed but rather that he has a mother who is distanced from him. He misses the women he remembers from his childhood and I wanted it to be as if she is not there, as if she had actually died but is simply detached from him: 'She still doesn't speak; it's as if his mother isn't even there. She remains silent and motionless, a pale imitation of the woman he once knew.' I think that the observations made about the mother are all the more affecting once the reader realises that the third person narrator is Charlie. I wanted there to be a distinct division of self in the piece, hence why I refrain from Charlie naming himself in third person. Once the narration shifts into first person I believe all the events, conversations and thoughts previously discussed become all the more poignant. We see how trapped Charlie is, both in his body and in his life.

22577696R00153

Printed in Poland
by Amazon Fulfillment
Poland Sp. z o.o., Wrocław